A Promise

A NOVEL

AMELIA MARTIN

5 HAWKS PUBLISHING

Book Cover designed by Betty Martinez @bettymar88.

ISBN - Ebook 979-8-9900934-0-9

ISBN - Paperback 979-8-9900934-1-6

ISBN - Hardback 979-8-9900934-2-3

Library of Congress Control Number: 2024902001

First edition published 2024.

To Aaron

1

Elisabeth Ehrler

If you thought only love was blind, you haven't witnessed the true darkness of hate.

Elisabeth stands at the window watching the clouds float past the full moon. The clouds remind her of the smoke that billows from her father's cigarettes. Hartwig Ehrler, a man born and bred to hate. Hartwig's hate has an insatiable hunger for light and goodness. He has always been determined to extinguish the light from his family and anyone that fell into his grasp along the way. His daughter didn't know it, but her light uld not be extinguished. Hartwig had tried for years. He tried beating it out of her. He tried brainwashing her to believe she was worthless and unlovable. He even tried ignoring her to the point that any normal person would have questioned their own existence, but to no avail. For some reason, unbeknownst to Hartwig, Elisabeth remained impervious to his tactics. Her light is her heart. Hartwig Ehrler doesn't have a heart, and if he does, it's black as night. This black heart is where he feeds his hate. He has spent years nurturing it, dutifully feeding it ignorance, judgment, and intolerance. Yes, this darkness shuts out the light, and most don't even know that it's happened. The light just slowly burns out. It begins with unhappiness. Unresolved, it turns into bitterness. Finally, little by little, hate seeps through the cracks, and you relent to the darkness. It's all rather expected; yet, most rarely see it coming. They're too busy enjoying the spoils of their superiority. In the end, they simply succumb to the darkness. There are many like Hartwig Ehrler. Some lurk in the shadows, but most live amongst us, armed with good manners and welcoming faces. Make no mistake. They carry an unwavering determination to bring everyone into the darkness with them. They will feed on the light of goodness until every light is extinguished. We must guard against them. Our light is our most powerful weapon. Funnily enough, most don't even know that they have it. They can't see their own light, but to those that live in the darkness, that light is blinding.

Elisabeth glances down to the street. She spots Hartwig drunkenly strolling towards their building. He's been at the beer hall, where he spends most of his evenings. He spends countless hours pickling his brain with his like minded National Socialists, or Nazis, as some call them. They sit in the beer halls plotting the return of the glory days of the Fatherland. They dream of a wealthy, prosperous, albeit intolerant, Fatherland. It's a dream that wakes them from the nightmare of this depression brought on by the war and the Treaty of Versailles. was plunged into darkness, and that dark cloud refuses to move. Some Germans succumb, having lost hope of ever finding happiness again, others search for a solution. The Communists and Socialists are convinced that their way is the only way out, but it only brings violence and division to the German people.

Elisabeth slips into bed as Hartwig opens the heavy wooden doors of their building. The stairs creak under each step as he makes his way up to their flat. Fear dances in her stomach. One never knows what kind of mood Hartwig will return in after a night of drinking, or who will be the recipient of his beatings or rage. It's not something you can gauge. It's just another one of Hartwig's special surprises, like the one he gave Elisabeth earlier that morning. He announced at breakfast that he, alone, will be choosing her husband. He's decided that it is his duty to find a true German for his daughter, and a Nazi is the only true German.

Hartwig quietly makes his way to his bedroom. One would think that you could breathe easy now, but that could be a mistake. Elisabeth listens intently until she hears the creak of the bed in her parents' room. She waits a few more minutes for the reassuring sound of Hartwig's snoring. Now, she can breathe a sigh of relief.

Lying awake in the darkness she envisions her new life with her new husband. Much like her mother's life, she will endure pain and suffering. Hartwig Ehrler will not choose a kind man. He sees kindness as weakness, and he won't allow it in a son in-law. After all, he'll be welcoming this man into his family, and there are strict regulations for admittance, none of which are good.

Elisabeth sits up in bed. She looks up to the ominous sky. The light of the moon is now hidden behind the clouds.

Elisabeth steps back for a final check of her reflection in the mirror. It's her first day back to school after a long summer. A warm breeze flutters the lace curtains as the sun streams through her window. Her father's cigarette, burning in the dining room, stifles the fresh summer air. His usual morning cough, brought on by a night of countless cigarettes, beckons her to the breakfast table.

Elisabeth slices a piece of bread unnoticed by her father. He continues to complain about the lack of food, and demands to know what her mother is doing with the money. Erna Ehrler ignores him, as she always does. Everyone in the Ehrler family knows, except Hartwig, that he spends most of their money at the beer halls.

Elisabeth spreads a thin layer of jam on her bread as Hartwig takes another drag from his cigarette. A cloud of smoke billows from his lips as he strokes his snow white beard.

"Tomorrow begins your rigorous training. You will get up early and prepare breakfast. After school, you will continue your training until bedtime. If I find one dirty dish, one speck of dust, one hem not sewn properly, you will be met with a punishment that you will never forget. I won't tolerate a lazy swine of a daughter. Only a fool would agree to marry you in the state that you're in." Hartwig presses his cigarette out in the ashtray. "Erna, she must learn her role to perfection. I understand that you're not the ideal teacher, but you will both work hard to ensure that I have my choice of candidates. She must be a true testament to our Fuhrer." Hartwig stands up and heads off to work, leaving fresh fear in his wake.

Erna continues to dry the dishes seemingly oblivious to her daughter's plight. Elisabeth searches her mother's face, but all she finds is the truth. No one can help her now.

"We're going to be late, Elisabeth." Henning breezes into the living room.

Elisabeth kisses her baby brother, Friedrich, before following Henning outside.

The sun is warm as they step onto the cobblestone road. Henning is the oldest of the three Ehrler children, two years older than Elisabeth.

"I have to pick up Olga. She's helping out at work until we find a new clerk."

Elisabeth rolls her eyes.

"Dad is right. You need to start readying yourself for a husband instead of hanging out with that troublemaker, Hannah."

"Hannah isn't a troublemaker."

"Olga told me that she picks on her, and she tried to cut her hair."

"Olga started it, and if anyone is a bully it's your girlfriend."

As they turn the corner Elisabeth spots Olga waiting for them outside her flat.

"Be nice," Henning whispers.

"You look pretty, Elisabeth." Olga steps toward them.

"Thanks, I have to go. I'm going to be late."

Elisabeth follows the sound of children playing. She rounds the corner to find Hannah and Adam waiting under the tree in their usual spot. There are a couple of teachers outside gathering their students, but there's still time before everyone has to be in their classrooms.

"Why didn't you walk with us today?" Hannah said.

"Henning asked me to walk with him to pick up Olga. I really don't know what he sees in her. He thinks that we're going to be friends."

"Can you imagine?" Adam said.

"No, I can't." Elisabeth said tersely. "We've been enemies our entire life. Why would she think that we could ever be friends? I'll be nice to her for Henning's sake, but that's it."

"Maybe she's changed," Adam said.

"Someone like Olga doesn't change," Hannah said.

Elisabeth sighs. "My father informed me that he will be choosing my husband."

"I can't even imagine the man that Hartwig will choose for you. Oh, Elisabeth..." Hannah's voice trails off.

Adam remains silent as they step inside the school, but Elisabeth sees the fear that he makes no effort to hide. They all know what Hartwig Ehrler brings.

The school days pass quickly as the warm days of summer are slowly eclipsed by the chill of fall.

In late autumn, Hannah delivers a bag of clothes to Elisabeth. The bag contains clothing that she no longer wears, or in some cases, has never worn.

"My mother forced me to clean out my wardrobe."

"Why don't you want them?" Elisabeth said.

"My grandmother sends me dresses. She says American dresses are more stylish. She thinks everything in America is better than us lowly Germans." Hannah walks to the door. "I must go. I don't want your father to find me here," she whispers before quietly closing the door behind her.

Elisabeth empties the bag onto the floor and studies its contents.

"She's such a nice girl." Elisabeth's mother stands over her.

Elisabeth sifts through the dresses in front of her. "They're not really my style or Hannah's. They're very American."

"I like this one." Erna picks up a pink dress with white flowers.

Elisabeth wrinkles her nose before turning her attention back to the dresses scattered out in front of her.

"I like this one." Elisabeth holds a powder blue dress against her chest.

"You can make good use of the ones that you don't like. They would make a beautiful quilt for your bed," Erna said.

Work on the quilt begins that evening. Elisabeth's brother, Friedrich, sleeps peacefully in his blanket on the floor between her and her mother. Henning is sprawled out on the settee reading his book. The only sound to be heard is the tearing of seams on Hannah's dresses.

Elisabeth and her mother work on the quilt every day, finishing it a week before Christmas. Elisabeth's skills as a seamstress are greatly improving, and her mother is impressed with her work. Erna is a skilled seamstress. She's even proficient in sewing lace, an intricate process that can take years to perfect.

On Christmas Eve, Elisabeth's father presents her with a gold necklace. A small cross dangles from it.

"It's a reminder that Jesus died for all of your sins, Elisabeth," Hartwig said.

Elisabeth thanks her father before setting it to the side. She plans to leave the necklace in a drawer, never to be seen again.

Hartwig lights a cigarette before directing his attention to his eldest son.

"Olga's father told me that she's been filling in at work."

"Yes, she's doing well."

"When are you going to marry that girl?"

"When I save up enough money."

"Oh, so we starve while you save money?"

"Henning pays me every week." Erna steps out of the kitchen.

"He's not a baby. He can stand up for himself. Why isn't dinner on the table?" Hartwig takes a gulp of beer. "Are you sure you want to get married? You could end up with a woman that's as useless as your mother."

"Leave her alone," Henning warns.

"Who the hell do you think you're talking to?" Hartwig stands up, eyes blazing.

"Hartwig, it's Christmas," Erna pleads with her husband.

Hartwig grabs Henning by the throat.

Friedrich screams. Elisabeth picks him up and rushes him into their bedroom, closing the door behind her.

Friedrich's screams fail to drown out their mother's pleas for Hartwig to stop. Friedrich holds Elisabeth tight as the fight in the living room rages on. She wraps her brother in a blanket and cradles him in her arms.

"Don't worry. It'll be over soon."

In the morning, Elisabeth wakes to her father's loud snoring. Friedrich is smiling up at her, his tiny hands playing with her braid. She scoops him up in her arms and carries him to the kitchen.

Henning smiles down at Friedrich before sitting down to eat. He has a small cut above his eye, but that's the only injury that's visible.

"Are you alright?" Elisabeth said.

"I'm not the one you should be worried about."

Henning finishes his breakfast in silence.

"I'm going to Olga's."

Later that afternoon, Hartwig emerges from his bedroom.

Elisabeth looks up from her book and watches him move carefully to the table. His every step seems painful. He sits down and mutters something under his breath.

He lights his cigarette before opening the newspaper. His face is bruised and swollen. His lip is cut, and blood is caked onto the inside of his nostrils.

Elisabeth slips away, unnoticed, to her bedroom. The excitement is coursing through her veins as she quietly closes the door.

Hartwig Ehrler has finally been defeated.

In February, they celebrate Friedrich's birthday. Hartwig celebrates at the beer hall.

Henning presents Friedrich with a small wooden horse that he had been working on for months.

At dinner, Henning talks incessantly about Adolf Hitler and his plans to restore the Fatherland.

"We can't continue to live in this depression. People are starving. Children are starving. We need things to change. Herr Hitler has plans for the German people. He's clever. He's disciplined. He's exactly what we need to restore our country to greatness."

Elisabeth rolls her eyes. "Yet, he and his Nazis are hateful and lawless. They commit violent crimes, and you know it. Adolf Hitler claims to be a law abiding citizen, but his actions are his truth."

"What do you know about politics? You're a girl."

"Being a girl doesn't make me blind."

"You don't know what you're talking about, Elisabeth. Women aren't meant to understand politics. Lawlessness is the only way to restore peace. It's the Communists who should concern you. They incite the violence. The Jews aren't blameless either. Don't you find it odd that this depression hasn't affected them? They're only getting richer, including your friend Hannah. You and mother were so grateful to receive her old, unwanted dresses. The filthy Jews have been stealing from us all along and you fools are grateful to receive their hand-me-downs."

"What about Adam? His family is just as poor as ours." Elisabeth locks eyes with her brother.

"Maybe Adam's family is an exception. Maybe they're just not as clever and devious as the rest of the Jews. Give them time." Henning grabs his coat. "Never trust a Jew, Elisabeth. I'm going to the beer hall."

Just after midnight, Elisabeth wakes to voices outside. She steps out of bed and tiptoes over to the window. Careful not to be seen, she peers out to the street below. Hartwig and Henning are just returning home from the beer hall.

Suddenly, Henning ducks behind a building as Hartwig stands in the road laughing.

Moments later, Henning reappears, wiping vomit from his mouth. He stumbles back in Hartwig's direction.

Elisabeth shakes her head.

Friedrich stirs as she slips into bed, but she's able to soothe him back to sleep.

She listens to Hartwig and Henning quietly making their way to their beds before drifting off to sleep.

2

Adam Herschel

Adam's father, Ivan, sits down at the table for dinner. He rubs his forehead with his fingertips as he stares down at his bowl.

"Is everything alright?" Adam said.

"We had to let more people go today. The shop isn't making enough money to be able to afford a full staff." Ivan takes a deep breath. "It feels like we're never going to stop paying for that war."

"Not if the Treaty of Versailles has anything to do with it," Adam said.

They finish their soup in silence.

The following morning, Adam has to be at the shop early. Easter is Sunday, and there's extra work that needs to be done. Herr and Frau Lenger own a tailoring shop. It has been in Herr Lenger's family for years. Adam was initially hired to clean, but Frau Lenger has been teaching him how to sew hems. Adam is doing well, although, his work still needs improvement.

After work, Adam follows the tree lined streets towards school. Hannah is waiting for him on the corner, so he quickens his pace. The sun is bright in the sky, but the air is still cool. Buds have emerged on the trees, the first signs of spring. It won't be long until the warmer weather returns.

"Don't forget they're Nazis." Hannah removes a stray thread from his coat.

"She's not." Adam feels protective of Frau Lenger.

"Well, her husband is, and everybody knows it. Be careful, Adam."

"He's old and senile. I'm not worried. I just do my job and go home."

Elisabeth catches up to them moments later.

As they walk past the butcher shop Hannah puts her arm out for them to stop so she can peer inside.

Adam glances into the large windows, but there is no one to be seen.

"You're so lucky that you get to see Dieter all of the time because of Henning," Hannah says to Elisabeth.

"Henning spends all of his time with Olga. I rarely see Dieter."

"Olga has fancied Dieter for as long as I can remember." Hannah glances back one more time.

"So have you." Adam smiles at Hannah. "Every girl fancies Dieter."

"I don't," Elisabeth said.

"That's probably because he's your brother's best friend," Adam said.

In the distance, they spot Henning and Olga crossing the street. Olga is laughing with her arm linked in Henning's.

"I think she's jealous of you," Hannah said.

"Why would she be jealous? I don't have anything," Elisabeth said.

"Yes, but you're pretty and she's not," Adam said. "Olga could be pretty, if she wasn't so ugly on the inside."

“Maybe she’s afraid you’ll take Dieter from her,” Hannah said.

“I can’t take Dieter from her because Dieter isn’t her boyfriend.” Elisabeth stops for a moment. “I wonder if Henning suspects that Olga fancies Dieter.”

“Love is blind.” Adam kicks a pebble across the road.

That evening, at dinner, Adam’s father addresses his family.

“My hours at work have been reduced.” Ivan directs his attention to Else, Adam’s mother. “I know that you have wanted to work outside our home for a long time, and it seems that I am now forced to relent. God will take care of us, but we must also take care of ourselves.”

Adam’s shoulders drop as he stares down at his bowl.

“Summer will be here soon. We’ll plant extra vegetables at the farm. I don’t know why I didn’t think of that before. We will get through this.” Ivan tries to reassure them.

The grandfather clock in the living room chimes, signaling an end to the family meeting.

In July, the last day of school finally arrives. Adam strolls to work as the sun rises in the distance.

It’s your last day of school.” Frau Lenger sets bolts of fabric onto the chair next to him.

“We’re picnicking at the lake tomorrow to celebrate.”

“Adam, I was wondering if you might be able to work some additional hours over the summer. Actually, it would be full time. If you don’t want to, that is fine, but I’ll need to hire someone. Herr Lenger isn’t well, as you know. He can’t keep working. His heart can’t take it.”

“I can do it.”

“Good, there will be a raise of course.”

Adam smiles as excitement swells in his stomach. “I need to finish cleaning the windows before I go.”

"Thank you Adam. It's such a relief. I didn't want to have to hire a stranger."

"You're welcome. I like working here." Adam picks up his rag and heads off to the front of the shop.

Adam spends the summer working, but he still has plenty of time to enjoy hours by the lake with Hannah and Elisabeth. Although it's a relaxing summer, he spends much of his time contemplating his future. By summer's end, he has finally reached a decision.

Adam waits quietly in the chair beside Ivan's desk.

"Yes, Adam." Ivan finally sets his pencil down.

Adam takes a deep breath. "I've decided that I'm not returning to school."

Adam's heart begins to race as he struggles to find the right words–convincing words.

"I've learned all that I can from school. I'm already ahead academically of what they'll be teaching this year, and I will continue learning on my own. Frau Lenger needs me, and my family needs me. I've always been respectful, Father, but I am a man now, and I am going to do what I think is right."

Ivan stares down at his desk for a moment.

"Well, you need to do what you think is right."

Ivan looks defeated as he rises from his chair and pushes it back under the desk. He disappears down the hallway leaving Adam stunned. He had prepared himself for a debate, an argument; instead, he was met with submission. However, this is no victory.

The following day, Adam meets Elisabeth and Hannah at the lake.

"This has been a weird summer." Hannah unpacks their lunch.

"Yeah." Adam and Elisabeth agree.

"It feels like it's all coming to an end. I think my father has found a husband for me," Hannah said.

"My father keeps reminding me that I can't live at home forever," Elisabeth said.

Adam averts his eyes. "I'm not returning to school."

"What?" Hannah said.

"My family and Frau Lenger need me."

"Does your father know?" Elisabeth said.

"I told him yesterday."

"What did he say?" Hannah's eyes are wide.

"He said ok."

"Just ok?" Hannah studies Adam.

"I think it hurt him deeply. He wanted me to go to University. I think he feels that he let me down."

"We need to promise, that happens, we'll always stay together," Elisabeth said.

"I promise." Adam looks up at Elisabeth, then Hannah.

"I promise." Hannah meets their eyes.

In October, Frau Lenger's husband passes away from heart failure. They don't have children, so she only has the help of an older sister in the wake of his death. Adam meets Frau Lenger's sister, Klara, and finds her to be just as kind as Frau Lenger. Klara insists that he call her by her first name and Adam obliges. Klara stays only a few weeks due to her husband's insistence that she return home to her own family. This leaves Adam to care for the grieving Frau Lenger on his own.

One afternoon, Frau Lenger leads Adam to a bookcase in her living room.

"There is a secret room behind this wall," she whispers. "My husband built it to keep the money safe." Frau Lenger helps Adam move the bookcase.

Adam peers into the dark room as Frau Lenger lights a candle. A small suitcase sits on top of a large one that takes up most of the tiny space.

"If anything happens to me these belong to you. You know where I keep the key at the shop."

"I don't understand," Adam said.

"I am leaving this to you when my time comes. My sister Klara is wealthy. She doesn't need, nor want, my money. You are my family now, so I would like you to have it."

Adam moves the bookcase back against the wall.

"Are you sure? You must have other relatives."

"Adam, please. I don't want to discuss this any further. These are my wishes."

She disappears into the kitchen.

Adam listens to the tea set clang softly against the tray as Frau Lenger prepares tea.

He sits down at the table across from her. Sunshine streams through the windows as he slowly stirs his tea.

"Adam, please don't tell anyone."

"Don't worry, I won't." He pauses for a moment. "I don't deserve it."

"You've been very kind to a lonely old woman. You're like a son to me. Now, let's enjoy our tea."

3

Hannah Berkowicz

Hannah glances down at the newspaper before taking her seat at the breakfast table. “How can people listen to Adolf Hitler’s speeches?”

“He has quite a following.” Hannah’s mother, Lena, sets the table.

“His brown shirt thugs enjoy terrorizing people,” Hannah said.

“Adolf Hitler is a fearful man, and fear breeds hate,” Lena said.

Hannah finishes her breakfast before helping her mother with the dishes.

“I would like to become a nurse.” Hannah hangs her towel to dry. “I could work with father.”

“I think you will find that being a wife and mother is plenty of work. It leaves little time for anything else.”

“I would find the time.”

“Your husband may feel differently, Hannah.” Lena drapes her rag across the sink to dry.

Hannah walks to her father's den. Wooden shelves lined with books fill the room.

"Hannah, your father doesn't want anyone in his study." Lena stands in the doorway.

"You just don't want me to look at his medical books."

"It's a waste of time. You'll be married soon, and you still need to practice mending."

"Mending? How hard is that?"

"Hannah, your father is going to be upset if he finds out that you're entertaining these wild ideas?"

"How is being a nurse a wild idea? I would be helping people."

"Hannah, this discussion is over."

Hannah brushes past her mother in the doorway. She heads to her bedroom and sits down on the bed, crossing her arms in front of her.

Wild ideas she repeats under her breath.

She slips on her shoes and grabs her coat.

"I'm going for a walk," she calls out to her mother.

She closes the door behind her and heads out to the street.

A thin layer of snow covers the cobble stone road as she quickens her pace to Marienplatz.

She's reminded of the time that Olga tried to cut her hair. Fresh anger sets in as she keeps a steady pace on the slippery snow.

Hannah's mind flashes back to that day. The silence of the falling snow was interrupted by the approaching footsteps behind her. Hannah turned to see Olga and her friends trying to sneak up on her. The road was slick as she tried to walk faster.

Just when she was finally gaining momentum she slipped, and before she could get up they were dragging her into a small alley behind the butcher shop.

Hannah struggled to break free, kicking and punching the boys holding her down. Olga laughed as she walked up behind them, pleased to see the fear in Hannah's eyes. The three boys had been in Olga's class, a couple of years older than Hannah. It was impossible to break free from their powerful grip. They turned Hannah over as one of the boys held her face against the ice covered ground. Hannah turned her head to the side in an effort to breathe, but his knee was still pressing hard on her back. She tried to scream, but it just left her breathless. She then felt Olga above her grabbing a clump of her hair. The dull scissors pulled on her hair as Olga struggled to cut it.

Suddenly, out of nowhere, a tall shadow towered over them. At that moment, Hannah felt the air rush back into her chest as the weight of the boys was lifted off of her. The scissors were ripped out of Olga's hands. She could hear the boys running in the other direction. Hannah looked up to see Dieter Kiesling towering over her.

"Are you alright?" Dieter held out his hand.

"Why don't you mind your own business, Dieter?" Olga scolded as she stood up and brushed the snow off of her skirt.

Instantly, Hannah rose up, and with all of the force that she had she punched Olga on the nose. Blood instantly gushed from her nose and mouth. Olga was too afraid to fight back because she was now alone. She waited for Dieter to come to her rescue, but he just stood beside Hannah.

"I'm going to tell Henning about this, Dieter!" Olga screamed.

"Tell him whatever you want...just stop bleeding all over my alley," Dieter laughed, unmoved by her threat.

Dieter gently dusted the snow off of Hannah's face and walked her home. Hannah had always fancied him, but she had never told anyone. Almost every girl fancied him, but Dieter seemed oblivious to it. He was a couple of years older than Hannah, and he was close friends with Henning, Elisabeth's brother. They had been close friends since they were young. Henning said that Dieter didn't have time for girls because his mother was ill. He quit school to work at the butcher shop full time. No one knew what had happened to his father.

Hannah's breath fogs the air. A crowd gathers ahead of her, returning her thoughts to the present. She makes her way to Rathaus-Glockenspiel. She peers up at the clock before scanning the crowded square.

She stands back with the others and stares up at the majestic building.

Finally, the bells ring out. She waits for figurines to ceremoniously act out their story. She stands alone in the crowd, under the dreary sky, watching their story unfold. Her own story is about to unfold, and there is no way of escaping it.

4

Elisabeth

Olga sits at the table with Henning. They're laughing at a silly face that Friedrich is making.

"Hello, Elisabeth." Olga smiles sweetly.

"Hello, Olga." Elisabeth quickly disappears into her bedroom.

"Why can't they spend their time at Olga's flat?" Elisabeth sits down on her bed while her mother folds one of Friedrich's sweaters.

"Olga doesn't have a good relationship with her parents. She doesn't like to be at home."

"Has she met Hartwig?"

"Elisabeth, that's enough. Put your clothes away."

Elisabeth sighs. "She never offers any money for food."

"Elisabeth, enough." Erna closes the door behind her.

"Are you busy?" Olga opens the door slightly and peers inside.

"No, you can come in." Elisabeth closes the book she's reading.

"Henning would like us to be friends. I'm going to be your sister in law, so maybe we should try to get along." Olga sits down next to Elisabeth. "I don't care about you and Dieter. I love Henning."

"Me and Dieter?" Elisabeth shakes her head. "There was never a *Me and Dieter.*"

"The way he always comes to your rescue. I thought..."

"My rescue?" Elisabeth interrupts her. "Do you mean the time that I fell out of the tree, and Dieter carried me home because I twisted my ankle? I was eight."

"He also protected you from that dog that tried to bite you," Olga adds. "And he always sticks up for you when Henning picks on you."

"So, that's why you've always hated me? You think that Dieter and I are having a secret romance?" Elisabeth stands up and quietly closes her door. "I don't want Dieter." Elisabeth narrows her eyes to Olga. "Why are you marrying Henning? Why don't you go after the man that you really want?"

"You've got it wrong, Elisabeth. Henning is the man that I truly want, not Dieter." Olga stands up toe to toe with Elisabeth. "I was hoping that we could be friends, but I can see that's not going to happen."

"No, it's not."

"I should get back to Henning." Olga closes the door behind her.

Elisabeth bundles Friedrich up before grabbing her own coat. She heads outside into the frigid air.

Half way to Hannah's she scoops him up in her arms because he's too tired to walk.

Elisabeth turns the corner and spots Dieter. He takes Friedrich from her arms, and sits him on top of his broad shoulders.

"I had to get out of there," Elisabeth said.

"Which one is it this time...your father or Olga?"

"Olga."

"I don't know what Henning sees in her," Dieter said.

"She fancies you. That's why she's so jealous of me."

"What are you talking about?" Dieter laughs.

"Do you remember when I fell out of the tree?"

"Yeah."

"Well, Olga believes that you carried me home because you're madly in love with me."

"You sprained your ankle."

"It seems she's fancied you for a long time. That's probably why she's with Henning. She couldn't have you, so she settled for the next best thing. I don't know, maybe I'm wrong, but I don't trust her." Elisabeth sighs. "How is your mom doing?"

"She's doing alright. She's been well enough to do some sewing for extra money. I think it lifts her spirits to know that she's not leaving the entire burden on me. That's the only reason that I let her do it. She still has bad days, but they're fewer than in the past."

"I always liked your mother. She was so kind to Henning and me. I would like to visit with her sometime when she's feeling better."

"You can come over anytime. She would love to see you and meet Friedrich."

They stand in front of Hannah's flat as Dieter lifts Friedrich off of his shoulders.

"If you ever need a ride let me know." Dieter smiles down at Friedrich.

"Maybe I'll stop by on Monday to visit your mother."

"I'll be off of work in the afternoon. We can walk together."

Friedrich claps his hands, excited by the prospect of riding on Dieter's shoulders again.

Elisabeth smiles down at Friedrich before turning to watch Dieter heading down the street towards home.

Hannah opens the door and smiles down at Friedrich. She is clearly surprised to see him.

"It's so nice to meet you. Come in, I have lots of toys!"

Friedrich follows Hannah inside to her brother's bedroom.

"I think Leon keeps his old toys under the bed. Let's see what we can find."

Friedrich watches Hannah intently as she pulls out a box.

"I think this is it." Hannah carries the box to her bedroom and dumps it out on the rug.

Friedrich's eyes are wide, but he doesn't move.

"Go ahead, you can play with them." Hannah sits down on the floor. "You can sit down here by me."

Friedrich takes a few cautious steps in Hannah's direction. Hannah holds out her hand for him to take it and he does, much to Elisabeth's relief. He sits down next to Hannah and picks up a toy. It's not long before he is lost in Leon's toy collection.

"Dieter walked with us. He says his mother is feeling better." Elisabeth sits down on Hannah's bed. "We're going to visit her on Monday."

"That will be nice."

"Is something wrong?" Elisabeth said.

"No, it's just that I'm running out of time before my parents marry me off."

"What did they say?"

"They don't say anything. They're being very secretive. It's only a matter of time."

"Are you scared? I would be."

"I'm not ready to be a wife."

"What are you going to do?"

"There's nothing I can do."

"Your parents will choose someone deserving of you. They will choose a good man. They love you."

Elisabeth stares out the window. "My father will choose a monster."

Monday afternoon, Elisabeth bundles Friedrich in his coat and heads to the butcher shop to pick up Dieter.

He isn't ready when they arrive, so they wait inside the shop. Elisabeth watches people come and go. She wonders what they do for a living to be able to afford meat.

"Sorry about the wait." Dieter interrupts her thoughts.

"It's okay." Elisabeth smiles up at him as he holds the door open.

Outside, Dieter lifts Friedrich up on his shoulders.

"My mother has been looking forward to this all week. She's preparing a special dinner for you, so I hope you can stay."

"Does she have cake?" Friedrich said.

"I don't know. If she doesn't, we'll stop for a treat at the bakery on the way home."

Elisabeth smiles up at Friedrich. She's pleased to see the excitement on his face. Dieter watches Elisabeth for a brief moment before she catches his eye.

"We're here." Dieter announces to Friedrich, who is growing increasingly anxious to find out if there's cake.

Dieter opens the door to the flat and leads them inside. The comforting scent of roast chicken is the first to greet them. Elisabeth is relieved to see Dieter's mother looking so healthy. The last time that Elisabeth had seen Frau Kiesling she had been quite ill.

Friedrich is pleased to find out that she's prepared a cake. Elisabeth gently reminds him to mind his manners and not show too much excitement.

Dieter stacks a few large books on the seat of Friedrich's chair to help him easily reach the table.

The roast dinner is delicious. Elisabeth could have devoured everything on the plate within minutes, but she is mindful of her manners. Friedrich eats too much dinner and forgets to leave room for cake, so Dieter's mother wraps the remaining pieces for him to take home.

After dinner, Elisabeth helps clean the dishes and prepare tea. Dieter plays with Friedrich on the floor in the living room as the women work side by side in the kitchen.

Frau Kiesling is surprised to find out that Henning is a Nazi.

"He was always such a nice boy. It's so hard to believe that he would have anything to do with people like that."

"It seems it's a bond that he and my father share."

"Yes, a son strives to make his father proud." Frau Kiesling sighs.

"What about you, Dieter?" She turns her attention to her son. "Do you have much interaction with the Nazis?"

"I hear people talking, but I usually keep to myself."

"What about Henning?"

Elisabeth can see the worry on Frau Kiesling's face.

"Mother, I don't see Henning. More importantly, he knows that I don't agree with the Nazi ideals."

"He was your best friend."

"Yes, he was, but things change."

Frau Kiesling takes a deep breath before relaxing back in her chair. She seems content with Dieter's answer, so she turns her attention back to Elisabeth.

"How is your mother?"

"She's tired, but she's always tired. I help her as much as I can." Elisabeth can see that Frau Kiesling is growing weary. "We should return home before it gets dark."

"Don't forget your cake, Friedrich." Dieter's mother places the parcel in Friedrich's small hands.

Friedrich is looking more tired by the minute. Elisabeth helps him with his coat and thanks Frau Kiesling again for the delicious food.

It's snowing softly as Dieter walks them home. Friedrich sleeps peacefully in his arms.

"Make sure you hide the cake. I don't want your father eating it."

"Don't worry, I wouldn't let that happen."

When they arrive home, Dieter gently lays Friedrich on the bed before slipping off his shoes. Elisabeth places the cake in the top drawer of her desk.

"Please thank your mother again for visiting with us," Elisabeth whispers.

"She was pleased to see you and meet Friedrich. We should do it again sometime."

Elisabeth watches Dieter through the window as he disappears down the street.

The following morning, Elisabeth sits down at the table for breakfast. She glances at the front page of the newspaper that Hartwig is holding. Splashed across the front page, in bold letters, the headline reads: *Adolf Hitler, Chancellor of* . Elisabeth eats her bread and jam. Adolf Hitler means nothing to her.

That evening, Hartwig, Henning, and Olga celebrate Adolf Hitler's new appointment as Chancellor of Germany. The rest of the family seeks sanctuary in Elisabeth's bedroom. Hartwig and Henning are drinking and singing victory songs loud enough for the neighbors to hear, but no one complains. Elisabeth reads to Friedrich while their mother sits at the desk writing a letter. It is easy to ignore the frivolity– they've had much practice throughout the years.

In early February, Hartwig gathers his family into the dining room. Adolf Hitler gives his first address to the German people. Germany's new leader makes promises of a bright future for the German people. Elisabeth listens intently to his words as they stream loudly from the small radio next to her father. Hartwig and Henning are so proud of their beloved Adolf. Elisabeth stares at the smoldering cigarette in the ash tray. Her father pushes the ashes around with his cigarette before lifting it to his beer-soaked lips.

Adolf Hitler finally ends his speech. It is clear, from the sound of the enormous crowd in the background, that everyone is a Nazi now. Elisabeth wonders if Dieter, Adam, and Hannah are listening to their radios too.

In late February, the Reichstag building in Berlin is set on fire. A Communist party member is reported to have been found at the scene and arrested, along with other members of the party. Adolf Hitler and the Nazis appear enraged by the supposed hate crime, but some people question their involvement. Elisabeth reads the newspaper, unmoved by the fighting between the Nazis and Communists. This is nothing new to the Germans.

The following day, Elisabeth and Friedrich visit Hannah. As they stroll past the butcher shop Dieter calls out to her. She turns back to see him jogging towards her.

"Did you hear what Adolf Hitler has done now?"

Elisabeth has never seen Dieter so angry.

"No." She stares at up at him.

"He's taken away our rights!"

"What are you talking about?"

"The Reichstag Fire Decree, Hermann Goering said the laws have been put in place just for the Communists, but it clearly states that even the right to an opinion has been abolished. Anyone who speaks out against the Nazis, even the press, will be jailed."

Elisabeth's body stiffens as she continues listening to the list of new laws created by the Nazis.

"They can read our mail and search our homes. There is nothing that we can do about it! They have stripped us of our constitutional rights! Can you believe this, Elisabeth? We no longer have a democracy! Adolf Hitler and his Nazis can do whatever they want to us now, we're no longer protected!" Dieter stops for a moment to catch his breath. "The people of Germany that support Hitler don't understand what it means to live under the rule of a dictator. They don't understand the importance of a democracy. Now, one man has the power to do whatever he wants, take whatever he wants, and destroy whatever he wants. The voice of the German people has been silenced."

The door to the shop opens, and Dieter's boss orders him back inside.

"What time do you get off of work?" Elisabeth said. "I'll be waiting in the back for you."

Elisabeth walks quickly to Hannah's flat. Friedrich struggles to keep her pace, so she carries him the rest of the way.

Hannah answers the door and smiles down at Friedrich before flashing Elisabeth a serious glance.

"So, you heard?"

"Yeah, it was in the newspaper." Hannah leads them to her bedroom where Leon's toys are already scattered on the rug.

Friedrich runs over to the toys and sits down. Elisabeth sits down on the floor next to Hannah and numbly watches Friedrich play.

"I bet they set the whole thing up."

"The fire?" Elisabeth said.

"Yeah, I don't trust them."

Later that afternoon, Hannah and Elisabeth walk with Adam to the butcher shop to meet Dieter. He's waiting for them outside when they arrive. They walk in silence. Elisabeth walks in step with Dieter as Hannah and Adam follow close behind.

Dieter's mother is sleeping in her bedroom when they arrive. Dieter checks on her before quietly closing her door.

"We have to be quiet. I don't want my mother to know that you're here or what we're talking about. It will only worry her."

Elisabeth prepares tea as they quietly discuss the possibility of an uprising.

Adam, as usual, is the voice of reason to the angry passion that fills the room. "We must remain calm. Anger will cloud our judgment, and we need to be clear and concise in our planning. I'm sure there are others like us, other Jews, Communists, just to name a few, but they won't be easy to find.

"Actually, I know Jews who support Adolf Hitler," Hannah said. "So, we really need to be careful. The enemy is all around us."

"You know Jews who support Adolf Hitler? He's made it clear that he hates the Jews. How stupid can you be?" Dieter shakes his head.

"I guess they've fallen under his spell," Hannah said.

"My father says that Hitler has charisma. I don't see it," Elisabeth said.

"People are going to feel compelled to stand up. They will also be fearful of what will happen if they do," Adam continues. "The police are lawless now. They don't need a reason to arrest you, and there are no laws protecting you while you're in their custody."

"I can't believe that President Hindenburg is allowing this," Hannah said.

"Elisabeth, it would be a good idea to keep a close eye on your father and brother. Maybe it will help to keep us a couple of steps ahead. They are members of the Nazi party and friends with Adolf Hitler. I'm sure that they know more than the rest of us," Adam begins. "At the very least, it will allow us to avoid places that they will be, and maybe give us information to help us rise up against them. Hartwig drinks a lot, and when he's drinking you said that all he talks about are the Nazis and their plans to save Germany. That information can be helpful to us."

"Alright, I'll start paying attention to what he says." Elisabeth sighs angrily.

"You have to be discreet, Elisabeth. If Hartwig suspects that you're spying on him the consequences could be grave," Dieter warns.

It's a sober warning they all know to be true.

In the following days, Elisabeth listens to every word that Hartwig Ehrler has to say. She listens to his fascination with all things Hitler, and his hatred of the Jews. Hartwig has never made it a secret that he hates Jews, but now he speaks wildly about what Germany needs to do with them.

One morning, at breakfast, Elisabeth finally receives some information that they can use.

"This is not their homeland. It belongs to the German people. This is our Fatherland. They need to go back to where they came from." Hartwig speaks to Henning, seated across the table. "And, they will."

Elisabeth acts as aloof about their Nazi ideas as she usually does, but fear swells in her stomach.

Hartwig continues to talk as if Elisabeth isn't there, but she hears every word. She is now certain of what the Nazis are planning to do with their power, and she has little faith that anyone can stop them.

Later that afternoon, Elisabeth calls a meeting at Dieter's flat.

Dieter's mother is sleeping in her bedroom as they sit down at the table. Hannah quietly pours the tea.

Elisabeth waits until Hannah is seated before she begins to speak.

"They're going after the Jews. My father said that the Jews have to go home. They are forcing them out of Germany by whatever means necessary."

"Home? This is my home. I was born here. My parents and grandparents were born here. How is this not my home?" Hannah said.

"How do they plan on accomplishing this? Will we be arrested like the Communists?" Adam's voice is barely a whisper, but his fear is audible.

"I don't think so. I know that everyone is supposed to start boycotting Jewish shops. My father said that they're going to start separating the Aryans from the Jews. I don't know how yet. He didn't say, but I think the boycott is happening very soon. Another thing...one of his Nazi friends brought over some paint last night. Hartwig has never done any work around our flat and I doubt that he would bother, so I'm still not sure what that's all about. Have any of you heard anything?"

"No one's talking," Dieter said. "People are too afraid."

Elisabeth and Dieter watch Hannah and Adam. Hannah is angry, and Adam looks terrified. The room remains silent until they hear Dieter's mother stir in the next room. Elisabeth, Hannah, and Adam quickly slip on their coats and head outside.

Dieter grabs Elisabeth's arm, pulls her back, and whispers in her ear. "We will start meeting once a week in a new place. I'll give you further instructions later. Tell them."

Elisabeth waits until they are in the stairway, out of view, before whispering Dieter's message. Hannah and Adam nod in agreement before silently making their way home in separate directions.

A week later, they find out why Hartwig was in possession of the paint. Large Stars of David are painted on all Jewish businesses. Signs that read *Abstain from all Jewish shops-buy only at German* are posted everywhere.

Dieter finds a discreet new meeting place. He is very close to his uncle, and he confides in him about their secret meetings. Klaus Schweiger despises the Nazis and volunteers his flat. He also promises not to tell Dieter's mother.

Adam and Hannah meet on the corner near the shop where Adam works. It's a warm Saturday afternoon as the sun shines bright in a cloudless sky. Elisabeth jogs towards them, her blond braids bouncing against her shoulders.

"Sorry, my mother hasn't been feeling well. I had to help her with Friedrich before I left."

They climb the stairs to Dieter's uncle's flat. The wood creaks softly with each step, no matter how hard they try to be quiet. The building is old, and the faded white paint on the walls has dulled over time. It's a stark contrast to the dark wooden staircase. Elisabeth glides her hand along the wooden banister as she follows the stairs up to the third floor.

They're all waiting to hear what Elisabeth has learned from Hartwig and Henning after their trip to Berlin. They were supposed to meet two days ago, but her father and brother drank too much and ended up returning home later than expected.

Elisabeth sits down at the table and waits for Hannah to finish pouring the tea.

Elisabeth lightly rubs the handle of the blue floral teacup sitting perfectly on its matching saucer.

"They're going to make it a law that Germans are not allowed to have relations with Jews. Hartwig threatened that those that disobey will be sent to a labor camp that they're building in Dachau."

"How bad is this going to get before someone puts a stop to this insanity?" Hannah said.

"I've been reading Hitler's book." Dieter opens it on the table in front of them.

"Why?" Elisabeth said.

"He believes that it is the work of the Lord to fight the Jews," Dieter begins. "He also believes that the Jews are actually the devil in human form. He also believes in the purity of blood. That's probably why he is outlawing relations with Jews."

"When are people going to stop hurting each other in God's name? Can't they see that it's wrong?" Adam sits back in his chair.

"They see what they want to see," Hannah said. "The bible, and even God, can be used as a weapon. People have been doing it since the beginning of time."

"I don't think it's that simple. If this is what you're taught, then this is all that you know," Dieter said.

"What about your own conscience? Hurting others is wrong, no matter what your reason," Elisabeth said.

"I'm just trying to understand all of this," Dieter said.

"By reading his book?" Elisabeth shakes her head. "Adolf Hitler is a hateful human being."

"It gives a lot of insight into to his beliefs. We need to be armed with all that we can if we are going to fight the Nazis."

On May 10, 1933, university students all over Germany burn books they deem un-German. Joseph Goebbels addresses the crowd in Berlin. Thousands of un-German books are burned in the fires, including the works of German poet Heinrich Heine who wrote

"Where they burn books, they will ultimately also burn people." The list of un-German authors ranges from Nobel Prize winning author Thomas Mann to American authors Ernest Hemmingway and Helen Keller.

June ushers in blue skies and the warm summer sun. Elisabeth and Friedrich spend the afternoon swimming. Friedrich's wet hair is matted against his head as they stroll down the cobblestone roads towards home. Vegetable gardens are just beginning to show life and flowers are overflowing from the window boxes.

As soon as they reach the flat, Friedrich races up the stairs.

Elisabeth opens the door to find Dieter's uncle sitting at the table with her mother. An uneasy feeling settles in her stomach. She fears that he told her mother about their secret meetings. Erna Ehrler doesn't subscribe to the Nazi ideology, but planning to rise up against them would not be tolerated either. She may even alert Hartwig to their plans.

"Friedrich, go put on dry clothes. I need to speak with your sister." Elisabeth's mother waits for Friedrich to leave the room. "Please sit down, Elisabeth. We have some bad news."

"Dieter's mother passed away this morning," Dieter's uncle said. Tears fill his red puffy eyes.

"Where's Dieter?" Elisabeth said.

"He's at home. I think we should leave him alone, Elisabeth," Herr Schweiger said.

"Well, I disagree. He shouldn't be alone right now."

"Elisabeth, mind your manners," Erna scolds her daughter.

"Maybe she's right," he sighs. "I must go and finish making arrangements. Thank you, Elisabeth." He pats her shoulder before straightening his suit to leave.

Elisabeth walks quickly to Dieter's flat. She pushes open the heavy wooden door and makes her way up the stairs. She knocks softly and waits. No one answers. She knocks again, a bit louder. Elisabeth listens to hear if someone is inside, but it's quiet. She slowly turns the door knob to see if it's locked. The door opens easily as she steps inside.

Dieter is sitting at the table with his head in his hands, a cigarette burns in the ashtray in front of him. He seems unaware of her presence. She walks over to the table and sits down in the chair next to him.

"We don't have to talk, but I'm going to stay with you," Elisabeth said.

The room remains silent. Dieter doesn't lift his head to acknowledge her. The cigarette burns down to ashes.

Elisabeth remains with him until late in the evening. She doesn't care about her father's rule to be home before dark. She doesn't care about anything, but the pain that Dieter is feeling.

Before she leaves, Elisabeth turns down the bed and leads Dieter to his room. He looks exhausted as he sits down on the edge of the bed. He removes his shoes, but doesn't bother to change into his night clothes. He rests his head on the pillow and closes his eyes. Elisabeth turns out the light.

"I'll be back in the morning."

Elisabeth is relieved to find that her father isn't home. She changes into her nightgown and climbs into bed next to Friedrich. She can feel Friedrich's warm breath on her shoulder as he snores softly. It isn't long before she drifts off to sleep.

The following morning, Elisabeth wakes early and quickly finishes her chores before walking to Dieter's flat. He is still asleep when she arrives, so she cleans as much as she can, being careful not to wake him.

When Dieter finally wakes, he walks sleepily to the kitchen and sits down.

"Are you hungry?"

"No."

"Can you try to eat a slice of bread with jam?"

Elisabeth prepares Dieter's bread and tea as he stares out the window. His blond hair is scruffy, his blue eyes empty. Elisabeth watches him sip his tea.

"Not that I'm complaining, but you should get cleaned up just in case you have visitors."

"I don't want to see anyone."

"Okay, but I still think you would feel better after a bath."

Dieter doesn't reply.

"I'll draw your bath."

Dieter finishes his breakfast, walks silently to the bathroom, and closes the door.

Elisabeth finishes tidying the flat before sitting down at the table with a cup of tea.

Moments later, there's a knock at the door. Dieter's Uncle Klaus stands in the doorway looking just as bereft as he had the day before.

"How is he doing?"

Elisabeth just shakes her head. "He said that he doesn't want to see anyone, but I don't think he means you."

Elisabeth pours him a cup of tea.

"He probably does, but I'll only stay a minute."

"Please stay long enough to finish your tea. He's in the bath. He should be out shortly. How are the arrangements going?"

"Everything is done. Now we grieve."

Dieter greets his uncle before sitting down at the table across from him. Elisabeth disappears into the kitchen to peel potatoes.

Elisabeth serves soup and bread in the afternoon. They eat in silence.

Elisabeth spends the rest of the summer at Dieter's flat, from dawn until dusk every day. Dieter only missed a couple of days of work, and every day when he returns home Elisabeth is there to greet him.

One evening, as Elisabeth clears the table, she can feel Dieter's eyes upon her. She smiles down at him and tousles his hair as she brushes past him to the kitchen. She sets the dishes in the sink, and sensing that something is wrong, turns back to him. He drops his head into his hands as tears stream down his face. She puts her arms around him and holds him while he weeps. Silent tears fall from her eyes.

In September, the green leaves on the trees change to warm shades of gold, orange, and brown. It has been a long summer, and Elisabeth is enjoying the cooler air of autumn. She still spends much of her time at Dieter's flat, and they are growing closer. Friedrich is Elisabeth's constant companion as well. He relishes his time with Dieter. Adam and Hannah now visit her at Dieter's flat, and life seems to be returning to normal.

Dieter has toys for Friedrich at his house, and Hannah brought some of Leon's old toys for Friedrich to play with as well. Elisabeth and Friedrich are eating better now that they're with Dieter, and Friedrich is looking much healthier.

Hartwig bought a bed from a friend, but Friedrich refuses to sleep in it. He waits at night until it's safe to climb into Elisabeth's bed. He tiptoes over to his sister waiting with the blanket lifted for him to climb inside.

By October, the air is growing colder. Elisabeth is working on a sweater for Friedrich because he's quickly growing out of his clothes. Dieter is working longer hours, so Elisabeth and Friedrich spend less time at his flat and more time at home. Hartwig and Henning are either working, or at the beer hall most days, so the Ehrler home is quiet much of the time.

One evening, Henning arrives home unusually early. He isn't drunk, but he isn't sober either.

Henning sits down at the table and lights a cigarette. Elisabeth sits quietly reading. Henning watches her intently as the smoke billows from his lips. Elisabeth can feel his eyes upon her, but she pretends not to notice as she turns the page of her book.

"I hear that you've moved in with Dieter."

"Leave her alone, Henning." Erna steps out from the kitchen.

"So, are you a whore now?"

"Henning, I will not allow that kind of language in this house. He needed a friend, and your sister was there for him."

"I bet she was. Aren't you embarrassed that everyone knows that your daughter is a whore?"

Erna Ehrler slaps Henning so quickly that it takes him a second to process what has happened.

Henning's shock quickly turns to rage as he grabs his mother's arms and pulls her to him. "Don't ever do that again."

Friedrich screams and Elisabeth rushes him to their bedroom. She knows that Henning isn't done with her yet.

Before Elisabeth can return to the living room, she sees Henning rushing towards her. She has already closed the door to the bedroom, and she is just outside when Henning grabs her by the hair and drags her to the living room. She doesn't make a sound for fear that Friedrich will hear. Henning pulls harder on her braid as he continues to question her about Dieter. Their mother hits Henning with her fists in an effort to force him to let go of Elisabeth. Henning swiftly pulls back and slaps his mother violently with the back of his hand, knocking her to the floor. As she lies on the floor, she pleads with Henning to unhand Elisabeth.

"Do you have any idea how your actions affect this family?" Henning jerks Elisabeth's head back by her hair and glares down at her.

"I've done nothing wrong, Henning, please!"

"Stay away from him, Elisabeth! If I hear that you've disobeyed me I will beat you and him!"

With that, he throws Elisabeth to the floor, next to her mother. He walks back to the table to finish his dinner.

Elisabeth helps her mother up and retrieves a cold rag from the bathroom for her swollen face. They both hurry to Elisabeth's bedroom to console Friedrich. They find him hiding under the blankets on Elisabeth's bed. After much coaxing, he finally emerges from his hiding place. Elisabeth holds him in her arms as tears stream down her cheeks. Erna has her arms around both of them.

Later that evening, Henning knocks softly on their bedroom door. "Can I come in?"

Friedrich hurries back under the blankets. Henning opens the door and stands in the doorway.

Elisabeth stares numbly at the floor beneath her feet.

"I'm sorry. I shouldn't have called you that, Elisabeth. Olga told me that people are starting to talk about the two of you. All I can think about is our father finding out and what he would do to you. You have to stay away from Dieter. Don't you understand that?"

"Yes, I understand."

Friedrich peers out from the blankets. Henning plays with him for a while before tucking him into bed.

That night, Elisabeth looks up at the stars from her window. The crescent moon dimly lights the night sky.

Elisabeth's thoughts are interrupted by Hartwig staggering home from the beer hall.

Elisabeth lets the lace curtain slip from her hand. She climbs into bed next to Friedrich and pulls the blanket to her chest. Henning's fear was concealed by his anger. She can see that now. If the rumors had reached their father's ears–she shudders at the thought. Henning was right; she must keep her distance from Dieter.

Elisabeth is now keenly aware that Olga is watching her, and no one keeps a closer eye on you than your enemy.

5

Adam

Adam places two steaming cups of tea on the lace covered table. Frau Lenger stirs in a teaspoon of sugar before carefully lifting it to her thin lips.

"My grandmother warned me, when I was a girl, to never get old." Frau Lenger carefully sets her cup down with shaky hands.

She folds her hands in her lap and stares out the window. The winter sky is indigo blue in the early evening light, but Frau Lenger is too lost in her own thoughts to notice.

"I can't remember a time that I wasn't in bed before 9 o'clock. When you work in a shop you must always keep early hours, as you know. It never bothered me. Morning is my favorite time of day. It's peaceful to be awake while the rest of the world is sleeping. Every morning begins a new day, full of promise and hope. Nothing is behind you. Everything is ahead of you...unlike old age." Frau Lenger presses her fingers down to smooth the lace tablecloth. "Are you still having your meetings?"

"No, nothing has been the same since Frau Kiesling's death. Dieter doesn't really socialize with anyone, and Elisabeth has been banned from seeing him."

"Who banned her from seeing him?"

"Her brother says that it's not appropriate for a girl to be alone with a man in his flat. He said that Elisabeth is giving their family a bad reputation, but she and Dieter are just friends."

"How old is Dieter?"

"He's only a couple of years older than Elisabeth."

"Well, maybe her brother is right. You know how people talk."

Frau Lenger clears the table before switching on the lamp in the sitting room. Adam volunteers to clean the tea cups, but she doesn't allow it.

"You work hard enough. I will take care of that."

Adam slips on his coat and turns to leave. Frau Lenger gently pats him on the back and opens the door for him.

"I'll see you in the morning, Adam."

Adam arrives home just before dark. His mother is busy in the kitchen. The scent of cabbage soup fills the air.

Adam takes a deep breath as he slips off his coat.

"Your uncle is here. Dinner will be ready soon."

Adam follows the voices to the living room.

"What are you doing here?" Adam hugs his aunt and uncle.

His uncle sighs and shakes his head in frustration.

"They're going to be staying with us for a while," Ivan said.

"Why? Why aren't you staying at the farm?"

"Jews are no longer allowed to own land." Nysen Herschel reclines back in his chair. "I did all that I could to stop them, but in the end there was nothing that I could do."

"Dinner is ready," Adam's mother calls from the kitchen.

"They can't just steal your land," Adam said.

"They can do whatever they want. We are powerless to stop them. They've waged war against us. They're going to steal everything and leave us destitute."

"Alright, that's enough." Ivan stands up. "Let's eat."

Spoons clank softly against bowls of watery cabbage soup.

"Dieter read Adolf Hitler's book *Mein Kampf*. Adolf Hitler believes that we are the devil in human form. He believes that we have evil plans to destroy all that is good in the world," Adam said.

"Us?" Uncle Nysen looks up from his soup.

"The Jews."

"Adam, that's enough," Else said.

Adam stares down at his bowl. Silence fills the room for a moment before everyone returns to their steaming bowls of soup.

That evening, Adam sleeps on the floor in the living room, allowing his aunt and uncle to share his bed. The floor is cold as he curls up inside his blanket. His stomach growls as he listens to his uncle snoring in the next room.

The following morning, the smell of yeast fills the air as Adam walks past the bakery to the shop. Frau Lenger is busy at her sewing machine when he arrives.

"We have a busy morning, Adam."

Later that afternoon, Adam finishes the last of his work and sweeps the floor of stray threads and fabric.

"You look tired," Frau Lenger said.

"My uncle is staying with us for awhile. He snores."

"Is he visiting?"

"He and his wife are staying with us until they have the documentation that they need to travel to America."

"That could take a long time," Frau Lenger said.

"The government stole their farm. It has been in our family for generations."

"Oh yes, the new laws, Jews cannot own land." Frau Lenger shakes her head. "Do they have any children?"

"They have a son. He lives in Berlin."

"Is he going to America with them?"

"No, his wife won't leave Germany."

"Well, I agree with your uncle. Germany is no place for a Jew." Frau Lenger pauses for a moment. "Adam, my husband was a member of the Nazi party, but I did not share his opinions. I am disgusted at what our government is doing and the people going along with it."

"I wish my parents would leave, but they won't. My uncle has tried to convince my father for months, but he refuses."

"They are doing what they believe is right. It's not easy leaving your home to start over in another country."

Adam arrives home early to find his uncle and father sitting at the table sifting through paperwork.

"We're having roast chicken with vegetables this evening. Your uncle bought it," Ivan said.

"If I had known how you were living I would have helped more," Uncle Nysen said.

"We're alright," Ivan reassures his brother.

"Why don't you come with us? It's only going to get worse here."

"We're not leaving our home. We can't afford it anyway."

"I will help you."

"You can't help. It's taking everything that you have to travel to America."

"What if I can help you once I get there? Would you leave?"

Ivan sits back in his chair. "Let's take it a step at a time."

The following week, Frau Lenger's sister arrives for a visit, and Adam spends much of his time with them. Klara prepares dinner for Frau Lenger every afternoon. However, her sister continues to eat very little.

"She doesn't eat much," Adam admits to Klara. Frau Lenger had disappeared into the kitchen.

"Her husband had other women," Klara whispers. "He told her that she wasn't thin enough, she didn't smile enough, she was boring, and many other unkind things. He even told her that she didn't take the time, like other women, to look pretty for him. He constantly reminded her that she wasn't good enough, and she believed every word. He treated my sister terribly." Klara shakes her head. "Not like my husband is much better."

"Why don't you leave? You could come here and live with your sister?"

"Oh no, I couldn't do that. I made my bed, now I must lie in it."

Adam finishes his tea before placing his cup and saucer on the counter.

"I'm meeting Elisabeth at Hannah's house tomorrow, and I've still got chores to do at home."

"Enjoy your day off, Adam," Frau Lenger calls out from the kitchen.

The following afternoon, Adam moves carefully through the fog enveloping the city. In the distance, he hears police sirens, so he quickens his pace.

Adam arrives at Hannah's flat and knocks softly on the heavy wooden door. Hannah opens the door and motions for him to come inside.

Dieter is sitting in the living room with Hannah's brother, Leon.

"What are you doing here?"

"I can go anywhere in this fog," Dieter said.

There's a knock at the door as Adam sits down.

Hannah opens the door to Elisabeth and ushers her inside.

"What are you doing here?" Elisabeth smiles at Dieter.

"Hannah came over this morning and advised that we're having a meeting."

"We haven't had a meeting in a long time, and I thought it was time that we did," Hannah said.

Hannah stands near the window and peers out. "I thought with the fog it was our only chance."

Hannah carries in a tray of hot tea as Dieter lights the fire.

"I've always loved your mother's tea set." Elisabeth carefully hands everyone their cup and saucer.

"My aunt sent it to her from America."

"My uncle is moving to America. He says the streets are paved with gold," Adam said.

"My father said that too. I'm going to live there someday. I just have a feeling." Hannah opens a tin of cookies and places them in the middle of the coffee table.

"Maybe you'll be a movie star." Elisabeth carefully chooses a cookie from the tin. "Just like Marlene Dietrich."

"You should go to University. Your parents can afford it," Adam said.

Hannah rolls her eyes. "My father has only one aspiration for me and that is to be married. Women belong in the home, raising children and taking care of their husbands."

"That's right," Dieter laughs.

"You're hilarious, Dieter." Hannah pretends to laugh hysterically.

Later that evening, Adam walks home with Dieter.

They are a block away from Adam's building when Adam stops and turns to Dieter.

"I see what's going on with you and Elisabeth, the way that you look at her, the way that she looks at you. You're both nervous, almost formal, around each other. I hate to say this, but you're only going to hurt her and yourself. You know how her family is, and unless you can protect her twenty four hours a day you're putting her at risk."

Dieter is silent.

Adam's heart races, he's beginning to regret his words. He has never been this frank with Dieter.

"I love her," Dieter said.

Adam takes a deep breath. "I know."

They walk in silence until they arrive at Adam's flat.

"You're right. I can't take any more chances. I need to let her go." Dieter turns to leave.

"Dieter, there's one more thing. Watch out for Olga."

"Olga?"

"I heard her talking to her friends a couple of months ago. They were in our shop. She didn't know that I was in the back. She fancies you. She's the one that told Henning about you and Elisabeth."

Adam steps inside his flat, closing the door behind him.

That evening, Adam thinks about Dieter and Elisabeth as he makes his bed on the floor. His thoughts are interrupted by his uncle's snoring. Adam pulls the blanket over his head, and slowly drifts off to sleep.

Days later, Adam sees Elisabeth walking with Friedrich. He calls out to them as he runs to catch up.

"We need to talk," Adam said.

"What is it?"

"Can you meet me at Hannah's this afternoon?"

"Okay, let me drop Friedrich at home. Is everything alright?"

"Yeah, don't worry. I'll meet you there."

That afternoon, Adam is relieved that Elisabeth hasn't arrived yet.

Adam quickly tells Hannah about his conversation with Dieter and what he had overheard Olga telling her friends.

Hannah ponders the situation for a moment before she speaks. "You're right, we need to warn her. Olga is at Elisabeth's flat every day. Elisabeth and her family believe that Olga wants to marry her brother. How could Olga even think about marrying Henning when Dieter is the one that she really wants? She's probably been keeping a close eye on Elisabeth this whole time just to ensure that she stays away from Dieter," Hannah said.

"That's a scary thought."

"Here's another scary thought... Olga knows that Elisabeth is friends with us and if Hartwig finds out..." Hannah's face flushes with worry. "Herr Ehrler would kill Elisabeth for befriending Jews."

"So far, Henning hasn't said anything, and I know that he knows about us," Adam said.

"Henning doesn't care about us. Olga does. She will do anything to hurt Elisabeth if she gets angry. Elisabeth has to stay away from Dieter."

"Your mother let me in." Elisabeth stands in the doorway.

Adam and Hannah look up.

"How much did you hear?" Hannah said.

"I heard enough."

"I'll get some tea. Sit down," Hannah said.

"Are you alright?" Adam said.

"Yes."

Adam and Elisabeth sit in silence until Hannah returns with the tea.

"What's going on with you and Dieter?" Hannah said.

"I don't really know, but everything has changed between us. Now, when I'm in the same room with him I feel nervous, and I think about him all the time."

Hannah reclines back in her chair. "Olga is out to get you. You need to keep an eye on her. As I'm sure she's keeping an eye on you."

"I would tell Henning, but he wouldn't believe me," Elisabeth said.

Adam rubs his forehead. "So, you have two choices: Tell Henning and deal with Olga's wrath, or let him marry a woman who doesn't love him."

"Well, when you put it that way, I have no choice. I can't let him marry Olga, even if I have to sacrifice myself to save him."

"Yes, but there's a good chance that you're going to sacrifice yourself for someone who won't believe you anyway," Hannah said.

"I know. I wish Dieter was here. He would know what do. Dieter knows Henning better than anyone," Elisabeth said.

"What are you going to do about Dieter?" Hannah said.

"Does he know about all of this?" Elisabeth said.

"Yeah, he knows," Adam said.

"What did he say?"

"He said that he is going to stay away from you. He doesn't want to put you in harm's way when he can't protect you. He knows how your family is, Elisabeth." Adam pauses for a moment. "He also said that he loves you."

Tears fill Elisabeth's eyes.

"I'm sorry, Elisabeth," Adam said.

"Me, too," Hannah said.

Adam walks Elisabeth half way home. They say their goodbyes, and Elisabeth heads in the direction of her building. Her face is serious as the cold wind tousles the strands of hair that have escaped her braids. She walks tall, but Adam knows that she has the weight of the world on her shoulders.

Adam is lost in his thoughts when he hears footsteps behind him. He turns to see Dieter jogging to catch up to him.

"You just missed Elisabeth. She's going to tell Henning about Olga."

"You have to stop her from telling Henning. He won't believe her, and he'll tell Olga. In the end, they will both be against her," Dieter said.

"I can't just go over there! Herr Ehrler might be there!"

"Just let me think for minute," Dieter said.

They sidestep down a narrow street where they can't be seen.

"This time of day it's unlikely that Herr Ehrler or Henning will be home. They're probably at the beer hall already. You can listen by Elisabeth's door before you knock."

"I'm not going there!"

"You're the only one that can save her right now, so yes, you are going there."

Adam takes a deep breath.

Adam and Dieter make their way towards Elisabeth's flat. Dieter waits a few buildings away to ensure that he isn't seen.

Adam cautiously approaches Elisabeth's building. He can see the light in the living room as he moves closer. He opens the heavy door. The wooden steps creak as he ascends the staircase to her flat.

Adam reaches the landing and presses his ear against the door. He listens for a few minutes. The only sound to be heard is Friedrich playing.

Adam's hands are sweating as he knocks softly.

Slowly, the door creaks open. Elisabeth stands before him.

"Dieter said not to tell Henning. He won't believe you," Adam whispers.

Elisabeth nods before quietly closing the door.

When Adam returns home, his mother is preparing dinner.

"Chicken soup?"

"Yes," she smiles. "It will be ready in a little while. You should try to study while it's quiet."

Adam steps into his bedroom. His aunt and uncle's trunks are sitting next to the bed.

Adam walks back to the kitchen.

"Where is uncle Nysen going?"

"They are going to Berlin, and then they are going to America." Adam's mother drops potatoes into a pot of water.

"How did it happen so quickly?"

"I'm not sure, but you know your uncle. He has ways of getting what he wants most of the time."

"Why don't we go with them to America?"

"Germany is our home."

That evening, everyone sits down at the table for their last dinner together. There is plenty of food for everyone and baked apples for dessert. Everyone is in high spirits for the first time in a long time.

In the morning, Adam and his parents walk his aunt and uncle to the train station. The sky is overcast as rain drizzles from the sky.

Adam's aunt and uncle wave as the train pulls out of the station. Adam watches the train heading down the track, slowly gaining momentum. Suddenly, the rain begins to pour down. The Herschel family doesn't run for cover like everyone else. They stand in the rain watching the train disappear down the track.

6

Hannah

Hannah sips her tea while her father reads his newspaper. Rain tumbles down the green leaves of the oak tree outside.

"I've made a decision regarding your husband." Hannah's father folds his newspaper. "Things are changing in Germany. I think you already know this."

"Josef, let her finish her breakfast. We'll talk about this later," Lena said.

"Adolf Hitler is now the most powerful man in Germany," Josef continues. "He's made his hatred of the Jews undeniable, and it seems our fellow Germans feel the same. I fear we are in danger."

An uneasy feeling swirls in Hannah's stomach.

"Otto Kirchner has agreed to marry you. I know that he will take care of you and protect you."

Hannah stares down at her steaming cup of tea.

"I know this is difficult, Hannah, but the situation is dire. We are hated by many. Our government has stripped us of our rights, and the police are hunting us in the streets. You need to think of your future. If he should decide, Otto has the finances to flee Germany. He also has more connections than anyone I know, so that is power too. Otto can keep you safe, whereas, I don't know if I can anymore."

Hannah stares out the window as her father gathers his newspaper. Josef withdraws to his den, not to be heard from again until the next day.

A week later, the Kirchners are invited for dinner. Otto, his parents, his older brother and his wife, will all be there to celebrate the engagement. It is the merging of two families. Even Hannah's older sister, Irma, and her family, will attend the celebratory dinner.

Hannah's mother cooks all afternoon while Hannah cleans every inch of the flat to ensure it is spotless when their guests arrive.

"You will learn to love him. You've been friends with Otto for many years. That's a strong foundation, Hannah." Lena peels potatoes.

Hannah nods and walks numbly to her room. She wants to cry, but no tears come.

Later that evening, the two families converge for their special dinner. Hannah helps her mother place steaming dishes of food in the center of the table.

Hannah glances across the table to Otto. He kindly, but it looks more like pity.

That evening, as everyone gathers to leave, Otto brushes past Hannah. He discretely slips a note into her hand. Hannah conceals the note as she says her goodbyes. Otto gives her one last glance before walking outside behind his parents. Hannah closes the door behind them and walks solemnly to her bedroom. She slips the note under her pillow before joining her mother in the kitchen to finish cleaning the dishes.

Later that evening, Hannah falls into bed and tucks herself under the blankets. Suddenly, she remembers the note. She reaches under her pillow and unfolds the paper. Otto's handwriting isn't easy to read, but she is able to decipher it.

I know this isn't easy for you. I just wanted you to know that when we are married nothing between us has to change. I know that, to you, I am just a friend, and that's the way it will remain for as long as you wish. I hope you understand what I am saying to you. Please know that the decision for us to marry was made with your best interest at heart.

Otto

Hannah feels the sun on her face as she slowly wakes from a deep sleep. She glances around her bedroom and is quickly reminded that today she will be married. Warm air breezes through her window as she sits up in bed. It's not easy to set a wedding date in the springtime when you're Jewish, but the date had been set, and the day had arrived. Otto's mother had insisted that it fall on a Tuesday, and Hannah didn't care enough to mind.

Hannah numbly makes her way to the living room and stands at the window. She peers out to the people below strolling down the sidewalks. She's grateful that she is required to fast before the wedding. Her stomach is upset, and she can only hope that she will be able to hold down food after the ceremony.

Hours later, Elisabeth stands in Hannah's bedroom doorway.

"Can I come in?"

"Sure."

"Are you alright?"

"I wish we could run away to our secret place, just you, me and Adam."

"I know. It all seems to be happening so fast. Everything is changing. Remember our promise. We're going to stay together, no matter what happens."

"I remember. I have dinner obligations every day for the next week, so I probably won't see you. Oh, and I'll be living with my husband... so, there's that, but you're welcome at my house anytime." Hannah smiles, but it quickly fades.

"It's going to be alright, Hannah."

Hannah cordially greets her guests before taking her seat on the opposite side of the room from her future husband. Adam and his family are seated only a few rows away. Adam gives her a reassuring smile.

"Mazel Tov!" The crowd shouts in unison. The ceremony is finally over.

Hannah joins Otto in their private room.

"Are you alright?" Otto looks down at Hannah.

"Yeah."

"You look beautiful."

"Thanks."

"Hannah, I meant what I said in the note. You don't have to be afraid. I'm not going to hurt you, or force you to do anything that you don't want to do. This is our life. We both knew that one day we would be expected to marry the person of our parents' choosing." Otto smiles down at her. "Let's make the best of it."

Hannah takes a deep breath.

"You're right. Let's make the best of it."

Hannah and Otto are invited to a special dinner every night the following week by their closest friends and family, allowing Hannah little time to acclimate to her new surroundings.

Otto purchased a large flat near Hannah's parents' home so that she would be able to remain close to them. The furnishings are limited, and the walls are bare, but in time he knows that she will make it their home.

Every evening, when they return to their flat, Hannah discreetly disappears into the bathroom to change into her nightgown. At night, they stay up late talking.

Otto is an attorney and works long hours during the week, occasionally spilling into the weekends. Much of Hannah's time is spent alone. Otto buys her plenty of books. She spends some of her free time reading, but much of her time is spent decorating their flat.

Hannah received cookware, flatware, fabric, and many other household gifts from their friends and family, but her most cherished gift is from Elisabeth. Elisabeth had given her the quilt that she had made out of Hannah's dresses.

As spring turns to summer, Hannah works tirelessly in the garden. Adam and Elisabeth visit a couple of times a week, and they still enjoy picnics in their secret place. Life is returning to normal, a new normal, but they remain true to their promise to stay together.

One evening, when Otto returns home from work, he sits down at the table as Hannah finishes dinner.

"I like the flowers. Did you buy them from Frau Schleiker?" Otto said.

"Yes, they were freshly cut this morning."

"Enjoy the flowers now; autumn will be here soon." Otto takes a bite of his sandwich.

"It can't get here fast enough. I would love to feel some cooler air blowing through the windows."

"Well, it won't be long. Why don't you take a cool bath? I'll clean up the dishes tonight?"

"That's alright, when you get home from work I prefer that you rest."

"I don't mind helping you. I would help my mother with dishes when I was young."

"I'm surprised your mother let her little prince do housework."

"She wouldn't allow it as I got older, but when I was very young she was alright with it."

The following morning, Hannah prepares Otto's breakfast. The sun is streaming through the windows, and the air is already warm. Hannah wipes her brow with the back of her hand before sitting down at the table.

"What are your plans for today?" Otto slices a piece of bread.

"Well, I need to do a little shopping, and I might even buy a new dress," Hannah smiles.

"Don't spend too much money," Otto teases.

Hannah finishes the dishes and walks Otto to the door.

"I'll see you tonight." Otto closes the door behind him.

Hannah steps over to the window and watches him disappear down the street. She's reminded of her mother's words–*you will learn to love him.*

Later that morning, Hannah walks to the shops a few blocks from their flat. It will take most of the afternoon to choose the fabric and be fitted. She turns the corner onto the street of her tailor. A large yellow star is painted on the window. She tries to open the door, but it's locked. She peers inside. Bolts of fabric are strewn across the floor, and the cash register is open on the counter.

"He was arrested a couple of days ago." A passerby informs her before continuing down the street.

She turns to ask what happened, but the stranger has already disappeared.

Hannah walks a few blocks away to the shop of another tailor.

"Can I help you?"

"Yes, I am in need of a summer dress."

"Alright, if you follow me I will show you our fabrics."

The back room is filled with fabrics from the floor to the ceiling. Hannah is astonished and excited to be able to choose from such a vast array of fabrics and patterns.

"I'll be in the front with another customer. Just let me know when you are ready."

Hannah is so lost in all of the fabric that she doesn't hear the tailor return with another customer.

"Are you seeing anything that interests you?"

Hannah turns to face him. The customer next to him is eyeing her intently.

"It's such a large selection. I think that it might take a while."

The well-dressed woman eyes Hannah disapprovingly. She whispers something to the tailor before disappearing out of the room. The tailor hurries after her, leaving Hannah alone again.

The tailor returns, seconds later, with a look of disgust. "We don't sell to Jews!"

Hannah's cheeks burn as she hurries past the tailor. She can feel the eyes upon her as she makes her way to the door. She can still feel their glares as she walks past the store window.

She rushes past shops and businesses, careful to keep her distance from the Aryan Germans. She averts her eyes from the yellow stars painted on the Jewish businesses. She follows the streets back to her flat, closes the door, and locks it securely.

That evening, when Otto returns home, Hannah says nothing about what had happened to her.

"Did you buy a dress today?"

"No, I got busy and lost track of time."

Otto sits down at the table and sips his soup. Hannah quietly finishes her meal and disappears into the kitchen.

Later that night, as they lie awake in bed, Hannah is unusually quiet.

Otto lights the candle on the nightstand.

"Are you going to tell me what's bothering you?"

"I don't want to tell you. It's too embarrassing." She turns away.

"Hannah, you don't ever have to feel embarrassed. You can tell me anything."

Finally, Hannah tells Otto everything that had happened that afternoon.

"The woman looked at me with such disgust. I have never been so embarrassed."

"They are the ones that should be embarrassed. When did everyone become so full of hate?"

"I think it was always there. People just kept it hidden, but now hate is acceptable, and Adolf Hitler is their shining example."

"I've been thinking about leaving Germany," Otto said.

"Where would we go?"

"We could go anywhere. We could go to America. I have family there."

"What about my parents? I could never leave them, Otto."

"I know, but if it gets worse here we need to go. Your father and I have already discussed it. I can't deal with this hate anymore. I didn't want to tell you this, but my law firm may be closing. There is no judicial system anymore. The Nazis have filled the courts with their own judges. There are no laws governing this country anymore. I have people in my office everyday reporting torture and murder at the hands of the Gestapo, and I can't fight for them. People are dying, Hannah."

Hannah allows Otto to hold her until she falls asleep.

The following morning, Otto sits quietly at the table eating his bread and jam.

"Why didn't you wake me?"

"I wanted to let you sleep."

"I enjoy making your breakfast and spending time with you before you go off to work." Hannah sits down across from him.

"I like it too."

Later that morning, Elisabeth and Friedrich arrive for a visit.

"It's cooler today." Elisabeth sits down in the chair next to the window.

"I'm so happy to see you." Hannah smiles down at Friedrich.

Friedrich laughs excitedly and follows Hannah into the kitchen for a treat.

"I overheard Henning talking to my father about marrying Olga," Elisabeth said.

"She'll probably insist that they move next door to Dieter." Hannah laughs from the kitchen.

"I just wish that there was something that I could do to make Henning see what kind of a person she really is."

"Love is blind," Hannah said. "Have you seen Dieter?"

"No."

"Do you still think about him, or have you moved on?"

"I still think about him, but I try to push him from my mind."

"Has your father given up on finding a husband for you?"

"I doubt it. My father has been busy with his fellow Nazis. They've been basking in the glory of their plans finally coming into fruition. I'm sure he's still in search of the perfect Nazi to marry me."

September ushers in cooler temperatures, much to everyone's relief. Otto doesn't seem as stressed about work, and Hannah's transformation of the flat is finally complete.

One evening, as Hannah watches Otto at the table working, something in her stirs.

That night, when they slip into bed, Hannah moves closer to Otto. He gently pulls her to him and kisses her softly...

The following morning, Hannah fixes her hair into a neat braid and slips on a dress that she knows is Otto's favorite.

Otto finishes his breakfast before gathering his paperwork to leave. Hannah is clearing the dishes when he pulls her close and kisses her tenderly.

"I love you," Otto whispers softly.

"I love you, too." Hannah smiles up at him.

Hannah watches Otto disappear down the street and smiles.

In late October, the leaves crunch under Hannah's feet as she walks home from visiting her parents.

"Why are you home so early?" Hannah eyes Otto seated at the table.

"Hannah, please sit down." Otto pulls out her chair and takes a deep breath. "We're leaving Germany. I don't want to hear any arguments. The decision has been made."

"Where are we going?"

"My family in the States wrote that they still haven't recovered from the Wall Street crash, but I have family in Paris. I received a letter from them today. They have invited us to stay with them. They are well to do and have many friends. We will be safe there."

"When will we go?"

"Soon."

7

Elisabeth

Icy rain taps against Elisabeth's window as she snuggles under the blankets. Her mother is running water in the kitchen and Hartwig is snoring loudly. Friedrich yawns and stretches under his blanket.

"Do you like your new bed?" Elisabeth said.

"Yes." Friedrich pulls the covers up to his chest.

"Let's go stand by the oven." Elisabeth throws back her blanket and steps onto the cold floor.

Elisabeth sits down at the table as Friedrich stands next to the oven.

"I've got a surprise." Erna slips back into the kitchen and returns minutes later.

"Sausages!" Elisabeth said.

"There's also fresh bread with mustard."

Erna sets the plate down in front of Elisabeth.

"Happy Christmas," Erna said.

"This is the best Christmas we've ever had!" Friedrich climbs up on his chair.

"Don't tell your father. There's not enough for him," Erna whispers.

Elisabeth bites into the crusty bread and sausage. Hartwig sleeps off his hangover while his family is being treated to the best meal they've had in years. Elisabeth can't help but smile.

A week later, Elisabeth walks home from Hannah's with Friedrich. Her breath fogs the air as the snow falls silent from the sky. Friedrich holds out his tongue to catch the icy snowflakes as Elisabeth stares off into the distance. Dusk is quickly fading to darkness as they quicken their pace. Hartwig had been adamant that she be on time for the party.

Elisabeth opens the door to the flat. Olga is seated next to Henning in the living room.

"Hi Elisabeth, look what I brought." Olga stands up and walks excitedly towards her. "It takes pictures like a movie!"

Elisabeth studies the camera.

"Instead of taking still pictures, it records your every move, just like the cameras they use in Hollywood," Olga said.

Elisabeth glances over at the table to the other guests before slipping off Friedrich's coat.

"Elisabeth, this is Manfred Becker and his son Reinhard." Hartwig stands up. "This is my daughter, Elisabeth."

Elisabeth smiles kindly as she removes her coat.

"Elisabeth would you like a drink?" Olga offers.

"No, thanks." Elisabeth sits down in her mother's chair in the living room.

Reinhard is quick to sit down on the arm of the chair next to her. "Your father tells me that you're almost finished with school."

"Yes, it's fast approaching."

Reinhard spends the evening conversing with Elisabeth. She remains polite, but she has little interest in him. She isn't attracted to men that can't hold their liquor, and it's clear that Reinhard is getting drunker by the minute.

Hartwig and Reinhard's father sit at the table discussing the Nazis. They are proud of the changes already taking place in Germany. They also discuss the Nuremberg rally, which both had attended in September.

Hartwig even quotes some of Hitler's speech. Elisabeth is surprised that Hartwig can remember enough to quote anyone with his beer soaked brain, but he clearly respects and adores Adolf Hitler. It's obvious that he hangs on his beloved leader's every word.

It's also obvious that Hartwig has something to hide.

A few beers later, Elisabeth finds out by eavesdropping from the kitchen.

"Well, I know that there were at least a hundred unmarried girls that returned home pregnant," Manfred begins. "I'm sure there's many more that we don't even know about. I'm pleased that everyone is doing their part to build a bigger and better German population. We need to do this immediately."

"That's why I feel that it's time for Elisabeth to marry." Hartwig speaks in a hushed tone.

Elisabeth stands silent in the kitchen as her mind struggles to process what is happening. Finally, it all becomes clear. Reinhard Becker is here to court her for marriage. The thought horrifies her.

Elisabeth returns to the living room as she struggles to forget what she has just overheard.

Elisabeth returns to her seat, prompting Reinhard to continue his conversation about being a loyal Nazi. His confidence in Adolf Hitler is unwavering. He is certain that his leader will elevate the German people to greatness once again. Elisabeth pretends to listen, but she already knows enough about Reinhard Becker. She has no interest in learning more. Elisabeth also has perfect clarity when it comes to their beloved leader. Adolf Hitler may fool some, but he doesn't fool all.

Reinhard is short in stature and chubby. He has a moon face with squinty eyes and weirdly small feet. There is nothing attractive about him. More important, Elisabeth's instincts are alerting her that he's not good. Reinhard may seem nice, but she senses that underneath that smile lies something sinister.

Henning is recording everyone on the camera while Olga joins Elisabeth and Reinhard's conversation. If anyone can dominate a conversation, it's Olga. It seems Reinhard isn't the only one who is self-obsessed. It isn't long until Olga and Reinhard are talking over each other, both attempting to dominate the conversation with their thoughts and opinions, which no one is interested in anyway. Elisabeth wonders if Reinhard is actually the perfect man for Olga. They have a great deal in common, and they both seem to have a mutual admiration for the other. Henning is not impervious to their flirtation. He reminds Olga, a few times, that she needs to slow down on the wine. She ignores him and turns her attention back to Reinhard.

Henning keeps a close eye on Olga and Reinhard. The more they drink, the more they flirt with each other. No one else seems notice but Henning and Elisabeth.

At the end of the night, Elisabeth excuses herself and helps her mother in the kitchen. Her mother had spent the evening working tirelessly to keep the flat clean, the drinks flowing, and her impressionable youngest son as far away as possible, in his bedroom with the door closed.

It is bad enough that the Nazis control the schools and teach their brand of hate to each and every German child, but Erna Ehrler works diligently to control what is being taught to her children in their home. Not everyone in Germany subscribes to the hate that the Nazis are trying to program into them.

In Friedrich's first week of school, he was taught a song about the Jews that he was expected to recite the following week. Friedrich slept in Elisabeth's bed for two weeks after reading it because of the nightmares. Friedrich and the other children in his class were being told terrifying stories about the Jews. In the song, Jews were killing Christian children.

In addition, all schools are now required to show the movie *Triumph of the Will,* which was filmed at the Nuremberg Rally. The propaganda and constant brainwashing are a part of everyday life in Germany. There is no escaping it.

The following morning, at breakfast, Hartwig broaches the subject of marriage to Elisabeth.

"You're getting a bit old to be living at home."

Elisabeth stares down at the slice of bread on her plate.

"That's why I brought Reinhard to meet you last night. He's a good man and would be a good provider. I would like to see you spending more time with him."

Erna stands behind Hartwig with a look of sheer terror. Her mother looks exactly how Elisabeth had felt the night before when she found out about Hartwig's plan.

"There is no rush, Elisabeth," Erna reassures her.

Hartwig turns around. "This conversation is not for your ears. Get back in the kitchen where you belong." He glares up at her, still towering over him. To Elisabeth's surprise, her mother glares right back.

Hartwig flies out of his chair, grabs Erna by the throat, and pins her against the wall.

"What happened the last time that you disobeyed me?"

Henning flies into the room and grabs Hartwig by the throat, hurling him to the floor. Hartwig attempts to get up, but Henning restrains him with his foot on his father's throat. Hartwig's face turns crimson as Henning stares down at him in a silent rage.

Finally, their mother talks Henning into letting Hartwig go, although it isn't easy.

Henning leaves Hartwig lying on the floor gasping for air.

Erna disappears back into the kitchen, Henning returns to the living room, and Elisabeth hurries to her bedroom to comfort Friedrich. It's just another day in the Ehrler home.

In early February, Elisabeth wakes in the middle of the night. Outside her window there are men shouting and barking dogs. The Gestapo is entering the building across the street with their trained attack dogs. Elisabeth opens her window slightly to listen as she peers discretely from behind the curtains.

The uniformed officers make their way into the building. The lights suddenly switch on in every room of the 3rd floor flat across the street. The Gestapo shouts orders, but she can't decipher what they're saying. Children are screaming, and a baby is crying. Her heart races as she strains to see what is happening inside the flat across the street. A policeman standing guard outside looks up towards her window. She ducks back out of sight.

Elisabeth opens the curtain slightly and peers across the street. The officer has returned his attention back to the building with the Gestapo inside.

Suddenly, glass shatters as an object flies out of the 3rd floor window. A piercing scream sounds from inside the flat. The Gestapo continues to bark orders, and the woman continues to scream as though they are torturing her. A barrage of gunshots unloads inside the flat. Elisabeth drops the curtain and straightens back against the wall.

In seconds, the shooting is replaced with an eerie silence.

Elisabeth waits for a moment before peering back outside.

Shadows are now moving quickly in and out of the light of the flat. Elisabeth can't discern if it's the officers or the people living inside.

Within minutes, Gestapo men climb back into their cars and speed away, but no one is taken into custody.

As the cars pull away their headlights illuminate the object that had been thrown from the window. The lifeless baby lies in a puddle of blood covered in shards of glass. Her pink blanket loosely wrapped around her tiny frame.

Elisabeth stares down to the scene below.

Tears stream down her face as she chokes back a sob. She stands silent in the window as her breaths began to steady.

Elisabeth dresses and slips on her shoes. Quietly, she opens the door to her flat and steps out into the foyer. As she carefully descends the stairs her legs tremble.

In her haste to rescue the baby it hadn't occurred to her what she would be risking. She finally has the presence of mind to consider what would happen if someone sees her. She would surely be reported to the Gestapo.

Elisabeth's mind races as she continues quietly down the stairs. She is certain that the infant is dead.

Finally, she opens the door to the outside, but only a crack. The lifeless baby lies still on the road.

She pauses for a moment before quietly closing the heavy wooden door.

Elisabeth makes her way back up the stairs to her flat. When she reaches her bedroom she sits down on the bed and stares out the window. The moon is bright in the night sky.

It becomes clear, as the shock wears off, that the entire family has just been murdered by the Gestapo.

A week later, Friedrich celebrates his birthday. Elisabeth bakes cookies to celebrate, but again, there are no gifts. Friedrich doesn't seem to mind. The Ehrler children are accustomed to it. Hartwig spends the day, and most of the night, at the beer hall with his friends. Elisabeth helps her mother with housework. She has been ill for a couple of weeks.

"I think you should see a doctor." Elisabeth rests a cool, damp cloth on her mother's forehead.

"I'll be fine, Elisabeth. I just need some rest."

The following week, Erna Ehrler looks even worse. Elisabeth pleads with her to see a doctor knowing that they can't afford it.

Elisabeth is desperate, so she goes to Hannah for help.

Hannah's father arrives at the flat, medical bag in hand. Henning keeps Hartwig busy at the beer hall. He mustn't be alerted to the fact that a Jewish doctor is in his home, caring for his sick wife. Although Henning hates the Jews, he makes an exception for his sick mother.

Dr. Berkowitz informs Erna privately of his diagnosis. She refuses the additional tests necessary for the doctor to be certain. He has no choice, but to respect her wishes.

"How long do I have?" Her voice is weak.

"I can't be sure, but I suspect, not long. This will help with the pain." He retrieves a needle and a small bottle from his bag. He waits by the window for her to succumb to the medication.

Dr. Berkowitz closes the bedroom door behind him. He hands Elisabeth a bottle of pills and writes down the dosage instructions.

"How is she?"

"She's resting now. You should check in on her later."

Elisabeth stands outside her mother's door. Somewhere, deep inside, she knows that she's losing her.

That evening, when Erna wakes, she confirms what Elisabeth had suspected.

"I'm ill and I don't have long, Elisabeth." Her mother holds her hand. "Take care of your brother. Stay at Grandma Heilwig's as much as possible. I won't be here to protect you. Not that I really ever did." Tears fill her eyes. "You deserved a better mother."

"Don't say that. I'm glad that you are my mother, and I wouldn't want any other." Elisabeth sits down on the bed next to her.

No one knows their secret yet. Friedrich is asleep, and Henning is at the beer hall with Hartwig. Elisabeth holds her mother in her arms while she drifts off to sleep. She wants to beg her to stay. She wants to tell her how much she loves her, so it will convince her to stay, but no words come.

The following morning, Erna informs the rest of the family. Elisabeth remains in her bedroom while the rest of her family gather by her mother's bedside. Elisabeth stares out the window. The sun is bright in the sky, but it shouldn't be. It shouldn't be a beautiful day. Elisabeth's face is blotchy and red from crying. Her lips are cherry red and swollen as she smears a bit of balm to soothe them.

Elisabeth listens for her father to scold her mother for dying, but she can't hear Hartwig, Henning or Friedrich. She walks to her parents' bedroom and stands in the doorway. No one acknowledges her presence. Hartwig holds his wife in his arms, Henning holds her hand, and Friedrich rests his head on her leg. Elisabeth walks back to her room. She already said her goodbyes. It's their turn now.

Erna Ehrler dies two weeks later with her family by her side. Erna's family kisses her one last time before Hartwig leads them out of the room, closing the door behind him.

Elisabeth keeps her word and spends most her time at her grandmother's flat with Friedrich. Grandmother Heilwig is lost in an ocean of grief. She barely eats and seems disoriented and distracted much of the time. She spends most days in her favorite chair staring out the window. Elisabeth is left to take care of her own household and now Grandma Heilwig's as well. Hartwig spends most of his time at the beer halls, while Henning and Olga spend their time at the flat getting drunk.

Olga eats with them every night, but she can't be bothered to help Elisabeth, even in the slightest of ways. Olga also can't be bothered to help pay for food, so Elisabeth is forced to sacrifice meals as well.

Elisabeth is alone, but she had seen this coming from the moment she found out that her mother was dying. There is no one to protect her now from the pack of wolves that surround her. She'll need to learn to protect herself.

One evening, after Elisabeth finishes the dishes and tucks Friedrich into bed, there's a knock at the door. She opens the door slightly and peers out.

"I saw them at the beer hall," Dieter said. "So, I thought it was safe to see you for a minute. Are you alright?"

Elisabeth opens the door and motions for him to enter.

Dieter steps toward Elisabeth and pulls her into his arms.

"Elisabeth, I want to marry you. I want you and Friedrich to come and live with me." Dieter kneels down on the floor beneath her. "I can take care of you."

Elisabeth just stares down at Dieter, unsure of what he is saying and too tired to care.

"Elisabeth, this is what I should have done when Henning forbade you from seeing me. I should have asked you to marry me."

"You'll need my father's approval, and I doubt that you will get it. You're not a Nazi."

"I'll become a Nazi."

Elisabeth scoffs. "In addition to that hurdle, we have Olga's obsession with you. I just have a feeling that she is going to do everything in her power to see to it that it doesn't happen. So, excuse me if I don't seem too excited. It seems that bad people like Olga and Hartwig always manage to get what they want."

Dieter kisses her softly.

"Just hold on, I'll be back tomorrow to talk to Hartwig."

Dieter kisses Elisabeth again before closing the flat door behind him. She sits down in her mother's chair. She knows that she should be happy that Dieter has asked her to marry him, but she has a feeling that Olga or Hartwig will find a way to keep them apart. One of the wolves will make sure that it doesn't happen, and she is almost certain that it will be Olga.

The following morning, Dieter is at the Ehrler's flat seated across from a Hartwig. He is nursing a hangover with a beer, but doesn't seem to mind Dieter's visit. It doesn't take much for Dieter to win his approval. Hartwig doesn't agree to the marriage because he likes Dieter, or because he wants his daughter to be happy. He agrees to their marriage because Adolf Hitler has made it clear that the German people need to procreate in order to grow the German population. Hartwig has given up on finding anyone that would be willing to marry an ungrateful girl like his daughter. He had hoped that Reinhard would have agreed to marry her, but it was clear that she didn't leave a good impression on him. Hartwig is disappointed that his daughter is a stubborn girl that refuses to submit. No Nazi man will have her. It's too much work to train a woman to be a dutiful wife. Elisabeth clearly lacks the understanding that her existence is to serve her husband and her country. Therefore, Hartwig believes that his daughter must do the only thing that she's capable of doing. She must utilize the womb that God gave her to give birth to future generations of pure-blooded Aryan Germans. It's the only way to ensure Germany's future. The German people must build an army of the best.

Elisabeth doesn't tell Olga or Henning when they return that afternoon from a meeting at the church where their wedding is to be held. Elisabeth prefers the element of surprise. She can't wait to see Olga's reaction when Hartwig announces their engagement.

Elisabeth and Friedrich pick up Adam before strolling over to Hannah's flat. It's a beautiful day as the sun shines bright in a cloudless sky. Happiness swells in her heart, but the grief returns instantly to dampen her spirits. She takes a deep breath and glances over at Adam. She wants to tell him her news, but she chooses to wait until Hannah is with them.

Hannah disappears into her bedroom and returns carrying a box of toys for Friedrich. She pours the contents out onto the floor and sits down next to Adam.

"I've been cleaning all day," Hannah said. "I wasn't expecting you. I look a mess."

"I have some news," Elisabeth said.

"What are the Nazis up to now?" Hannah said.

"No, it's not them. Dieter and I are to be wed."

Hannah and Adam remain silent, but bewilderment flashes across their faces. They glance at each other before turning their attention back toElisabeth.

"What about your family?" Adam asks.

"Hartwig approves and has given Dieter his blessing."

"What about Olga and Henning?" Hannah said.

"They don't know yet. We'll tell them tonight."

Hannah takes a deep breath. Adam remains stoic, his gaze to the floor where Friedrich is playing.

Elisabeth swallows hard and waits for one of them to speak.

"I have a bad feeling about this, Elisabeth," Hannah said.

"Me, too," Adam said.

"You must be cautious," Hannah warns. "Olga will surely be displeased about your engagement. She was your enemy before, but I fear that will be nothing compared to the enemy that she will become. Don't let it stop you from marrying the man that you love, but you must tread carefully." Hannah watches Friedrich for a moment. "I know I sound less than thrilled, but I am truly happy for you. You and Dieter belong together. We won't be able to attend the wedding, but we'll be thinking of you." Hannah smiles, but it's insincere. Elisabeth can see the fear in her eyes.

"Congratulations," Adam said.

Elisabeth is reminded of the fact that her best friends are Jews. They will not be permitted to attend her wedding, just as she had been unable to attend Hannah's. If Hartwig had found out that his daughter attended a Jewish wedding the punishment would be severe.

That evening, Dieter arrives early with some meat from the butcher shop along with extra potatoes and carrots. Hartwig is more grateful than anyone and he's quickly warming to Dieter's charms.

Elisabeth prepares dinner while Hartwig and Dieter talk at the table. Dieter listens to Hartwig talk incessantly about the Nazi's plans to rebuild Germany and nods in agreement. Elisabeth smiles to herself. Dieter pretending to be a Nazi–she never thought she would see the day. He must be seething inside, but his face remains stoic.

She is in the kitchen when Henning and Olga arrive. She hurries to Dieter's side in case Henning decides to start trouble. Henning stares intently at his best friend as he struggles to understand what Dieter is doing at the Ehrler home, with Hartwig. Olga looks equally confused.

"Your sister is to be married." Hartwig smiles proudly.

Henning remains silent as he eyes Dieter.

"Congratulations." Henning finally shakes Dieter's hand.

Olga steps forward next to Henning to congratulate them. Elisabeth can see the fear and confusion welling up in Olga's eyes as she's crushed under the weight of Hartwig's words. Elisabeth pours Olga a glass of wine before handing Henning a large mug of beer.

Henning sits down at the table and lights a cigarette. The three men talk as though Elisabeth and Olga are no longer there. It is clear that Henning has missed his longtime friend. Olga sits in the living room staring out the window.

Elisabeth continues to prepare dinner. Hartwig prefers to eat at the end of the night, so that the food doesn't soak up the alcohol too soon and ruin his blissful state of drunkenness.

"Would you like another drink?" Elisabeth stands over Olga seated in her mother's chair.

"No, thank you." Olga continues to stare out the window.

Dieter joins Elisabeth in the kitchen moments later.

"I don't think Olga's taking this well," Dieter said.

Hartwig is in the bathroom, and Henning is in the living room speaking quietly to Olga.

"No, she's not."

"Just ignore her and think about us." Dieter smiles before walking back to the table. He doesn't want Hartwig to catch him alone with his daughter. It would be inappropriate.

Elisabeth is grateful to be leaving the Ehrler household. She knows that it's only a matter of time before her father terrorizes her, the way that he had her mother. Hartwig's grief, and the regrets that accompany it, are keeping Elisabeth safe for the moment, but this reprieve is fleeting. The real Hartwig will soon return.

In March, Henning and Olga are married by the registrar. They have a small party afterwards, and both families attend. Dieter escorts Elisabeth and Friedrich to the small gathering while Hartwig shows up late after a few drinks at the beer hall.

Henning is happy. He is singing and dancing with the others while Olga entertains her guests by getting so drunk she can hardly stand.

It is late, and almost everyone is drunk, so Dieter insists on walking Elisabeth and Friedrich home. Although, Friedrich doesn't do much walking once they step outside into the chill of the night air. He is fast asleep in Dieter's arms within minutes of leaving the party.

Dieter walks them up to the flat and helps Elisabeth tuck Friedrich into bed.

"What time do you think your father will be home?" Dieter shakes his head. "He was done before he even started."

"What's new?" Elisabeth rolls her eyes. "Olga made a fool of herself."

"Which is a surprise to no one," Dieter said.

Dieter pulls her to him and kisses her.

"I don't know how much longer I can wait until you are my wife."

Elisabeth kisses him gently. "It won't be long."

The wedding is planned for April, leaving little time for anyone to stand in their way. Elisabeth's grandmother sews the dress and helps with the preparations. Elisabeth is pleased to see that her grandmother is finding her way back from her grief. Elisabeth still has yet to grieve fully. She's been so busy taking care of everyone else that there has been little time or space to grieve. Sometimes it hits her at the oddest moments, like cleaning the bathroom, or brushing her hair. Suddenly, she finds herself crying. Even at her busiest, Elisabeth thinks about her mother often. She still misses her terribly.

When he isn't working, Dieter spends much of his time at the Ehrler's flat. Hartwig is only home to pass out after a night at the beer halls, and Henning lives with Olga a couple of blocks away. It is as though Elisabeth and Dieter are already married. Friedrich loves having Dieter around and rarely leaves his side.

"Have you talked to Hartwig about Friedrich staying with us after we're married?"

"No, my father doesn't care what happens to Friedrich, as long as he doesn't have to take care of him."

"So, all we need to figure out is who's going to take care of Hartwig," Dieter laughs.

The wedding is days away. Elisabeth has organized everything with the assistance of her grandmother. The spring air is warm, and the trees are covered with bright green leaves again. The windows can finally be opened after a long winter.

It is early evening, and the sun is slowly melting into the horizon. Elisabeth sits in her mother's chair satisfied that all of the housework is finally completed. There is still time to enjoy what is left of the day.

Friedrich is quietly drawing in the bedroom, and the flat is peaceful as Elisabeth listens to the city outside her window. Dieter will be there soon, and they will take Friedrich for a walk to the park before it gets dark.

Friedrich runs ahead as Dieter and Elisabeth stroll casually to the park. The sun is slowly fading, and Friedrich knows that he doesn't have much time. He joins his friends while Dieter finds an empty bench.

Elisabeth sits down beside him and watches Friedrich play.

"If you had told me when we were young that I would marry you someday I wouldn't have believed it," Elisabeth said. "Not that I disliked you. I just never thought of you that way."

"Hartwig told me that he wasn't surprised," Dieter said.

"It's funny that someone with a brain pickled in beer could be more perceptive than the rest of us." Elisabeth shakes her head.

After Friedrich's bath, Elisabeth and Dieter tuck him into bed.

"I'm too old to get tucked in."

"Ok, this will be the last time." Elisabeth lifts the blanket to his chest.

It's dark outside, but a flickering candle lights the small living room.

Elisabeth walks Dieter to the door.

"I can't wait until we're married. I hate saying goodbye every night," Elisabeth said.

"Two more days." Dieter reminds her before leaning in to kiss her goodbye. "I love you."

The sun streams through the window of Elisabeth's bedroom. She sits up in bed and looks out to the city. Today will be the last time that she wakes in the bed that she has slept in all of her life. Today will be her last day in the Ehrler home, and the last day that she will have to listen to Hartwig's snoring as it vibrates the walls.

Elisabeth glances over at Friedrich sleeping peacefully in his bed. She steps out of bed quietly and tip toes to the kitchen. Hannah had given her the coffee as a wedding gift, and she can't wait to enjoy it.

It's early, and the birds are chirping outside the living room window. Elisabeth sips her coffee. She relaxes back in her mother's chair with the sun on her face.

Hours later, Elisabeth stands in front of the mirror wearing her wedding dress. It's a simple ivory dress that cascades down to her ankles. She adjusts the veil that flows down her back and spills onto the floor. She stands back to take one last look.

There's a knock at her bedroom door.

"May I come in?" Olga opens the door slightly and peers inside.

"Sure."

Olga sits down on the bed and leans back on her elbows as she watches Elisabeth in the mirror.

"What do you want?" Elisabeth finally asks.

Olga shakes her head and grins as though she has a secret. "You might want to sit down for this." Olga flashes a wicked smile.

Elisabeth sits down on Friedrich's bed. Fear swells in her stomach, but she's careful not to show it. Olga studies Elisabeth like a wolf circling its prey. Although Olga smiles, her icy blue eyes cannot hide the rage that she is barely able to contain.

"Did you really think that I was going to let this happen? Did you really think that I would just let you have him?"

Olga steps towards Elisabeth.

"Do you know who my father is? He's the Gestapo." Olga continues to speak in a hushed tone as she glares down at Elisabeth. "I will file a damning report full of lies about you. I will tell my father that you defy Adolf Hitler and despise Nazis. I will tell him about your Jewish friends and make up a story about a plan to rise up against the Nazis with other Jews. If you marry Dieter you will not only kill him and yourself, but your friends as well. I will paint all of you as traitors to our country and our Fuhrer." Olga's voice is hoarse and deep as the rage flashes in her eyes. "You're lucky that I don't kill you now as you stand there in that pathetic dress believing no one will see the whore underneath."

Olga's words burn through Elisabeth. The adrenaline courses through her at lightening speeds.

Elisabeth finally understands what is happening. She understands every word that drips from the wolf's mouth.

The room remains silent as Olga watches Elisabeth slowly accept her defeat.

"How do I know that you won't do it anyway?" Elisabeth finally speaks.

"What would be the point? You just play the game my way, and you'll be just fine."

"What game?"

"I thought I had squashed this little love affair, but the two of you just won't stop. I knew that I needed a plan that would ensure an end to you and Dieter. So, pay attention. You've decided to be with someone else. I know someone that owes me a favor, and you're the favor. Also, you must admit your torrid love affair to all, just to ensure that you are properly shamed. Dieter will finally see you for the whore that you really are. I will be here when you sit down with your father. You will tell him that you are in love with Walter Lutze and cannot marry Dieter."

"You are a truly disgusting human being." Elisabeth stands up.

"Be careful," Olga whispers. "You wouldn't want to wake your father."

"I should tell everyone who you really are. Henning would leave you if he knew."

"I don't care about Henning. Haven't you figured that out yet?"

"Why did you marry him?"

"It was better than what my father had planned for me. We will see how Hartwig would like you to deal with this whole mess. Oh, and just to ensure that Hartwig doesn't force you to marry Dieter anyway, you'll need to tell him that you are pregnant with Walter's child."

"You want me to get pregnant?"

"No, I just want you to say that you are pregnant. Hartwig won't force you to marry Dieter if you're pregnant with another man's child. Keep up, Elisabeth," Olga scolds her.

"What about Dieter?"

"I'll go home and tell Henning everything that happened. He will be the one to report the sad news to Dieter."

Friedrich opens the door and brushes past Elisabeth in search of his toy. Elisabeth and Olga stand motionless as he kneels down under his bed. Friedrich reaches underneath, grabs his toy, and disappears back into the living room.

In the silence that Friedrich leaves behind, Elisabeth hears Hartwig close the bathroom door. He's awake. Fresh fear races through her body.

Olga smiles at the terror on Elisabeth's face.

Elisabeth steps out to the living room and instructs Friedrich to play at the park.

"Don't come back until I come for you."

Friedrich runs to the bedroom to retrieve his shoes.

"Don't worry, I'll pick up Friedrich and take him to my flat if Hartwig kills you," Olga grins.

Disgust washes over Elisabeth's face, but she's quick to disguise it when Friedrich returns to the room.

"Walk to the park, and don't veer off our normal path."

"Okay." Friedrich closes the door behind him.

Elisabeth sits down at the table across from Hartwig. Olga remains in the living room, seemingly oblivious to what is about to unfold.

Hartwig is clearly nursing a hangover.

"Are you ready for your wedding?" Hartwig lights his cigarette.

Elisabeth searches for the words to tell her father.

"What the hell is wrong with you?" Elisabeth now has Hartwig's full attention.

Elisabeth takes a deep breath.

"I can't marry Dieter," Elisabeth begins. "I'm in love with someone else, and I'm pregnant." She says it quickly. She can only hope that hearing that she is expecting a child might deter her father from killing her with his bare hands.

Elisabeth watches Hartwig process her words with his alcohol soaked brain. Suddenly, she sees a flash in Hartwig's eyes and feels his large fist crash against her cheek. She's jolted to the floor. Hartwig jerks her up by her hair and pulls her to him. His alcohol steeped breath saturates the small space between them.

"You are a whore!" Hartwig shouts before violently throwing her back to the floor.

Hartwig walks to his bedroom, quickly dresses and leaves the flat. He needs a drink.

Olga sits in the living room watching Elisabeth struggle to stand.

"I thought that was going to be a lot worse," Olga grins.

Elisabeth doesn't try to talk. Blood trickles from the corner of her lip.

She finally stands and walks to her bedroom, closing the door behind her.

Olga smiles as she closes the door to the flat. Her work here is done.

Elisabeth picks Friedrich up at the park. Her face is hot and swollen as she makes her way to their grandma Heilwig's flat. Friedrich asks repeatedly what had happened to her, but Elisabeth remains silent as she hurries him down the street.

Once inside, Elisabeth instructs Friedrich to play in the bedroom while she speaks privately to their grandmother.

Elisabeth stands in the tiny kitchen going over every detail of what had happened. Grandmother Heilwig listens in disbelief. She can't believe that Olga could be so horrible.

She holds a cold, damp rag on Elisabeth's cheek as she sobs.

"Henning is probably on his way to Dieter's flat right now," Elisabeth said.

Her grandmother pours cups of tea before sitting down across the table.

"I have to tell Dieter the truth," Elisabeth said.

"I agree, but you must be certain that Olga will never find out. I believe that if Olga even suspects that you told Dieter she will carry out her threat. If you decide to tell him, you must also tell him goodbye."

That night, Friedrich sleeps peacefully on the floor in their grandmother's room. Elisabeth is in her mother's old bedroom. The night air blows softly through the window as she tries to sleep. She fears Hartwig or Henning will come to her grandmother's flat in a drunken rage.

Elisabeth's thoughts are interrupted by someone knocking softly on the door to the flat.

Elisabeth moves quietly to the door and opens it slowly. It's Dieter.

She holds the door open signaling for him to enter.

Dieter sits down at the table as she lights a candle.

"I'm so sorry, Dieter." Elisabeth begins to cry. "I love you so much, but I had to do it."

With that, Elisabeth begins to tell him the truth–every cruel detail of Olga's plan.

“Who hit you?”

“Hartwig, but it could have been a lot worse.”

“I’m going to take you away from here. These people aren’t going to hurt you anymore.”

“I can’t leave Friedrich.”

“I’m not letting you go, Elisabeth. I don’t know how to fix this yet, but I won’t let her win. In the meantime, we need to find a way of communicating.”

Dieter holds Elisabeth close until morning’s first light.

“I’ll never leave you,” he whispers.

Dieter kisses her once more before closing the door behind him.

8

Adam

Rain mists from the sky as Adam makes his way home from work. Frau Lenger's shop is doing well, and Adam receives another pay raise. His contribution to the Herschel household allows for them to eat meat twice a week now. In addition, Adam's father is doing well at work adding to the increase in finances for the family.

Adam opens the door to his flat and glances around to see if his mother is home from work. The flat is quiet. The only sound to be heard is the ticking of the grandfather clock in the living room.

Adam pulls back the blanket and falls into bed. He hasn't been sleeping well for the past week due to a tooth ache, but Frau Lenger had paid to get it repaired by a local Jewish dentist.

Adam closes his eyes and slips into a peaceful sleep.

Adam wakes an hour later to his mother clanging pans in the kitchen. He stretches out on the bed and yawns. His father will be home for lunch soon, and Adam plans on walking back to his work with him. He needs to stop at one of the shops for shoe laces. The laces on his shoes are so short from breakage that they're barely long enough to tie.

"I didn't know that you were home." Adam's mother looks startled when he walks into the kitchen. "I thought you were still at work."

"I was tired, so I took a nap."

After lunch, Adam walks with his father back to work. The sun is bright, and everyone seems to be outdoors enjoying the warm spring air.

Adam and his father are careful to stay off of the sidewalks with the Aryan Germans.

As they make their way down the street, Adam notices two Gestapo officers eyeing his father. Adam picks up the pace as his heart races. Suddenly, one of the officers calls out to them. There is no way to pretend that they didn't hear them, and everyone is now staring.

Adam's father walks back toward the Gestapo officers. Adam follows close behind.

"Did you not see that cigarette butt lying on the ground?" The officers glare at Ivan.

"No, I didn't see it," Ivan's voice trembles.

"I don't know why I ask these people questions; they never tell the truth." One officer says to the other.

The officer then pulls out his gun and begins beating Adam's father with it. Adam watches helplessly as the other officer joins in, and they mercilessly beat Ivan to the ground. The officers are shouting obscenities as they deliver blow after blow until Ivan's body is a motionless heap, bleeding in the street. One of the officers picks up the cigarette butt and shoves it in Ivan's bloody mouth.

"Eat it, you filthy Jew!" The officer demands, still out of breath from the beating.

Adam's father is barely able to understand what the officer is saying as he tries to move his mouth to chew. Blood and tobacco stream from Ivan's mouth as he struggles to follow the Gestapo's order. The officers watch with pleasure to ensure Ivan swallows all of it, before leaving him in a heap on the road. Some people stare in disbelief, but most seem unconcerned.

Adam struggles to pick up his father. Ivan is bleeding and barely able to stand. Adam is able to help his father to the alley, away from the passing onlookers that are still staring at them.

Adam removes his shirt and tips his father's head back. Gently, he presses it to Ivan's nose to stop the bleeding. Adam brushes the tobacco and blood from his father's chin as he struggles to sit him up.

"Just rest for a minute." Adam holds the shirt against Ivan's bleeding nose.

Adam sits alone with his barely conscious father resting in his arms. Tears stream down his face.

They spend the rest of the afternoon hidden away in the alley. They will make their way home as soon as it's dark.

Days later, Adam's father is healed enough that Adam feels comfortable leaving him alone in the flat.

Adam walks to Hannah's, careful to stay out of site by ducking down alleys and cutting through gardens.

Elisabeth arrives before Adam. She is seated at the table, and Hannah is in the kitchen preparing tea. Adam watches Hannah move awkwardly around the kitchen. Her pregnant stomach is enormous and it seems to get in her way with every move. Hannah pours Adam a cup of tea and adds a spoonful of sugar before sitting down at the table with them.

"This is the first time that I've seen you since your engagement was called off." Hannah directs her attention to Elisabeth. "It's rumored that you were having an affair. We know that's not true, so I suspect Olga is behind all of this."

Adam watches Elisabeth's reaction, and it's clear that she's choosing her words carefully.

"I can't tell you everything, for reasons too insane to even believe, but I can tell you that I'm living at my grandmother's flat until everything is sordid out. Friedrich is living with us. Hartwig and Henning do not have contact with me. They have made it clear that I have shamed our family, therefore, I am dead to them."

Adam stares at Elisabeth in disbelief. He tries to process it, but none of it makes sense. He glances over at Hannah to see if she might have been able to decipher the meaning behind Elisabeth's words, but it's clear that she is just as baffled.

"Elisabeth, whatever it is, you can trust us," Hannah said. "We have always kept each other's secrets."

Elisabeth looks at both of them. "There are no secrets when it comes to the Nazis, the Gestapo, and most of the German people. People are being tortured to death every day. It's not safe here."

"What are you saying? Has someone threatened you?" Hannah looks fearful and confused as she tries to decode her friend's words.

"I don't want to say anything more," Elisabeth said.

Adam keeps his head down and slowly stirs his tea while Hannah sits back in her chair and stares out the window. They understand. They don't know the details of what has happened to Elisabeth, but they understand the message.

"Is there anything that we can do to help?" Adam interrupts the silence.

"No."

"How long can you stay?" Hannah asks.

"I can stay for a while."

"I'm not leaving until it gets dark." Adam glances out the window. "I don't care about the curfew. It's safer in the dark."

"I have some news." Hannah pauses for a moment. "After the baby is born we're moving to Paris."

"Paris?" Elisabeth said.

"You're right, it's not safe here," Hannah said.

"Yeah, I wish I could leave," Adam said. "Why don't you go to America? Why Paris?"

"Otto has family there, and they invited us to stay with them."

They finish their tea in silence.

Two days later, Otto rushes into Frau Lenger's shop to notify Adam that Hannah has given birth to a healthy baby girl named Helena. Adam promises to visit in a few days to allow Hannah some rest. On his way home, he stops by Elisabeth's grandmother's flat to tell her the news.

Adam doesn't stay long; his father has called a family meeting.

Ivan is sitting at the table when Adam arrives home. Adam washes his hands before sitting down across from him. Ivan leans back in his chair and stares down at the lace table cloth as Else ladles steaming cabbage soup into their bowls.

Ivan waits until Else is seated before he begins.

"We are going to America. We have to get out of here before they kill us all."

Adam nods his head in agreement.

"We have some money saved but not enough. We need to make cuts wherever possible, including food. If my calculations are correct, we will have the money that we need in a little over a year. I know that sounds like a long time, but traveling to America is expensive. Your uncle has reassured me that he can help us once we get there. In the meantime, we have to stay under the radar of the Gestapo. We will continue to only leave the house when necessary. We don't want to attract any attention. Your uncle also said that he has a friend there that owns a printing shop. A job will be waiting for you, Adam."

That evening, Adam drifts off to sleep thinking of America. He has dreamt of going to America most of his life. He can hardly wait until the day comes when they can finally leave Germany and live in a place where they aren't hated and persecuted.

9

Elisabeth

Elisabeth hasn't heard from Dieter in weeks. She worries that she will be living with the stranger that Olga has chosen for her before Dieter can find a way to save her. She is expected to move in with Walter by the end of the week. Olga made all of the plans and is determined to see her plans through. Elisabeth will *live in sin*, as Olga calls it, and there is no way out.

Elisabeth continues to have no communication with Henning or her father. Olga destroyed those relationships as well.

Elisabeth rarely leaves the flat since she now has the reputation of being promiscuous. Olga had been sure to tell everyone the sordid details of Elisabeth's broken engagement.

Elisabeth now spends much of her time with Friedrich preparing him for school to start at the end of summer. Grandma Heilwig does most of the shopping and takes Friedrich to the park every day.

One morning, before dawn, there is a knock at the door. Elisabeth quietly slips out of bed and rushes to answer it.

She opens the door slightly and peers out to see Dieter standing in front of her. He quietly steps inside.

"I'm sorry I couldn't get here sooner." He quickly kisses her.

Elisabeth leads him to the table and lights a candle.

"This has just gotten more complicated. Henning has joined the Reich Labor Service. He will be gone for a while to train. Olga's been to my flat a couple of times, but I don't let her in."

"She wants you to have an affair with her while Henning's away, and she calls me the whore."

"I told her that my uncle is not well, and I have to care for him. I just need to be careful about the way that I deal with Olga."

"Your uncle isn't well?" Elisabeth interrupts.

"He's been ill for over a month now, but the doctors are still unsure of what is wrong. It started out as a spring cold, and it has slowly worsened. I think that he'll be fine, don't worry. What I was saying is the situation with Olga is delicate. I can't see her dealing well with rejection, so I need to keep my distance until Henning returns."

Elisabeth sits quietly at the table watching the flickering flame on the candle.

"I have been getting information on Walter Lutze, and here's what I know about him." Dieter looks somber. "Whatever Olga has on him it must be pretty serious because his loyalty to her is unshakeable."

"How do you know?"

"I just know. Don't worry; I've done nothing that could implicate me."

"I'm going to have to live with him. There's no way out of this."

"I wish I could take you away, Elisabeth."

"This isn't your fault." Elisabeth looks up at Dieter. "I know that you thought you could save me, but no one can."

"I was able to do one thing. The night that your brother beat Walter up I had a friend of mine visit him in the hospital and relay a message. He told him that the message was from Henning. My friend told Walter that he could never touch you in any way. He was warned not to even sleep in the same bed as you. If he does anything stupid Henning will have him killed. Walter was also warned not to tell Olga about Henning's message or he would not only be killed, but tortured as well. My friend told him that this was his punishment for tainting your reputation. Walter agreed, and to ensure his compliance my friend will pay him regular visits just to let him know that we are watching. It bides us time to find a solution, Elisabeth, and it keeps you safe."

The sun is just peeking over the horizon. It's time for Dieter to say goodbye.

"I wish that I was clever enough to find a way out of this but I'm not." Dieter stares down at the table.

"You should know by now that there are things that happen in life that we can't control, no matter how clever we are. I think that we would be safer if we just said our goodbyes now and moved on with our lives. I love you. I will always love you." Elisabeth fights back tears.

Dieter remains silent.

"It just isn't meant to be. Can't you see that?" Elisabeth said.

"I'll do as you wish and stay away, but I'm not giving up." Dieter kisses her softly before he leaves.

Elisabeth doesn't watch him through the window this time. She blows out the candle and watches the sun slowly rise in the distance.

A few days later, Elisabeth packs her belongings, says her goodbyes to her grandmother and Friedrich, and follows Olga's written directions to Walter's flat.

Elisabeth arrives at the time that Olga had instructed. Walter answers the door. He isn't at all what Elisabeth was expecting.

Walter's parents are sitting in the living room. It is obvious that they are aware of the rumors of Elisabeth's promiscuity. Olga left no stone unturned in her devious little plan.

Walter's mother looks Elisabeth up and down with disapproval. To her, Elisabeth is nothing more than a tainted woman that has shamed their family.

When Walter finally speaks, it's quite clear that he is nothing like his parents. At one point, Elisabeth even feels sorry for him. His parents couldn't be colder towards their own son.

Walter's parents only stay a short while, much to Elisabeth's relief.

Walter's mother glances back at Elisabeth with a final reminder that she disapproves of her, before closing the flat door. Walter and Elisabeth remain silent, both unsure of what to say about their mutual predicament. Elisabeth is curious to find out what Olga has on Walter.

"You can stay in the guest room. It's comfortable and looks out to the garden." Walter leads her down a small hallway. "I'll let you unpack. If there's anything that you need, just let me know." Walter offers before closing the door behind him.

Elisabeth steps over to the window and peers out to the garden.

Later that evening, as the sun disappears into the horizon, Elisabeth walks out to the sitting room where Walter is reading.

"Are you hungry? I can make you a sandwich." Walter looks up from his book.

"No, thanks." Elisabeth sits down across from him.

Walter places a small piece of paper inside his book to save the page.

"The room is nice. Thank you," Elisabeth said.

"We will get through this much easier if we both concede that we're in this together. I don't blame you, and you shouldn't blame me. Olga was the mastermind of this awful situation. I'm not your enemy, but we do have an enemy in common which automatically makes us friends."

"That true," Elisabeth said.

Walter nods in agreement. "Someday, I will get my chance to make Olga pay, and I'm going to take it."

"I'll help."

"Would you like a glass of wine?" Walter heads to the kitchen.

"I don't usually drink, but I think I will today."

Elisabeth wants to ask Walter what Olga has on him, but it doesn't feel right to ask. It's not her business.

On August 1, 1936, the Olympics open in Berlin. All of the anti-Jewish propaganda and graffiti is wiped clean, leaving visitors with the impression that Nazi Germany is a tolerant country.

"They know what they are doing is wrong, or they wouldn't be trying to hide it from the rest of the world," Elisabeth said angrily as she peels potatoes.

Walter is setting the table, as he does every night. "Well, consider it a reprieve for the Jews."

After dinner, Walter and Elisabeth sit in the living room reading, as they do most evenings. Their worlds are combining, and they are becoming friends. Elisabeth feels that she can tell Walter anything. He feels the same, except for the one secret he swore he would never tell anyone.

10

Hannah

The spring of 1937 ushers in new life to the trees and gardens outside and a promise of a brighter future for Hannah, Otto and Helena.

Hannah carefully packs their trunks for the move to Paris as Helena sleeps peacefully on the bed beside her.

Helena begins to stir. Hannah watches her slowly wake from her slumber.

"Hello, my beautiful girl." Hannah smiles down at her.

Elisabeth and Adam are coming over for a visit today, and Hannah is looking forward to being with them one last time. She still can't imagine her life without them. She rocks Helena in her arms as her mind drifts back to the warm summers by the lake. The carefree days of youth are now a distant memory.

Their promise to stay together will be sealed in each and every letter until they meet again.

Hannah prepares a special dinner with baked cinnamon apples for dessert.

"It smells so good in here." Elisabeth sits down on the floor and plays with Helena.

"I brought you an early birthday present." Elisabeth stands up with Helena in her arms and walks over to her satchel. She reaches inside and pulls out a small doll. Helena eyes it suspiciously. After a brief moment, Helena relents to her curiosity and reaches out for it. Elisabeth and Hannah laugh. It is Helena's first doll, and she isn't sure what to think of it, but she quickly makes friends with the homemade doll that Elisabeth has sewn.

Adam arrives shortly after Elisabeth with another present for Helena. He presents outfits for Helena's doll that his mother had sewn. Helena is too young to know how to change the dresses now, but it won't be long.

They sit in the living room as the warm air breezes through the windows.

"How's Walter?" Hannah said.

"He's doing well. How's Otto?" Elisabeth said.

"He'll be home later. He's angry about what he sees in the courts now. Democracy is long gone. The judges are corrupt and lawless. There is no one to ensure that they are fair, honest, or decent. Most are cruel Nazis ushered into the courts by Adolf Hitler's new form of government, which Otto has aptly named 'Demonocracy.' He won't offer details, he says that it's too disturbing, but he has said that the Gestapo is committing heinous crimes against the German people. Our country is governed and run by criminals, and there's nothing that we can do about it."

As they enjoy the dinner that Hannah has prepared, they reminisce about growing up and the good times that they had together. The memories remain fresh in their minds and safe in their heart.

"I'm going to miss you," Elisabeth said.

"I know that we promised to stay together," Hannah said.

"This isn't your fault. It's not safe here," Adam reassures her. "We're going to America. We're leaving, too."

Hannah and Elisabeth are silenced by the admission.

Otto arrives later that afternoon, but only stays for a short while.

"I'm going to take Helena to see my parents." Otto smiles as he gently scoops his daughter into his arms.

Elisabeth's eyes fill with tears as she looks at Helena sleeping peacefully in Otto's arms.

Elisabeth kisses her softly on the head as the tears stream down her cheeks. Adam kisses her too.

Later that evening, after the kitchen had been cleaned and the tea cups put away, the three friends stand together in the living room to say goodbye one last time. No words; just tears that say *we'll never forget* and a promise that remains dear in their hearts.

Days later, the Kirchner's arrive in Paris. It isn't, at all, as Hannah had pictured it. Paris is not conservative and old fashioned like her beloved Munich; in contrast, it is much more modern and artistic.

In May, the cafés spill over with Parisians relaxing in the warm air. The parks are lush green with brightly colored flowers. The city is filled with artists and writers that came for inspiration, but stayed because it became their home. It definitely didn't feel like home for Hannah, but Paris is an exciting place to be, and she is quickly falling under its spell.

Otto's family reside in a flat high up in a building near the center of the city. The flat is bright and cozy. The windows stretch from the floor to the ceiling. Every room is drenched in sunlight. The exquisite buildings surrounding them stretch out across the city. Some buildings are adorned with wrought iron terraces. The architecture stands simple, yet elegant. Cobblestone streets wind through the city. Surrounding the city is a vast countryside with quaint villages. Hannah's journey to France has ignited a light of hope. She feels the strain release its grip from her stiff muscles.

Otto and Hannah carry their luggage, as directed by Otto's aunt, to the last bedroom at the end of the hallway. Marie Kirchner speaks very little and seems ill at ease that Otto and Hannah are in her home.

"Welcome, it's nice to meet you," Hannah whispers sarcastically when they are alone in the room. "You're mother was right about her; she is rude."

"She's French, that's how they are." Otto sets Helena down on the bed.

Hannah rolls her eyes. She unpacks the trunk and organizes their clothes in the drawers that Marie had emptied for them.

"Why did your uncle marry a French woman?"

"How would I know?"

Hannah and Otto are exhausted from the trip, and the tension of living in someone else's home isn't helping. Helena, however, is full of energy. She slept most of the way.

An hour later, Hannah is fast asleep, and Otto is feeding Helena in the kitchen. Otto's uncle, Itzhak, has just arrived home from a long day at work. He takes Helena from Otto's arms and introduces himself to her. Helena is enamored by the old man as he talks excitedly about the children's books in his shop.

"You look tired, Otto. Why don't you rest? We can take care of the little one." Itzhak smiles at Helena.

"She'll be fine," Marie reassures him.

Otto finally relents and tucks into bed for a short nap. He rests his arm around Hannah before falling fast asleep.

Later that evening, Marie serves a late dinner. Itzhak and Marie's daughter, Giselle, joins them. Hannah really takes to the young woman. Giselle is a year younger than Hannah, but Hannah seems much older. Giselle is animated and jovial. She's an artist, much to Marie's dismay. Marie wanted Giselle to marry well and have children, but Giselle isn't ready for that kind of commitment. Itzhak respects his daughter's free spirit and never pushes her into marriage. He believes we all must be who we want to be.

Otto works and saves money all summer so that they can afford a flat of their own. His salary from his uncle's bookstore allows for them to live comfortably, but without all of the luxuries they were accustomed to in Munich.

In September, Otto and Hannah move their family into a small flat only a few blocks from his uncle's home. Hannah has grown to care for Otto's family, but she is relieved to finally have a place of her own again.

The first night in their flat, as Otto and Helena sleep peacefully in their beds, Hannah sits in the living room staring out the window. She wonders if this charming city will ever feel like home. She sent letters to her family and Elisabeth and Adam, notifying them of her new address, but no one has replied yet. She can't help, but wonder, if the Nazis had intercepted them.

11

Elisabeth

Winter is slowly warming into spring, and the days are getting longer. Elisabeth is working in a clothing store as a seamstress. Her mother had been a gifted seamstress and taught Elisabeth everything that she knew. The owner of the clothing store adores Elisabeth and pays her well.

Adam spends much of his time with Walter. They have become close friends, and he's usually at their flat. He continues to work full time at Frau Lenger's shop. He has also been working part time cleaning horse stalls on a farm outside of town. Adam and his family are saving to go to America, and his father is close to securing the necessary documentation.

Elisabeth was saddened by the news that Adam would be leaving, but she understands that Germany is no place for a Jew. It's not a safe place for a German, either. Adam needs to get out as soon as possible. Walter and Elisabeth offered to help financially, but Adam's father is adamant that his family make their own way.

On March 12th, 1938, Adolf Hitler marches Nazi troops into Austria and seizes control of their government. No one seems to mind, including the Austrian people. An Anschluss is proclaimed the next day. Austria is now annexed to Germany.

Elisabeth, Adam, and Walter are shocked. It's as though the world has fallen under Adolf Hitler's spell.

Walter plans a special picnic for Adam's birthday in June. Elisabeth packs a lunch for them as Walter finishes wrapping the gifts that he bought.

"I'm so glad that you and Adam have become friends. Although, I can't imagine anyone not liking him," Elisabeth said.

"Yes, you would really have to try hard to dislike him," Walter said.

Elisabeth leads Walter to their picnic spot. The grass is lush and the wild flowers are in full bloom. Elisabeth walks through the tall grass with Walter close behind. The soft blades brush against her bare legs as she holds her dress up past her knees. The grass is warm and soft under their bare feet as they carry their shoes in their hands. Adam jogs up behind them, removes his shirt, and tosses it over his shoulder.

Finally, they reach their spot near the bank of the lake. Elisabeth unpacks the food and wine as Walter and Adam check the temperature of the water with their toes.

"I miss Hannah." Adam sits down next to Elisabeth. "Do you think we'll ever see her again?"

"I don't know. I hope so. I've thought about going to visit her, but I don't want to travel alone. I received a letter from her last month. She says they're doing well."

"Yeah, I got one, too, but I haven't made the time to write back. I hate that our letters have to be so superficial. If I am honest about what is really going on here I would be arrested," Adam said.

"I feel the same. I know they read our letters and we are allowed no privacy. I keep mine pretty superficial, too, and there is so much that I wish I could tell her," Elisabeth said.

Walter strolls back from the lake and sits down on the grass next to Adam. Elisabeth lies back in the grass, closing her eyes to the sun, as Adam and Walter follow. It's so peaceful listening to the water gently splash against the rocks while the tall grass rustles in the soft breeze. The sun is warm, and there isn't a cloud in the sky. Elisabeth and Adam are silently thinking the same thing–the day would have been perfect if only Hannah could be there with them.

The summer of 1938 ushers in celebrations and parades honoring Adolf Hitler. Along with the usual sea of Nazi flags, the city is buzzing with excitement and frivolity.

One hot afternoon, Elisabeth and Walter stand in the window of their flat watching the people lined up outside for another one of Hitler's parades.

"It's stuffy in here. Do you want to go for a walk?" Walter said.

"Do these people really love him that much?" Elisabeth stares in amazement to the crowd gathering outside.

"Apparently."

"I don't get it."

Elisabeth and Walter walk to a park off the main path of the parade, distancing themselves from the excited crowd. A growing sea of people, right arms elevated in a Nazi salute, chant in unison *Heil Hitler*. It is the law that you must say *Heil Hitler* and salute as you pass someone on the street or when you walk into a business. Everyone is expected to greet each other with *Heil Hitler* at all times. Pictures of Adolf Hitler adorn the walls of homes, businesses, and government offices.

"One day I counted how many times I said *Heil Hitler*. I counted over forty times in one day," Walter said. "It's insane."

"All of this is insane."

Hours later, Walter and Elisabeth return from the park, just in time to see the Nazi soldiers goose-stepping, in perfect formation, for a cheering crowd. Elisabeth watches Adolf Hitler, the soldiers, and the captivated crowd around her. She is careful to hide her disdain for the spectacle that is now her government and its people. An uneasy feeling settles in the pit of her stomach as she watches the soldiers. She has a feeling that Austria isn't the only country that Adolf Hitler wants to control.

In September, Elisabeth learns that her premonition was correct. Adolf Hitler sets his sights on the German speaking territory in Czechoslovakia as well. He makes it clear that he wants all Germans to belong to Germany, and he is determined to see it through, by any means necessary.

Adolf Hitler is given permission, with the Munich Agreement, by the end of September.

"The other countries looked the other way while Adolf Hitler formed a military. They did nothing when he invaded Austria, and now he's invading Czechoslovakia. Have they forgotten Germany's part in World War I or the Treaty of Versailles?" Elisabeth pours wine into their glasses. "Germany is not allowed to form a military and here we are...military formed, countries invaded, evil dictator at the helm...it doesn't take a genius to figure out where this is headed."

"It seems he's cast a spell over everyone." Walter sips his wine.

"Not everyone." Elisabeth sits back in her chair.

The night sky is full of stars, and the moon is full and bright as Elisabeth walks home from work. It's been a long day, and she's looking forward to a late dinner and an early night to catch up on some much needed sleep.

Suddenly, she sees a drunken Hartwig walking down the street. He is with friends, and they look as though they are heading home after a long day of drinking. Not one of them can walk straight. They seem to weave back and forth as they laugh and talk animatedly to each other.

Elisabeth turns around and swiftly follows the street back to the shop. Her hands tremble as she fits the key into the lock. She steps inside, locking the door behind her.

The shop is dark, with only the dim street lights glowing through the windows. She stands back against the wall and waits for the men to pass. She remains still, careful not to make any shadows in the dim light. She can hear their laughter as the men get closer. She doesn't think that her father saw her go into the shop, but one can never be sure when it comes to Hartwig Ehrler.

Elisabeth waits for them to pass. She is reminded of what it was like to grow up with Hartwig. She hasn't felt that kind of fear in a while, and it brings back a flood of memories she wishes to forget.

Finally, the men pass by the shop and continue down the street. Elisabeth takes a deep breath and lets it out slowly. She waits a few minutes and peers outside. She stands there for a moment, watching them walk happily down the road. There is a silver lining to the cloud that Olga has placed over her life–Hartwig Ehrler is no longer in it.

Elisabeth smiles to herself...and what a silver lining it is.

12

Adam

Crisp autumn leaves carpet the ground, and the sky is gray. It is early November, 1938. The summer seemed to pass quickly. There is a chill in the air as Adam walks home from work.

Ivan is sitting at the table with Else when Adam arrives.

Adam hands his father the money that he had earned that week before heading to his room to change clothes.

"Did you get a raise in pay?" Ivan asks as Adam sits down at the table across from him.

"No, we just worked more this week. Christmas is coming, so we'll be putting in a lot of hours."

"Thank you, Adam. It won't be long until we can go to America. I turned in the final documentation today, and we almost have all of next year's taxes. Hopefully, we will be in America by summer." Ivan looks happier than he has in years.

"It's ridiculous that we have to pay taxes for next year, and they know that we won't even be living here." Adam has had a long day.

He's too tired to hide his frustration. "They want us out of Germany, but they want to steal from us before we go."

"Once we are out of here, we are safe. That is all that matters now," Ivan said.

The following day, Adam walks to Walter and Elisabeth's flat for dinner. The sun is bright in the sky, but it won't be for long. The days are getting shorter as winter descends upon them.

When Adam arrives, Walter pours him a cup of tea and the two men talk while Elisabeth prepares dinner.

Almost an hour later, Adam and Walter join Elisabeth at the table as she serves their plates. The flat is filled with the aroma of freshly baked bread as they enjoy their dinner.

Adam spends the night, as he usually does if it's late. The only space available to sleep is on the floor in the living room, but he doesn't mind. Adam knows that the Gestapo will arrest him if he is caught outside after dark. Jews could be beaten, arrested, or even killed for being out in the streets at night, or during the day for that matter. The Gestapo really didn't need a reason to beat or kill a Jew.

The following evening, Adam is working in the shop when Dieter bursts inside. He rushes past Frau Lenger and runs straight to the back of the shop where Adam is busy sewing.

"You have to get out of here! They're coming for the Jews!" Dieter grabs Adam's arm and pulls him up from his chair.

Frau Lenger hurries behind Dieter to see what's happening. She quickly retrieves Adam's coat and tosses it into his hands.

"Where will you go?" Fear washes over Frau Lenger's face.

"I'll take care of him." Dieter reassures her before leading Adam out the back door.

"What about my parents?" Adam's heart is beating wildly as he struggles to keep pace with Dieter.

Dieter turns to Adam and motions for him to be quiet as he leads him into a building just a few blocks from the shop. Dieter unlocks the door to the first floor flat. Adam follows him inside.

""I'm going to get your parents. Stay here." Dieter quietly closes the door to the flat and disappears outside.

The flat is dark as Adam huddles in the corner of the dining room listening to the chaos outside. He buries his head in his hands. Fires light up the night as crowds form in the streets. Fear swells in his stomach as he thinks about his parents. He prays that Dieter can save them.

Close to an hour later, Dieter steps back inside the flat, locking the door behind him. Adam is still huddled on the floor in the dark. The dim light from distant fires scarcely illuminates the darkness.

"Where are my parents?"

Dieter sits down on the floor next to him. "They've been arrested."

"No! What is going on out there? Why have they been arrested?"

"You need to stay calm. You need to think clearly right now," Dieter warns him.

"I'm never going to see them again."

"You don't know that."

Adam remains silent. He can only imagine what his parents are going through at that very moment. He suddenly has the urge to vomit. Adam stands up quickly and runs to the sink.

Adam sits back down on the floor and leans his head back against the wall. "Do you have a plan?"

"Not yet, but you will be safe here. The flat belongs to a friend of my uncle. She's visiting family in Berlin for a few weeks." Dieter stares out the window into the madness of the streets. "I need to tell Elisabeth that you're alright. I'll be back."

Adam sits alone as the fires rage throughout the city. He stares into the dancing light of the flames outside. His stomach threatens another upset, but he is able to contain it.

Dieter returns to find Adam still huddled in the same spot.

"I have a note from Elisabeth."

Adam inches towards the window and holds the letter to the light.

Do you know where your father hid the money for America? We will get it for you. Stay safe.

13

Elisabeth

"I forgot about the money. It's under the floorboard of the doorway to the flat. My father thought it would be a good place. People usually look inside the flat. No one ever looks in the doorway as they enter." A sob breaks free as he thinks about his father.

Dieter hands him a pencil. "You can write her back. I'm going to your flat."

Adam sits alone in the darkness with the paper in his hands. He writes simply *thank you.*

Dieter returns with a large box.

"I had to make it look like I was looting your house. I just grabbed anything that I thought you might want." Dieter reaches into his pocket. "Here's the money. I brought your parent's blanket to keep you warm and to keep them close. I grabbed the pillow from your bed and a book from your nightstand. I also got your mother's address book and all of the family pictures that I could find."

Adam looks up at Dieter as tears fill his eyes. "Thank you."

"I have to get back to Elisabeth. I'm afraid she might do something foolish. I will be back tomorrow evening with food. There is some food in the kitchen, but be very quiet. We are lucky that my uncle's friend lives in the basement flat; no creaking floors, but you still have to be undetectable."

"Alright," Adam whispers as he hands Dieter the note. "I don't know how I can ever repay you for what you have done for me." A tear slides down his cheek. "Thank you, Dieter."

That evening, in the darkness, Adam huddles inside his parents' blanket listening to the chaos outside. He thinks about his father's laugh and the silly songs that he would make up. He thinks about the way his mother smiles at him, the way she would hum when she cleaned the flat. He thinks about how much he loves them, and prays that he will see them again. He prays over and over that his parents will be spared from the hands of evil.

14

Hannah

In the spring of 1939 flowers are in bloom all over the city. Bistro tables are outdoors again, and the cafes are full of people soaking up the sun or just enjoying a perfect cup of coffee or glass of wine.

The sun is bright as Hannah walks Helena to the park. It's refreshing to be outside after being stuck in the small flat all winter.

"Are those for me?" Hannah smiles at Helena as she holds out a hand full of flowers.

Helena lies in the grass beside Hannah and rests her head on her lap. Hannah strokes her hair as Helena closes her eyes to the sun. Hannah thinks about Munich and what their lives would be like if they would have stayed. They certainly wouldn't be allowed at a park or even to sit on a park bench. They would be hated and persecuted for being Jewish. Hannah wondered if they would still be alive. She is grateful that she had agreed with Otto to come to Paris.

Paris welcomed them and probably saved their lives. Hannah is accustomed to this vibrant city, but it is still quite a contrast to Munich.

Paris is unique. No one leads. No one follows. It embraces individuality. There is a true sense of freedom in Paris, and Hannah finds it refreshing.

That evening, Marie invites them for dinner. It's Itzhak's birthday, so they are celebrating with a small party of close friends and family.

Marie is preparing dinner when they arrive, and Hannah heads into the kitchen to help. The flat is filled with the aromas of delicious food, and Hannah can't wait to eat. Marie is a wonderful cook. Her meals can last for hours, with many different courses.

By the end of the evening, Hannah can barely stay awake. It is late, and a full stomach isn't helping her fatigue. She helps Marie clean up before walking back home with Otto and Helena.

When they arrive home, Hannah and Otto slip Helena into her nightgown and tuck her into bed.

Hannah climbs into bed and snuggles under the blankets next to Otto. He kisses her softly before they both fall asleep.

Hours later, Hannah wakes to a nervous feeling in her stomach.

She quietly steps out of bed and dresses. She decides a walk might help the feeling subside.

She slips on her shoes and steps outside into the night air. Everyone is sleeping and the city is quiet. The street lamps glow dimly through the fog as she sits down on a bench a block from the flat. This isn't the result of a bad dream, as she had first thought. This is a premonition. Something bad is coming her way.

15

Adam

Adam peers out a small window that looks out onto the alleyway between buildings. He shivers as he wraps the blanket around his shoulders. He leans back against the stone wall of the basement and breathes in the musty air. Staring down at Elisabeth's letter he searches for the words to write.

Dear Elisabeth,

Thank you for the letters. I am nervous about my trip to Hamburg. Not just for me, but for Klara. I'm grateful that she insisted on helping me, but I worry for her safety. Frau Lenger has continued to provide food and books. It's been lonely. I miss my parents terribly. We promised that we would stay together, and now I am the second one to break that promise. I know it's for the best, but it's funny the plans you make in life. You believe that you have some kind of control, but I'm not sure that we do. Life is taking me in a different direction, one far from what I had planned, and certainly not one that I could have predicted. I've enclosed a thank you note for Walter. Take care, my friend.

The following morning, Frau Lenger returns to collect the rent from her tenants and to visit Adam.

"Herr Halder doesn't have his rent again, so I'll be back next week with more food." Frau Lenger hands Adam a parcel that she has hidden in her apron. "There's another book in there too."

"Has Dieter heard any news about my parents?"

"No, nothing yet."

"Here are my letters." Adam pauses for a moment. "I really wish you'd talk to Klara. She doesn't need to accompany me. I will be alright on my own."

"Klara has always been like this, Adam. She's stubborn, like our father. No one can talk her out of it if she's got her mind made up."

Adam holds back tears. "I don't know what I would do without all of you. I would probably be dead." A tear escapes and slides down his cheek.

Frau Lenger pats his shoulder. "I have to go. I can't be down here long."

Adam watches her disappear around the corner before listening to her footsteps on the stairs. A warm breeze drifts through the window as he leans back against wall.

The following night, Adam wakes to police sirens outside the building. He leans back against the wall, out of sight, as the boot clad men race past the basement window. Adam's heart pounds against his chest as the Gestapo officers shout orders in one of the rooms above him. Adam's lip begins to quiver as he struggles to stop his body from shaking. Their footsteps pound the floor above. They seem as though they are searching for something or someone. Adam listens intently, but their voices are muffled as they continue to bark orders to Frau Lenger's tenants.

Moments later, the Gestapo's leather boots pound the cobblestone outside. The Gestapo officers move swiftly past the window of the basement. Their dogs bark ferociously as they are led back to the cars.

Adam cautiously peers out the window as soon as he's certain that all of the cars have sped away. He swallows hard as he stares up at the moon. The sky is black but the moon is bright and smiling down at him. He wipes the sweat from his brow as he returns to his seat on the stone floor. The city is quiet again as he listens for Frau Lenger's tenants above. Not a creak in the floor, not a muffled voice. He can only hear his own breaths, slow and steady now. An uneasy feeling settles in his stomach.

As Adam snuggles under his blanket, his thoughts return to his parents. He now understands the fear that they must have felt knowing that they were in the hands of the Gestapo. Hate fills his heart.

The following morning, sunlight trickles through the window beckoning Adam to wake from his slumber. He yawns and sits up against the cool stone. The spring air is already warm as he stands up and peers outside. He can hear children playing nearby. His mind drifts back to Elisabeth and Hannah, and the warm summer days spent by the lake.

Adam's thoughts are interrupted by footsteps descending the stairs. He stands motionless near the window. Again his heart races as the adrenaline courses through his body. He listens as the footsteps get closer. It's a woman.

"Are you alright?" Frau Lenger whispers.

"Yes, why was the Gestapo here?"

"They arrested Herr Halder."

"What did he do?" Adam asked.

"He's an alcoholic. I won't be able to bring food as often now. The other tenants pay their rent on time. I brought as much as I could hide in this dress." Frau Lenger hands Adam two parcels. "I talked to Dieter about clearing out Herr Halder's things and making the needed repairs to his flat. He will bring food when he is here."

"He was arrested for being an alcoholic?" Adam struggles to believe it.

"Yes, and that's all that I know." She furrows her brow as she glances down at Adam's blanket. "Are you staying warm at night?"

"Yes, my blanket keeps me warm."

"Dieter will be here tomorrow." Frau Lenger waves goodbye.

The following morning, thunder rumbles in the distance. Rain splashes into the puddles outside as Adam sips the tea that he had steeped in tepid water overnight.

"Good morning."

Adam's eyes are wide as he stares up at Dieter standing in the doorway.

"I didn't hear you come down the stairs!"

"I was trying to be quiet," Dieter whispers. "I brought you some food and books from Frau Lenger. I also have letters from Elisabeth and Walter."

"Have you heard anything about my parents?"

Dieter glances out the window and takes a deep breath.

"Your father is dead. I'm sorry, Adam. Your mother was sent to a labor camp."

"They killed him?"

"I'm sorry, Adam."

Adam stares out the window. Tears stream down his cheeks as the rain streaks down the pane of glass.

"What about my mother?"

"All I know is that she was sent to Dachau."

"What are the chances that they will let her go?"

"It's not good."

"When do we leave for Hamburg?"

"A week from tomorrow someone will be here to pick you up. You will be carrying German identification." Dieter hands Adam an envelope. "You look Aryan, so it will be safer for you to travel as a German, not a Jew. Keep your real identification hidden until you board the ship. Once on board, destroy the fake ones. Klara will be with you, and I'll have someone traveling at a safe distance behind. Once you're on board you can rest easy. I will give you more information later."

"How did you do all of this?"

"I have connections."

"Underground connections?" Adam said.

"We're forming a militia against the Nazis. I have to get back upstairs. I'll be back when I can."

Adam watches Dieter disappear around the corner. He shakes his head and stares out the window. Leave it to Dieter to stand up to the Nazis.

He doesn't give his parents another thought. Not now. Now he has to survive.

In May, Adam boards the SS St. Louis. His stomach is uneasy as the Nazi flags flutter in the breeze. He waves goodbye to Klara. He can see the tears in her eyes. He hopes that she can't see his. He follows the line of people walking up the ramp of the ship. He turns to see Klara one more time before stepping onto the ship. He hands his paperwork to an officer standing at the entrance. His heart races as the man studies his documents.

"This is your room key. Follow the corridor to the right until you almost reach the end."

Adam passes the grand picture of Adolf Hitler in the front hall before following the corridor to his room.

The cabin is small with two twin beds. Adam sits down on the edge of the bed and breathes a sigh of relief.

An elderly man knocks softly on the door before stepping inside the cabin.

"Hello." The man smiles as he sets his luggage on the bed across from Adam.

"My name is Ezekiel." He offers his hand to shake.

"I'm Adam."

"Where are you from?" Ezekiel begins unpacking.

"Munich."

"I'm from Augsburg. Are you traveling alone?" Ezekiel sits down on the bed for a rest.

"Yes." Adam continues to unpack. He has no interest in making new friends.

A week later, the ship sails into a storm. Powerful waves crash against the ship, plunging it in and out of the water. Adam holds tight to the metal bed as the boat rocks violently.

"Don't be afraid," Ezekiel reassures him. "Ships have been traveling these waters for hundreds of years. Have you forgotten the Vikings?"

The following morning, the sun shines bright in the sky. Adam sits up in bed and glances over at Ezekiel.

"Good morning." Adam smiles slightly.

"It sure looks like it." Ezekiel sits up and looks out the window. "Should we head down to breakfast?"

Adam sets his plate down and sips his tea.

"This is the best that I have ever eaten." Ezekiel bites into his toast. "My wife was a good cook, but we couldn't afford to eat like this."

Adam pushes the fruit around on his plate.

"You haven't had an easy time of it?" Ezekiel sets his toast down and turns his attention to Adam.

“No.”

Ezekiel slowly stirs his tea.

“Where are your parents?”

“I’m not hungry.” Adam stands up and gathers his dishes. “My stomach is still uneasy after last night. I’ll see you back in the room.”

Adam moves swiftly down the corridor to his room.

He sits down on the bed. He picks up his nightshirt and throws it toward the window before dropping his head into his hands.

That night, Ezekiel turns out the light. The moon is dim outside their window.

“The Gestapo killed my sons,” Ezekiel’s voice cracks. “They may as well have killed my wife. She died from a broken heart. She couldn’t live with the fact that her sons had been beaten and tortured to death. She just couldn’t.”

Silence fills the room.

“They killed my father, and they’re going to kill my mother, if they haven’t already.” Adam finally speaks.

They both cry silently in the darkness, but neither utters another word.

The ship finally reaches Cuba, and it is clear that something is wrong. The passengers are not allowed to disembark. Adam and Ezekiel sit in their room waiting for word, but no word comes.

“It has been days.” Adam stares out the window. “The rumors are probably true. Now that Cuba doesn’t want us, where will we go?” Adam turns to Ezekiel.

“Maybe the Americans will change their minds.”

“What if they send us back to Germany?”

“I can’t imagine that they would do that,” Ezekiel reassures him.

Days later, it is clear that the rumors are true. The ship turns around and heads towards America, but the American Coast Guard surrounds the ship to ensure the passengers don't disembark.

Soon, the SS St. Louis and its passengers are on their way back to Europe.

The people on the ship are quiet now. Everyone is visibly afraid, except the children. They play happily together oblivious of the danger that awaits them in Germany, but their parents know, and there seems to be no way out.

Adam and Ezekiel speak very little now. The hope that they once shared for a better life is now gone. It seems no one wants the Jews, not even America.

Days later, there is a knock at the door.

"All passengers must go to the meeting room." The officer instructs Adam and Ezekiel.

Adam glances at Ezekiel as they both step toward the door. They make their way down the corridor with the other passengers.

The meeting room is crammed with people as names are called out to the crowd.

Adam's name is finally called. He walks to a desk in the front corner of the room and sits down. The woman behind the desk hands him a stack of documents.

"Please read these carefully and sign."

Adam pores over the information printed on the documents. His hands hold tight to each piece of paper.

"I don't understand," his voice is barely a whisper.

" has agreed to grant you a visa. You will be disembarking in a couple of days."

"I'm not returning to Germany?"

"No, please keep your paperwork safe, as you will need it when you arrive. Do you have any questions?"

"No. Thank you."

Adam returns to the cabin to find Ezekiel sitting on the bed. Adam sits down on the bed across from him still holding tight to his paperwork. Ezekiel has documents as well.

"What did they say to you?" Ezekiel asks Adam.

"I have been given a visa by England. I don't have to go back to Germany. What did they say to you?"

"I'm going to Belgium!"

Both men dance around the room.

"Well, at least someone cares about us!" Ezekiel smiles through the tears.

Hours later, at dinner, the other passengers talk excitedly about their destinations. Some are going to France, others to the Netherlands, Great Britain and Belgium. It is rumored that their captain and organizations that help Jews made arrangements for the passengers to be provided visas. The captain had refused to return the passengers to Germany.

Adam thought about the German captain that night before he drifted off to sleep.

"Do you think the captain really did that for us?" Adam whispers to Ezekiel.

"If he did, we all owe him our lives." Ezekiel answers in the darkness.

Days later, Adam says goodbye to Ezekiel and boards a steamer to England.

16

Hannah

Hannah sips her tea and peers out the window to the city below. Otto sits down at the table and opens his newspaper.

"Germany invaded Poland." Otto reads the headline aloud.

"I knew they would. Do you think France and England will stand by what they said?"

"I don't know. They warned Hitl not to do it, and he did it anyway. We'll have to wait and see."

Days later, Hannah's fears are realized. France and Britain declare war on Germany September 3, 1939.

In October, the leaves begin to change, and there's a chill in the air. Otto is working less, allowing him to spend more time with his family. Hannah has finally convinced him that he needs to be home more.

Many of the younger men have enlisted to fight Germany, including Giselle's boyfriend. Giselle had been depressed, but it only lasted a few days. She quickly returned to her partying ways, enjoying the single life.

France is at war, but it isn't at their door yet. Most of the tourists have gone home, but Paris is still buzzing with its usual excitement.

Hannah is shopping for a new coat for Helena. She walks past the busy cafes and stores. It amazes her to see everyone living their lives as usual. No one seems aware that they are at war including Hannah.

Hannah prepares dinner while Helena plays on the floor. It has been a long day, and she still has sewing to do after she cleans the dinner dishes. As she peels potatoes, she thinks about Elisabeth and Adam. Now they are at war, as well. Her friends feel so far away now. She thinks about sending a letter home, but quickly dismisses the idea. It isn't safe.

When Otto returns home from work he is in good spirits. He kisses Hannah before joining Helena to play on the floor.

After dinner, Otto kisses Hannah softly before pulling her into his arms. "I know this is hard for you."

"I'm fine."

"I asked Marie to watch Helena on Friday. I'm taking you out for dinner."

"I'm so glad I married you." Hannah smiles up at Otto.

A couple of weeks later, Giselle arrives for a visit carrying a letter from Germany. Hannah rereads the name and address of the sender a few times before opening it. The name and address aren't familiar, but the handwriting is Elisabeth's. It had been sent to Otto's uncle's address.

Dear Hannah,

I hope all is well. Please give Otto and Helena my love. I know that we agreed not to write, but I had an opportunity to get this letter to you and I took it. I will not speak of what is happening between our countries. I am writing this letter so that you can help me find Adam. He had been on the SS St. Louis, but that is all that I know. The ship returned empty, and it is said that other countries rescued the passengers from a terrible fate here in Germany. I heard that one of the countries was France. Can you please help us find him? A lot has happened here. I cannot talk about it now. We will only be allowed one letter each. Take care. I miss you.

Alles Liebe,

Elisabeth

Hannah studies Elisabeth's handwriting. She cherishes holding the same letter that her friend had held.

Hannah turns her attention back to Giselle. "I need to see your mother. Can you stay here with Helena? I won't be long."

Hannah slips on her shoes and grabs a sweater. The sky is gray and nightfall is settling over the city.

"This could take a few days, maybe even weeks." Marie advises as she rereads the letter.

"I don't care. I just have to know if he's here. I need to know that he is safe."

"Alright, I'll see what I can do."

A week later, Marie arrives at Hannah's flat with news.

"I saw a complete list of the passengers that France accepted. I'm sorry, but your friend was not on it. I have no way of contacting any of the other countries that accepted passengers, except for . I have a friend with a contact there. She will let me know any information that she can find. Don't give up, Hannah."

It's been weeks and Hannah still hasn't received any news on Adam's whereabouts. She wonders how worried Elisabeth must be that she hasn't received a letter yet. Hannah can only hope that Elisabeth understands that something like this could take some time.

In November, there is an assassination attempt on Adolf Hitler, but he escapes unharmed.

Hannah continues to wait for news on Adam and the war. The Parisians slowly begin to hibernate for the winter as the cold winds blow through the city. All is quiet and ominous. Hannah can't shake this uneasy feeling.

In early December, Marie arrives at Hannah's flat with news.

"Here's what I found." Marie hands Hannah a piece of paper with a handwritten address. "This is Adam's address in ."

Hannah stares down at the address before smiling up at Marie.

"I don't know how to thank you. I knew that if anyone could find him it would be you." Hannah hugs Marie.

That evening, Hannah writes two letters. As she writes, she is filled with gratitude that her friends are back in her life. She writes to Adam that she hopes to visit soon. She sends Elisabeth's letter with Adam's information to the name and address that Elisabeth had instructed. She signs Elisabeth's letter with a small butterfly, but an escaped tear smears the ink.

17

Elisabeth

Christmas is weeks away, and Elisabeth is sewing a quilt for Friedrich. Walter has been working late for months now, and it seems he's only home to sleep. She hasn't heard from Dieter since she had given him the letter for Hannah. Elisabeth has no idea how he was able to get a letter to her, but he reassured her that they would be safe. Elisabeth still worries about Adam and hopes that Hannah will be able to find him.

Walter arrives home around eleven with a bottle of wine. "You're up late tonight."

"I need to get this done before Christmas. You're in good spirits." Elisabeth glances up from her sewing.

"Oh, I am. I finally have everything that I need to exact my revenge."

"Olga?" Elisabeth slides her needle into her pin cushion before turning her attention to Walter.

"I've been spending my nights spying on her. I have followed her every move."

"You're crazy," Elisabeth laughs.

"Dieter told me, months ago, that it was rumored that Olga was having an affair. That's how it all started. I wanted to find proof of the affair, and perhaps turn the tables on her. Fortunately, I found what I was looking for and now I'm finally going to exact my revenge."

"She'll hand you over to the Gestapo and have you tortured to death," Elisabeth warns soberly.

"She won't know it was me."

"So, what has Olga been up to?" Elisabeth asks excitedly as she pours the wine.

"She's been having an affair with Reinhard Becker. When your brother goes off to the beer halls, she sneaks over to his flat. They seem to have a passionate relationship. Their fights are brutal. They're both heavy drinkers, I overheard a neighbor talking about it. They don't seem to be trying to hide their affair. I'm surprised that no one has told your brother. "

The smile fades from Elisabeth's face. "My father wanted me to marry Reinhard."

"Well, you were smart not to, he's not a good man. He's a brute."

Elisabeth reflects upon the night her father invited Reinhard to their flat. She's reminded of how much her mother disapproved of him. Like Elisabeth, she must have sensed that Reinhard was trouble.

"So, what do you plan to do with all of this information?"

"I have a friend who is going to slip Henning a note. When Henning lays his coat down at the beer hall my friend will discretely slip the note into his pocket. The note will detail the times and places that Olga and her lover meet. How do you think your brother will react?"

"He'll go mad!"

"He wouldn't hit her?" Walter looks slightly worried.

"No, I think Henning would be too afraid of Olga's father to do anything foolish."

"I think that Reinhard hits her," Walter said.

"I wonder how she explains the bruises to Henning." Elisabeth takes a deep breath. "Am I a bad person because I don't feel sorry for her?"

"I've asked myself the same thing. She's so awful. It's hard to have any compassion for her, especially after she threatened to have the Gestapo torture me to death."

"She destroyed my life too, and I will never forgive her for it. I have the same amount of compassion for Olga that she has for me," Elisabeth said.

"Well, maybe Olga will finally get what she deserves. The sad part is that it won't change our predicament."

The following day, Walter puts his plan into action. The letter is slipped discretely into Henning's coat. Now, they wait. Elisabeth has no idea what Henning will do once he finds out that his wife has been having an affair.

Monday evening, there is a knock at the door.

Elisabeth opens it to find Dieter standing in front of her.

"I received a letter from Hannah today."

Elisabeth holds the letter for a moment, afraid to open it. She stares down at Hannah's handwriting on the envelope.

"Do you want me to read it?" Dieter asks.

"No."

Elisabeth carefully tears the envelope and removes the letter.

The smeared butterfly reminds her of the butterflies that Hannah would draw for her when they were young.

"What does it say?"

"I haven't read it yet." Elisabeth sits down.

Elisabeth reads the letter quickly. She doesn't want to worry Dieter more.

"They're alright! Hannah found Adam! He's in London! Hannah says that she is going to visit him as soon as she can!"

Dieter pulls Elisabeth into his arms and they hold each other tight.

Moments later, they silently reread the letter together. Elisabeth wishes that she could go with Hannah to England. She misses both of her friends terribly.

"I don't know how you did it, and I'm not going to ask, but thanks for getting my letter to Hannah. I'm so grateful."

"I'm just relieved that they are alright." Dieter walks to the door.

Elisabeth watches him, and it hurts that he wants to leave so quickly, but she is careful to hide it.

She waits for him to say something more. It seems that he wants to say something, but he remains silent.

"Thank you, Dieter."

Dieter suddenly looks crestfallen as he turns to face her.

"Take care, Elisabeth."

Elisabeth walks to the window and watches him until he disappears down the street.

Christmas candles warmly light the houses as Elisabeth walks down the cobblestone streets to her grandmother's flat. Friedrich is excited to see her. He spent weeks trying to guess what she had made for him, and now he can finally open his presents. Along with the blanket, Elisabeth also bought Friedrich a toy.

Christmas is bittersweet. It's peaceful because her father is no longer there to ruin it, but grief still fills her heart. While Elisabeth is grateful for all that she has and the people that remain in her life, she is still mourning the loss of her mother. She wonders if Friedrich and her grandmother are missing her mother too. If they do, no one shows it.

Elisabeth lights the candles before sitting down in a chair beside the fireplace. It's warm and cozy as she swigs down her shot of schnapps. Elisabeth and Grandma Heilwig watch Friedrich play with his toys as the radio plays in the background. The winter winds blow outside under a dark sky, but inside it's safe and warm. This is the first Christmas that Elisabeth doesn't have to worry about Hartwig. This is the first Christmas that she doesn't have to be afraid.

Elisabeth silently thanks God again that Hannah and Adam are safe. She prays that He keeps them that way.

That evening, when Elisabeth returns home, she finds Walter sitting alone in the dark.

"I thought that you would be staying at your grandmother's." Walter lights a candle.

"I didn't want you to wake up alone on Christmas. Why are you sitting in the dark?"

"I was at the hospital."

Elisabeth slips off her coat and sits down across from him.

"Your brother knows about Reinhard and Olga. Henning kicked Olga out of their flat. Olga had been living with Reinhard for a couple of weeks when he found out that she was pregnant and lying about it." Walter's face is pale. "Olga's in the hospital. The baby is gone."

"Did Reinhard beat her? Is that why she's in the hospital?"

Walter nods.

"Does Henning know?"

"I don't know. They don't know if Olga's going to make it. Her condition is quite serious."

"Is her family with her?"

"I have a friend that works at the hospital, and she said that Olga's family had refused to see her."

Elisabeth sits back in her chair. "I guess she can't blackmail people using her Gestapo father anymore."

"She can still make up lies to the Gestapo, and I'm sure she would if we make her angry," Walter warns.

"Yeah, I know. I hate that an innocent baby died. I feel bad for Olga." Elisabeth feels a twinge of guilt. Suddenly, a jarring thought eclipses her sympathy for Olga.

Walter eyes her. "What is it?"

"Was the baby Reinhard's or Henning's?"

"I don't know."

"How could I be so cold to care who the father was?" Elisabeth berates herself. She sits back in her chair, lost in thought. It isn't long before the realization of the situation begins to diminish her guilt. "I don't mean to be cold. Only, if it was Henning's it would make me the baby's aunt."

"They're not sure if Olga will survive and I can't say that I'm sad about it." Walter stares down at the floor. "I'm an awful person."

"You are not awful. You don't want her to survive because you would be free from the threat of being tortured to death. Your secret would go to the grave with her. What person would not secretly want that?"

"I should go to bed." Walter rubs his eyes. "It's been a long night."

Walter pats Elisabeth's shoulder before disappearing into his room.

Elisabeth slips on her nightgown and tucks herself into bed.

No one is losing sleep over Olga Ehrler.

A month later, Olga is again living with Reinhard. Although it didn't surprise Walter, Elisabeth is shocked. The Olga that Elisabeth knew wasn't the type of woman that would allow a man to treat her so terribly and go back to him, especially after he caused the loss of her unborn child. It just didn't make any sense.

"She has nowhere else to go," Walter said.

"If Olga was that desperate don't you think she would force us to take her in?"

"Maybe the thought never occurred to her." Walter sips his tea.

"Olga hasn't forgotten about us. She just has us where she wants us, so we are no longer a concern."

In January 1940, Elisabeth receives a letter from Henning. He had entrusted it with Dieter to give to her. After reading the letter it is clear that Olga admitted to him everything that she had done to Elisabeth and Dieter. Henning now knows the truth. He apologizes for disowning Elisabeth, and she believes that he is being sincere.

Sadly, it is a goodbye letter. Henning joined the military, and he is on his way to the front lines. He kept the letter brief and asked Elisabeth to take care. That's it. He's gone...again.

Elisabeth wonders why Henning wrote a letter instead of saying what he had to say in person, but she knows that her brother has too much pride to face her. He wrote in the letter that Hartwig also knows the truth about Olga, but that means nothing to Elisabeth. She is free of Hartwig Ehrler and has no intentions of allowing him back in her life.

Elisabeth wonders why Olga admitted everything. Did she have a guilty conscience? No, she doubted Olga even has a conscience. Elisabeth suspects that Olga probably told Henning to hurt him. She probably told him that she never loved him, and she only married him because she couldn't have Dieter. It doesn't matter. The damage is done.

Dieter tells Elisabeth that Henning had apologized to him as well.

Dieter now seems to have the weight of the world on his shoulders. His eyes are tired and he seems distracted. Elisabeth wants to help him, but she doubts that he would share with her what has him so consumed with worry. It hurts her that she still thinks of him every day. It is clear that he has moved on with his life.

By June, Germany has conquered Norway, Denmark, the Netherlands, Belgium, Luxembourg, and now France. Elisabeth worries about Hannah and Adam, especially Hannah. She can only hope that Hannah will find a way to keep herself and her family safe from the Nazis that now occupy France.

18

Hannah

On June 14th, 1940, Hannah wakes to the German military parading down her street. The goose-stepping soldiers, eyes forward, march in perfect step. Hannah stands at the window and watches their flagrant show of triumph over the French people. She now understands the meaning of her premonition.

Helena tugs at Hannah's nightgown, signaling she is ready for breakfast. Hannah scoops Helena up and holds her in her arms. Hannah knows that she must find a way to protect Helena. The Nazis will be coming for all of them soon.

Warm air blows softly through the curtains in the living room as Hannah prepares porridge. Helena watches the parade, fascinated by the sea of red flags and the marching soldiers.

Hannah's mind searches for any possible way that they can flee France, but she sees no way out. She wishes that the Americans would join the war, but that doesn't seem too promising. The United States isn't exactly staying neutral, but they aren't declaring war either.

Otto returns home from work, and they discuss the food shortages. Food is becoming scarce, but the Germans are living well from all of the counties that they have robbed, including France.

"We must be frugal. This will get worse before it gets better," Otto warns. "The Nazis are going to make France pay for the Treaty of Versailles."

"I'm scared, Otto. We have to find a way out of here. We have to go to America."

"We can't just go to America, Hannah. We don't even have the proper documentation to be living here yet. Just hold on. I'll think of something."

Helena squeals from her chair for Otto to pick her up. Hannah watches her husband as he scoops Helena up into in his arms. Hannah turns away quickly as the tears slide down her cheeks.

A couple of weeks later, Hannah asks Marie to watch over Helena so that she can do her shopping. It's imperative that Hannah does her shopping quickly without garnering attention from the Nazis.

It's a beautiful day, and the sun is bright in a cloudless sky. The flowers are in full bloom, and parks are filled with Parisians soaking up the summer sun.

Hannah is careful to seem casual as she strolls to the shops, but it isn't easy. It seems that Paris is the perfect holiday destination for German soldiers and Hitler's thugs. The Nazis stroll down the streets of Paris as though it belongs to them, and Hannah is quickly reminded, that it does.

Hannah finishes her shopping and rushes back to retrieve Helena. Marie seems worried as well, but neither of them broaches the subject.

The stress of living under Nazi rule again, the heat of summer, and the food shortages are quickly taking a toll on Hannah and Otto. The guilt of not being able to feed their daughter properly also weighs heavily on them. In addition, they fear that they won't be able to protect Helena from the Nazis. The Jews that witnessed the rise of the Nazis in Germany know the evil that they bring. Hannah and Otto know that it's only a matter of time until the Nazis come for the Jews of France.

19

Adam

September of 1940, the Blitz begins. Germany is bombing London relentlessly. Adam now resides in a neighborhood on the east side of London. He lives with an elderly Jewish couple that opened their home to him the day that he arrived in England. Adam had worried about what he would do once he actually set foot on British soil. He was grateful that there were people waiting to help the Jews when they arrived.

Fritz and Martha Scholz immigrated to Britain three years earlier from Berlin. Martha has distant family in London that offered to help them leave Germany. The Scholz's were tired of being persecuted, and they had enough money to allow them to escape from Germany to live a better life in a more tolerant place. Although, there are those in Britain that are not particularly fond of the Jews, any place is better than Germany.

Adam spent his first week at the Scholz's home digging. Every morning, after preparing breakfast, he would clean up and return to his chore of digging up the land needed for the bomb shelter. Adam and Fritz set up the shelter while Martha was responsible for following the guidelines of what should be stocked in the emergency box. Martha is a frail woman, but she does what she can to help.

Their bomb shelter is located steps away from the back door of the kitchen, so it is easily accessible during the bombings.

When Adam finished their shelter he volunteered to help the young mother next door. Nancy Deacon's sister and mother a live a few blocks away. They help Nancy as much as possible, but the majority of the time she's on her own. She is one of many, left alone while their husbands fight in the war.

The backyard of the Scholz's home is a small fenced area with a large garden. The ration cards don't allow for much, so it is essential to grow your own vegetables.

Adam helped to make all of the blackout blinds for the windows. It is against the law to allow any light to shine at night, even a lit cigarette. It is imperative that the bombers above are met with complete darkness below. The Scholz's were fined the first week of the blackout due to a report that light had seeped through one of the bedroom windows.

Although everyone lives in fear of their homes being bombed, or their friends and family being killed, life goes on. Adam fills his days cooking and cleaning for Martha and Fritz. Martha has heart problems, and Fritz knows little about housework or cooking. This is Adam's way of earning his place in their home. It isn't easy though. The rations allow them enough food to keep from starving, but most of the time they go to bed hungry. This is something Adam has been accustomed to most of his life. The only time that he had been allowed to eat until his stomach was full was on the S.S. St. Louis. There was plenty of food for everyone and it was delicious. Adam would have enjoyed it more if the situation had been different, but he was grieving the loss of his parents and on his way to a foreign land. The anxiety and grief didn't allow for much of an appetite, so he ate very little. He regrets that now.

Adam scrubs the tub with the last of the Vim. He shakes the can to empty out every bit of powder, but he is left with a tiny bit of dust. He wonders, as he scrubs, how often Winston Churchill bathes. Adam assumes that King George probably bathes every day. The King stated that they are rationing just like everyone else, but Adam isn't sure he believes it. He respects the Royal Family for remaining with their people and refusing to leave for a safer place. Adam is grateful to live in a country reigned by a Monarchy that stands by its people. He's grateful to be in England, even if they are getting bombed relentlessly.

The blaring sirens interrupt Adam's thoughts. He drops the rag in the tub, turns out the light, and moves carefully down the stairs. The house is dark as he makes his way through the kitchen and out the back door.

The thunderous planes loom overhead. The bombs began to drop as Adam steps inside the shelter. Fritz and Martha are already inside, as usual. They are terrified of the bombs and remain ready, at all times, to seek the safety of the shelter. Adam worries about Fritz, and especially Martha, in the middle of the night as they make their way down the stairs in the darkness. Adam is always in the lead just in case one of them should fall. They can't fall far if he's in front of them. Adam always reminds them to hold the rail as they carefully descend the steep staircase.

The bombs whistle out of the sky as the planes buzz overhead. Adam hates Adolf Hitler. It is his only thought as the bombs explode and the fires light up the night.

That night, Adam falls asleep to the sound of the planes above them and bombs destroying everything in their path. As he drifts off to sleep, he wonders if he will wake up. He thinks about the people who die in the shelters as they sleep. He finally relents to the exhaustion and drifts off to sleep.

Early the next morning, Adam wakes to the siren notifying them it that is safe to come out of the shelter. He rubs his eyes and steps outside. Fritz and Martha are close behind.

The kitchen door is open, and there is dust and broken dishes everywhere. Adam inspects the house before removing the blackout blinds from each window. As he opens the window in the sitting room he notices smoke down the street. A home is still on fire, destroyed by the bombs. Adam runs towards the blazing fire in an effort to help. The firemen are working to contain the blaze as it crackles and spits hot sparks into the air.

"Is there anything that I can do to help? Is everyone alright?"

The fireman glares at Adam. He has discerned his German accent. "They're dead."

He returns home to find Martha in the kitchen trying to clean up the soot that coats the floor.

"I'll do that." Adam takes the broom from Martha's hand.

Martha's doctor had given her strict orders that she do no physical work. Her heart is working hard enough dealing with the stress of the bombings, and it can barely handle that.

"I'm sorry that I wasn't here to help. I just wanted to check on the family down the street."

"Adam, don't worry about that. You do so much for us and we can barely even feed you. Are they alright?"

"They didn't survive."

It takes hours to clean up. Adam prepares dinner while Fritz and Martha nap in the living room. Adam doesn't have the best cooking skills, but he's learning. He had learned from his mother how to make the most out of so little, and he is always careful to waste nothing. Even the water used to cook vegetables will later be used for stock. It is a *waste not, want not* life in Britain during wartime, something Adam knows very well.

That evening, Fritz turns on the radio, and they relax in the living room listening to Churchill's address to the nation. The Germans want to devastate the morale of the British people, but the bombings have the opposite effect. The British people become even more resilient and resolute to stand and fight. *Business as Usual* is written on chalk boards in shop windows. Although they live in constant danger, they continue to carry out their daily life.

Adam is becoming fast friends with their neighbor, Nancy. When they first met, he felt sorry for the young woman because she was alone with two children, but the more time that he spends with her he sees a clever and capable woman. Her sons are polite young boys. Evan is seven years old, and Ben is five. The boys play well together and usually don't get into too much mischief. Nancy runs her home like a well-oiled machine. She teaches Adam some tricks in the kitchen and helps him understand the ration books, which can be quite confusing.

Adam speaks English, but he still struggles with it. He had never heard anyone speak the English language until he arrived in Britain. He had learned the basics from his uncle's books. He works on his accent as well. Practicing his English with Fritz and Martha is also a welcome distraction to the long nights in the shelter.

Adam stops by Nancy's house so that they can walk together to the grocer. The lines are long and it gives them someone to pass the time with while they wait.

"Where are the children?" Adam asks as Nancy steps outside.

"My sister picked them up this morning. They try to give me a break once in a while. It's nice to have the help. How is Martha feeling?"

"She's been feeling a bit better, but Fritz has been more tired than usual. It's probably the stress of it all. It feels like the bombing will never end."

"Do you ever miss Germany?"

Adam just shakes his head and changes the subject. He has told his story to Martha and Fritz, and that is the last time that he ever wants to talk about it. He hasn't even been to a synagogue since he arrived in England, even though there is one in walking distance from their house. Adam convinces himself that he is too busy taking care of Fritz and Martha, but the truth is that he can't bear any reminders of his past, especially the loss of his parents. Surviving is all that he can do right now, and that is enough.

That evening, the sirens sound during dinner. There is a chill in the air as they make their way to the shelter. Adam wraps a blanket around Martha as the city explodes outside.

Adam sits down across from Fritz and Martha in the darkness. He curls up against the wall and pulls the blanket over his head. He sobs quietly as the bombs continue to drop from the planes overhead.

By December, it is clear that the United States is not entering the war. Fritz tells Martha to hold on to hope, but between the food shortages and the seemingly constant bombings, it is getting difficult to hope for anything. Adam is angry at America for not helping.

"They know that we could use their help, and they're continuing to enjoy the good life while we suffer."

"It's not really their war." Fritz pours tea into their cups.

"America is a country of immigrants, mostly from Europe. Have they forgotten?"

"Well, were still holding our own. It's not over yet," Fritz reminds Adam.

He knows that Fritz is right. It is too early to tell how the war will end.

Adam washes the dinner dishes with the small amount of soap he has left, while Fritz carries in charcoal for the stove. Martha is napping in the living room. Adam looks forward to the evenings when the sirens are quiet, and the only sound to be heard is the BBC broadcasts on the radio.

Adam wakes in the middle of the night to the sirens wailing across the city. He slips on his coat and makes his way to Fritz and Martha's bedroom where they are waiting in the doorway. Fritz and Martha carefully make their way down the stairs with Adam in the lead. Martha holds onto Adam's coat with one hand and the railing with the other. Fritz has one hand on Martha and one on the railing. It is dark in the house, so, even though they need to move quickly, they also need to move carefully. Being plunged into darkness had its casualties. Some people lost their lives as they made their way to the shelters in the darkness, others to car accidents in the blacked out streets of London.

Adam, Fritz, and Martha walk in an orderly fashion through the kitchen and out the door to the shelter.

Inside the shelter, Adam pulls the blankets over his head and falls back to sleep. It isn't long before Fritz and Martha are sleeping too.

Later that night, a bomb hits so close that it jolts them from their slumber. Adam, Fritz, and Martha have grown accustomed to sleeping through the bombings, but this one feels as though it has hit their shelter. The sound is deafening, and the shelter shakes violently. Adam's ears are ringing as he peers outside. A bomb has exploded on the house across the street. The bright flames shoot up into the night sky as the roof of the house collapses. The bombing continues as the planes hover overhead.

Adam steps outside of the shelter, ignoring Fritz's warnings. He watches the flames light up the city. For a moment, he doesn't care whether he lives or dies. All that he can feel is hate for Adolf Hitler and his Nazis.

Adam stands tall as the planes buzz overhead and the fires explode around him. He can no longer hear Fritz or Martha pleading with him from inside the shelter.

He stands alone–without fear.

He is done giving anyone that power.

20

Elisabeth

Fresh snow crunches under Elisabeth's worn shoes as she makes her way back home. She has taken care of all of the arrangements, and now Grandmother Heilwig can rest in peace. Friedrich walks with Elisabeth in stride as the snow falls silent from the gray sky.

Friedrich had been the one to find Grandma Heilwig when he returned home from school. She had been suffering from seizures for over a year and the doctors were unable to find what was causing them, so they just kept her medicated hoping it would help. The medication helped for a while, but the seizures returned. On January 2, 1941, Grandma Heilwig had a seizure and hit her head on the table in the dining room. Friedrich came home to find her dead on the floor in a pool of blood.

Walter volunteers to share his room with Friedrich, but Elisabeth is adamant that Friedrich sleep in the living room. She shares her bedroom for his things. Friedrich still seems in shock, so Elisabeth limits any conversation about their grandmother until he has had some time to process it.

Elisabeth prepares dinner while Friedrich sits in her bedroom staring out the window to the frozen garden outside.

A week later, Elisabeth tucks Friedrich into bed.

"I'm too old to be tucked in, Elisabeth."

"I know." Elisabeth pulls the blanket up to his chest.

"I miss her," Friedrich said.

Elisabeth pats his hand. "I know."

That night, Elisabeth and Friedrich stay up most of the night talking. They talk about their family and reminisce about the good times and cry together remembering the hard times. Friedrich admits to Elisabeth that Henning had visited him frequently at their grandma Heilwig's.

"He would only come when he knew that you wouldn't be there. I hated that my family was so torn apart."

Elisabeth tells Friedrich about the letter that Henning had written to her before he left to fight in the war. She doesn't give him all of the details, but she makes it clear that they had resolved their issues.

"It's alright now." Elisabeth smiles through the tears.

"I'm sure he'll be back soon. My camp leaders say that the war will end quickly in a victory."

Elisabeth wonders what other things the Hitler Youth is telling her brother.

In late February, Elisabeth spots Olga on the street. Olga weaves back and forth, but still manages to remain upright. A woman pushing a pram stares at her in disgust. She is so drunk that Elisabeth wonders how she will make it home. It is early afternoon, which means Olga is still drunk from the previous night, or she started drinking early in the morning.

Elisabeth is relieved that Olga is too drunk to even notice that she is following her. Of course, Elisabeth remains a safe distance away.

Elisabeth watches Olga open the door to a building. She waits a few minutes before following her inside.

Olga knocks on the door of a flat on the top floor. Moments later, a man answers. Elisabeth thinks she recognizes his voice, but she isn't sure.

Elisabeth can hear Olga and the man arguing inside. She stands in the hallway listening. She's aware that she is too close. If they open the door she will certainly be caught, but she can't leave. She listens to the man call Olga names that she thought only Hartwig would call a woman. Suddenly, there's a commotion inside the flat. She is certain that their fight is now physical. Elisabeth's heart races; she needs to get out of there. She quickly descends the wooden stairs, pushes the heavy door open, and slips outside. She walks around the corner, and waits for Olga to come out. She knows that it could be days until Olga leaves, but she wants to stay for a little while longer, just in case she's wrong.

Twenty minutes later, Olga still hasn't appeared. Elisabeth decides to walk home. As she turns to leave, the door to the building opens.

Olga is pushed to the ground. Elisabeth ducks back and peeks around the corner just in time to see Reinhard Becker closing the door behind him. Olga yells obscenities in his direction. Elisabeth watches her to see if she can get up on her own. There is no way that she is going to help her. Olga would know that she had followed her, and that wouldn't be good.

Finally, Olga attempts to stand, but she can't. It is clear that she is badly hurt, and Elisabeth wonders if someone will stop to help her.

Almost ten minutes has passed, and no one has stopped to help. Olga is still lying on the ground, drunk and bloody. Elisabeth sighs angrily. She hates that she has compassion for this soulless creature.

Suddenly, an older woman appears. She struggles to help Olga to her feet, but Olga is too heavy. A man then stops to the help the woman, but he is unable to lift Olga as well. Finally, they are able to drag Olga inside the building to sleep it off.

Elisabeth decides that she should get out of there. She's seen enough.

That evening, Elisabeth thinks about Dieter. She feels alone without Hannah and Adam, and the loss of her grandmother. Walter is kind and he is a friend, but it isn't the same. She tries to push all of it from her mind as she slips on her coat. Friedrich is with friends and she wants to walk him home. It's not safe for him to walk alone in the city.

Friedrich is waiting outside his friend's building when Elisabeth arrives.

"Why are you waiting outside?"

"I just wanted to," Friedrich smiles. "I think we should stop at the bakery."

They walk along the cobblestone streets. Dim city lights illuminate their way. Elisabeth and Friedrich are almost to the bakery when they pass Dieter on the street. He looks pleased to see them.

"I guess you're probably not going to want a ride on my shoulders."

"I don't think so." Friedrich's cheeks turn slightly red. "We're going to the bakery. Why don't you come with us?"

Dieter glances at Elisabeth, and she smiles to let him know that he is welcome to join them. As they walk, it is clear that Friedrich still worships Dieter, just as he had when he was young. It is the first time that Elisabeth has been in public with Dieter since Olga began blackmailing her. She feels fairly certain that Olga won't see them tonight, but they still need to be careful.

Elisabeth purchases an apple strudel at the bakery while Dieter and Friedrich talk outside. Friedrich is laughing, and Dieter looks happy. It reminds Elisabeth how much she has missed him. The smile fades from her face. At that moment, Dieter glances at her through the window. His smile quickly fades. She sees the weight of the world return to his eyes.

Moments later, Elisabeth steps outside and hands Dieter a small package.

"This was your favorite."

Dieter opens the wax paper and peeks inside. The smile returns to his face, but his eyes hold their sadness.

Elisabeth and Friedrich say goodbye to Dieter. Elisabeth and Dieter know not to tempt fate. If Olga were to find out about this interaction, small as it may be, it could provoke her to exact her revenge on them.

"Why didn't you invite Dieter for a visit?"

"It's a long story. I'll tell you about it someday, but not now."

That evening, after Friedrich falls asleep, Elisabeth tells Walter about Olga.

"I hate that a drunk like her has been able to keep Dieter and I apart." Buried anger tightens in Elisabeth's stomach as she quietly closes her bedroom door. "I will never love another man." Elisabeth sits down on her bed, across from Walter, seated at her desk. "I know I'm too young to say that, but I have a feeling that it's true. Somewhere, deep down, I know it's true. Thanks to Olga, I will die a lonely woman."

The following morning, Elisabeth prepares breakfast for Friedrich before walking him to school. Rain drizzles from the gray sky as they stroll down the cobblestone streets. On the way to school Friedrich talks excitedly about the Hitler Youth.

As Elisabeth listens to Friedrich she worries that he will end up like her father and Henning. She also worries that if she tells Friedrich the truth about the Nazis that he may hate them as much as she does. If Friedrich doesn't agree with the Nazis it could get him into a lot of trouble, and he is too honest to be able to hide it. Elisabeth wonders if it would just be easier to let Friedrich believe their lies than to put him in danger with the truth.

"Now judgment has begun and it will reach its conclusion only when knowledge of the Jews has been erased from the earth." –Nazi Newspaper

Elisabeth sips her tea while reading the newest hate splashed across the newspaper. She wonders how the Nazis plan to erase the Jews. The Gestapo is already killing and torturing every Jew that they can get their evil hands on, but it seems that the German government is intent on erasing all Jews from existence. One could only wonder how they planned to do that.

In March, all Jews are ordered to forced labor.

Elisabeth walks to the market, past the lines of Jewish citizens, all wearing the required yellow Star of David badge with JUDE written in black letters. Small children hold their parents' hands as they stand in the long lines. Elisabeth walks past with her gaze forward. Showing sympathy for the Jews will certainly get you arrested. Adolf Hitler is very clear that anyone that isn't with him is against him, and the punishment for this dissension is severe.

Guilt plagues her as she walks past. Anyone with a conscience knows that what Adolf Hitler and the Nazis are doing is wrong. She thinks back to the crying baby thrown out of a window by the Gestapo. The Gestapo killed their entire family.

Anyone can be killed or tortured by the Gestapo. Olga is a perfect example of the Germany that Hitler has created. The hounds of hell roam the streets in search of prey, and it seems the majority of the

German people have accepted this new way of life. Everyone now has the ability to have anyone tortured or killed. All it takes is a report to the Gestapo, even if it's a lie. In the eyes of the Gestapo, everyone is guilty, and they will pay in the cruelest of ways. When Olga threatened Elisabeth's life, the day of her wedding, Elisabeth knew that it was not an idle threat. Elisabeth also knows that she has the power to destroy Olga's life, as well, even if her father is the Gestapo. It would take very little thought and planning to throw Olga into the evil hands of the Gestapo. Fortunately for Olga, Elisabeth wouldn't do anything that cruel, even to her enemy.

Elisabeth finishes her shopping and walks to Friedrich's school. As she waits outside, she thinks about Hannah and Adam. She's reminded of the times that they were tormented by the other students. The persecution of the Jews in the past is nothing compared to how the Jews live now. Elisabeth is grateful that her friends had found a way out of Germany. She can only hope that Adolf Hitler loses the war, even if she and the German people have to pay right along with him. Adolf Hitler needs to be destroyed before he conquers all of Europe.

That evening, after Elisabeth tucks Friedrich into bed, she pours a cup of tea and sits by the window listening to the sounds of the city. Every night, the blare of police sirens surprise innocent victims with an arrest. Surprising people is the Gestapo's favorite tactic. One important lesson that Elisabeth learned from Hartwig is that the weak love power and they always find ways to abuse it.

Elisabeth, Friedrich, and Walter spend most of their time inside the flat. They only leave when they have to go to work, school, or shopping for food. In the evenings, they read or just talk. Friedrich begs to hear Hitler's speeches on the radio, but Elisabeth will not allow it. She apologizes to Friedrich that the radio is broken...after she secretly breaks it. She can show no signs of defiance toward Adolf Hitler. So, to Friedrich, Elisabeth is a loyal Nazi and so is Walter.

Spring ushers in the warmth of the sun and new life to the garden outside Elisabeth's bedroom window. She opens the windows and cleans the flat, with the help of Walter and Friedrich. Spring is her favorite time of year. She loves opening the windows to allow the fresh air to clear the stuffiness of winter.

Elisabeth's job as a seamstress is going well, but she still doesn't make much money. It's enough to support her family, but that is only because Walter insists on paying all of the rent.

Friedrich is growing more and more infatuated with the Nazi ideology. He now believes that the Germans are the superior race.

"It's been proven. We must take it seriously and do our part to change the world." Friedrich preaches one evening as Elisabeth prepares dinner.

"What's been proven?" Friedrich now has Elisabeth's full attention.

"It's a fact that German blood is the blood of ancient Gods."

Elisabeth continues to peel potatoes as Friedrich talks incessantly about the German superiority. The anger wells up inside her, but she is careful to hide it. She is relieved when Walter steps in and reminds Friedrich that he needs to finish his studies.

Elisabeth remains silent, but her anger is clear as she clangs pots and pans around the kitchen.

"Did you hear what he said about the Jews?" Elisabeth whispers.

Walter pours her a glass of wine and forces her to sit down at the table.

"I can't do this anymore!" Elisabeth continues to whisper. "He needs to know that these people are evil!"

"If he believes you, it will change the way that he sees the Nazis and the world around him. It will put him in grave danger if they suspect that he's not loyal, and they will know. Friedrich won't be able to hide what he feels for them. That's if he believes you at all. Remember, he has been brainwashed by your father, your brother, his teachers, the Youth Leaders and everyone else, his entire childhood. This is all he knows."

"My mother did everything that she could to shield him from all of the brainwashing."

"Your mother wanted to protect him and that's exactly what you're doing." Walter reassures her. "Wait until he's older. Maybe then it will be safe to tell him the truth."

Elisabeth knows that Walter is right, but she hates watching her brother turn into a Nazi right before her eyes.

That night, Elisabeth wakes to a loud banging on the door. Walter opens it and two Gestapo officers burst inside. Friedrich watches the men with wide eyes. Elisabeth runs to be near him as the men bark orders at Walter.

Walter follows their orders and dresses quickly. Elisabeth holds Friedrich close as the men rifle through the flat. One of the men inspects the bedrooms while the other inspects the rest of the flat.

"Why do you sleep in different rooms?" The Gestapo officer eyes Elisabeth and Walter.

Walter looks terrified. "She's been ill, so I've been sleeping in her brother's room.

The officer doesn't seem to believe Walter, but he says nothing more. Walter is arrested and led outside to a car. Elisabeth watches out the window as the car pulls away and speeds down the street.

Moments later, when the shock wears off, fear sets in. Elisabeth needs to get to Dieter. He has connections with the Gestapo that can get them information. Elisabeth dresses quickly and slips on her coat.

"Stay here, I'll be right back. Everything is going to be alright. I'm going to get Dieter."

Elisabeth jogs at a steady pace as the rain pours down. When she arrives at Dieter's building she quickly climbs the stairs to his flat and knocks softly on the door.

It takes a few minutes, but Dieter finally answers.

"They arrested Walter." Elisabeth whispers as she steps inside.

"Where's Friedrich?"

"He's at home." Elisabeth is trembling now.

Dieter grabs his coat and walks out of the flat with Elisabeth. They move quickly through the city streets as the rain pours from the sky. It is almost midnight when they arrive back at her flat. Friedrich is sitting in the living room, visibly shaken, but he is relieved to see Dieter.

Dieter sits down beside him and reassures him that it will be alright while Elisabeth boils water for tea.

Her heart is still racing minutes later. She doesn't even notice that Dieter is now standing behind her.

Dieter holds her in his arms and reminds her that she needs to be strong for Friedrich. Elisabeth cries silently in his arms.

Moments later, Elisabeth gathers herself together and wipes away her tears.

She carries steaming cups of tea on a tray into the living room. She hands Dieter and Friedrich a cup. The rain taps on the windows as they sip their tea in silence.

Friedrich is the first to finish his tea and he's growing tired. Elisabeth tucks him in and asks Dieter to wait in her bedroom.

She closes the bedroom door behind her so that Friedrich can't hear their conversation.

Elisabeth sits down next to Dieter on the bed.

"Did the Gestapo notice that you and Walter sleep in different rooms?" Dieter looks worried.

"Yes, but Walter said it was because I had been ill. Why?"

"Did they say what he was being arrested for?"

"No, they just stormed in and took him. Why did you ask if the Gestapo noticed our sleeping arrangement?"

"Elisabeth, you know that Walter is a homosexual."

"No."

"He didn't tell you? You never suspected it?"

"No, I had no idea. Do you think that is why they arrested him?"

"I don't know." Dieter sighs. "Hopefully, I will find something out in the next couple of days."

Elisabeth sits quietly, still processing Dieter words. She wonders if Adam had known. She hopes that isn't the reason that the Gestapo arrested him. If it is, he is in a lot of trouble. She could be, as well, if they suspect that she covered it up.

"What if they come back and arrest me?" Elisabeth looks up at Dieter.

"Just tell the truth. You really didn't know. When you moved in he wanted you to stay in your own room. You never asked why because a woman shouldn't question those things," Dieter coaches her.

Although he doesn't show it, Dieter has concerns that the Gestapo might come back to arrest Elisabeth.

That night, Dieter stays with Elisabeth.

"I love you. I never stopped loving you." Dieter admits in the silence of the dark room.

Dieter pulls Elisabeth close to him and kisses her softly. Elisabeth doesn't pull away. She loves him, and that night, she gives herself to him. It no longer matters that they aren't married. Elisabeth knows that Dieter is the only man that she will ever love.

Dieter finally receives information regarding Walter a few days later.

"He was tortured and killed the night of his arrest. On the death certificate they documented the cause of death to be dysentery, but that was a lie." Dieter takes a deep breath. "Someone reported to the Gestapo that they thought he was a homosexual."

Elisabeth sobs as Dieter holds her in his arms.

"And, you don't have to worry. They aren't going to arrest you."

Dieter doesn't tell Elisabeth that, although they didn't arrest her, they did open a file on her. Anyone that the Gestapo has suspicions about has a file.

A month later, Elisabeth and Friedrich move into a more affordable flat. Money is tight and the flat is small, with only one bedroom. Friedrich volunteers to sleep in the living room so that Elisabeth can have the bedroom.

Elisabeth didn't know how to contact Walter's parents, so she sold the items that they couldn't take with them to the new flat. Elisabeth kept a few of Walter's personal items that were special to her in small box that Friedrich decorated in his memory.

Dieter visits as much as he can, but they still have to be careful. Although, it does seem that Olga is too preoccupied with Reinhard, and destroying her liver to pay attention to what Elisabeth is doing.

Elisabeth stands at the window looking out to the dimly lit city below. The moon is a white sliver in the onyx sky.

In the silence, she thinks about Walter. She wonders if Walter's homosexuality was what Olga had been holding over him. Tears fill her eyes. Walter was so kind and giving–why did it matter who he loved?

Elisabeth thinks about Adam. She wonders if he and Walter had been more than just friends. Walter had paid a large sum of money to help Adam, and she was certain that losing him had broken Walter's heart. The glances between them flash in her mind.

How could she have missed the clues that had been right in front of her? Why didn't Adam confide in her? Didn't he trust her? She is his best friend. Nothing could change that. Adam knew that she had no judgments regarding homosexuality. They had talked about it, in passing, a few times. Hannah felt the same way. Why didn't he tell us? The questions swirl in her mind. But shame rests heavy in her heart. What had she done, or said, to make Adam feel that he needed to hide who he was?

Elisabeth prays again for Adam and Hannah's safety. She also prays for forgiveness before crying herself to sleep.

21

Hannah

Ice glazes the leafless trees under a bitter cold sky. Power lines snap from the ice causing loss of power in many areas of the city. The Germans use all of the coal and fuel that they desire, leaving little to the Parisians. The same can be said for food. Meat is a rarity, as well as cooking oil. There are even shortages of cabbage and potatoes, which is a true indicator of the desperate conditions brought on by the Nazi regime.

Acts of French resistance are recurring more and more. German officers have been assaulted and underground movements are gaining new members every day. Even the communists in France are gaining a following.

Itzhak, Marie, and Giselle move in with Otto and Hannah. Otto and Hannah are undocumented Jews, so it is safer for everyone to stay at their flat. In the eyes of the law, Hannah and Otto don't exist.

Hannah is grateful that she hadn't turned in the documentation for their flat. Their last known address is Otto's uncle's flat. Their landlord didn't require them to submit documentation. The building is in disrepair, so the landlord accepts any tenants that are willing to live under such deplorable conditions. He doesn't care who they are as long as they pay the rent on time.

The flat seemed small before the rest of the family moved in, and now it feels even smaller.

Marie does what she can to keep everyone fed, but most nights they go to bed hungry. Itzhak's business had been stolen shortly before they moved in, so both he and Otto lost their jobs. One day, a man just walked into the store, accompanied by the French police, and advised that the business now belonged to him. He wasn't required to pay anything for it. The French police escorted Otto and his employees out within minutes. The Jews are hated in France, just as they are in Germany.

Otto and Itzhak now work at a factory on the outskirts of town. The owner of the factory is a Jewish sympathizer, and many of the Jews that have lost their jobs and businesses work there. Otto and Itzhak walk to work every day knowing that they could be arrested if they are caught, but they have no choice. They also know that it is only a matter of time until the factory is raided, but they have a family to feed.

The Jews are now hunted in Paris, not only by the Nazis, but the French police. They stop people on the streets demanding to see their papers in search of Jews. Raids are carried out daily on homes and businesses; many are arrested. Hannah, Marie, and Giselle rarely leave the flat. Otto and his uncle are always careful on their way to and from work to remain out of sight. It makes their journey much longer, but they have no choice.

On June 22, 1941, Germany invades the Soviet Union. Hannah is pleased to hear it. The more countries that are against the Germans increase the odds of beating them. Hannah knows that Adolf Hitler and his Nazis are arrogant enough to believe that they will take over the world, and that arrogance will be their downfall. Hannah hopes that it will only be a matter of time until the United States joins the fight.

The summer is hot and the living conditions have worsened. Helena only eats once a day, but it isn't much. Hannah, Marie, and Giselle are now eating every other day and it usually consists of watered down cabbage or onion soup. Otto and Itzhak are eating daily, but they are growing increasingly thin due to the lack of food and the arduous work at the factory. Hannah, Marie, and Giselle reserve their bread for the men, but bread and watery soup provides little nourishment.

Helena cries frequently due to hunger, and Hannah is helpless to stop it. She does everything that she can to feed her, including preparing salads out of grass from the park. She even thinks about stealing food, but the grocers watch everyone closely due to the starving conditions. People who are caught stealing are arrested and jailed. Hannah has heard rumors about how the French police treat their detainees, and it seems they abuse their power almost as much as the Nazis in Germany.

The family worries about Itzhak. He is too old to be living under these conditions. Marie does all that she can for her husband, but he is becoming increasingly frail. Itzhak also insists on going to work every day, without exception.

October ushers in cooler temperatures and fresh fears of the upcoming winter. Coal is scarce, and the flat is usually cold. Hannah still picks grass every day for the family to eat, but she worries about what they will do once the snow blankets the ground.

By mid-October, Itzhak is growing weak, and there are rumors at the factory that he is going to lose his job. Otto speaks to the Director and requests that he work Itzhak's hours, in addition to his own, if

Itzhak is to lose his job. The Director only authorizes Otto to work half of Itzhak's hours. Factory work is not easy, especially if you are barely eating.

The following day, the Director pulls Itzhak aside at the end of the day and informs him that he can no longer employ him. The Director thanks Itzhak for his work and gives him a little extra pay to help.

Otto works longer hours and he is only home to sleep. Hannah worries about him constantly. He is even too tired to play with Helena, which is something that he had always looked forward to when he returned home from work.

Hannah worries about Adam. She can no longer write to him, and she fears that he may have been hurt or killed in the bombings. She also worries about Elisabeth and her own parents. She is homesick, now, more than ever. She reminisces about the good times growing up in Munich to escape the hopelessness of her reality. It is a place in her mind where she can go to see her friends and family. In her mind, Hannah can return home any time that she desires. Her memories remain alive there.

In early November, a doctor checks on Itzhak. Marie worries that he is suffering from something more serious than just old age. The doctor is a trusted friend of the family, and Marie is relieved to see him.

Dr. Brodeur examines Itzhak and tells the family that he is alright. He advises that Itzhak is malnourished, but that is to be expected living in such poor conditions. The doctor visits for a short time and tells them about Drancy, the prison for Jews. Dr. Brodeur is saddened by the conditions in which the people detained there have to live, especially the children.

A week later, a flat in the building across the street is searched and the people are arrested. Hannah doesn't know any of her neighbors. She has no idea why they were arrested, but Marie has contacts. She was informed that they are Jews from Poland. The children are taken, along with the others, to Drancy.

The Germans are getting closer.

Hannah has another premonition that night that wakes her before dawn. Fear washes over her as her heart races. She sits up in bed and stares into the darkness. The nightmare slowly fades, but the message is clear–they are in imminent danger.

22

Adam

Adam rubs his hands together over the stove for warmth. Martha and Fritz are in the living room reading. The morning air is chilly as the rain taps on the windows. Adam numbly begins his chores as he does every day.

In the afternoon, Adam visits with Nancy. The sky is gray as he walks to her house next door. She is on her knees cleaning the kitchen floor when he arrives.

"A good excuse for a break." Nancy smiles up at him.

Adam is still not feeling sociable, but he needs her opinion on something that he has been contemplating for awhile.

"I am going to see if I can get a job at the factory where your husband worked."

"Will you have time to work?" Nancy asks, referring to Fritz and Martha.

"I have to do something. I can't join the military and abandon the Scholz's, but I can still try to find other ways to help. What are the chances that they would hire a German?"

"Not good. It's not going to be easy. I know your story, but they don't. They just know you're a German and the Germans are trying to kill us."

Adam has done all he can to assimilate to the British culture. He understands what is expected of him. He must not look or act too Jewish or German. He is again living in a country that dislikes or distrusts the Jews, and they despise the Germans even more.

That evening, after dinner, Adam cleans the dishes and sweeps the kitchen floor. Martha has gone to bed early, and Fritz is reading in the living room. Hard rain taps against the blacked out windows. They aren't experiencing the bombing anymore like the days of the Blitz, but one never knows when the Germans will pay them a visit. The blackout laws remain in place.

Adam sits at the kitchen table, alone in the darkness. He still wonders every day what fate befell his mother. He holds onto the hope that she has been released from the labor camps.

"I noticed it was quiet in here." Fritz turns on the light. "I'm sorry. Would you like to be alone?"

Adam just shakes his head and smiles; he enjoys being with Fritz. He reminds him of his uncle.

"I don't know what to do while I'm here. I am trying to help, but no one wants my help. Nancy says it's doubtful that anyone would hire a German and I understand it, I really do, but I feel like I should be doing more. This country took me in and saved my life. I owe them."

"It's not going to be easy, but if it's that important to you then you must continue to try. I think you do plenty, but I understand you wanting to do more. The English don't trust you because they hear the accent and they are reminded of the Germans–their enemy. It has nothing to do with you personally."

"Were people friendly to you and Martha when you moved here?"

"Not really. I haven't met too many people here that like the Jews either," Fritz sighs. "All of this hate..."

"I fear that hate will soon be all I have left."

"That's not hate. That's pain, and it will ease with time." Fritz pats Adam on the shoulder. "Goodnight."

The next morning, Adam prepares breakfast and completes his chores. He is going to follow Fritz's advice and keep trying.

He applies to every factory and shop that is in walking distance. He also stops at any place in his travels that might be hiring. He does this for weeks, but still has no luck finding a job.

On December 7, 1941, Japan bombs Pearl Harbor.

The United States enters the war.

Adam, Fritz, and Martha sit in front of the radio listening intently.

Finally, when they all have a chance to absorb what is happening Martha cries as Fritz and Adam struggle to keep composure. Adam breathes a sigh of relief as he listens to the rest of the BBC broadcast.

In January, Adam has a visitor at the house. It's an older woman that manages the library. Adam spends as much time there as possible, but he rarely has the time.

Adam is shocked to see her standing in the doorway.

"Please, come in." Adam motions for her to enter.

"I'm sorry, but I don't have a lot of time. I would like to discuss a position that you had applied for at the library. One of my employees thought that you might be right for the job. I would like to schedule an interview with you at your earliest convenience."

Adam is silent, stunned by the woman's invitation.

"I am available anytime."

"Alright, I will see you tomorrow morning at nine o'clock."

Fritz and Martha are listening in the living room. It isn't often that they receive guests.

"Things are looking up," Fritz said.

The following morning, Adam rises early to complete his chores and prepare breakfast for Fritz and Martha, but he is too nervous to eat.

When he arrives at the library, the older woman is waiting for him behind a large desk in the back. She motions for him to join her.

"I forgot to introduce myself yesterday, my name is Mrs. Martin."

Adam shakes her hand and waits for her to invite him to be seated.

Adam feels at ease with Mrs. Martin, and they spend most of the interview just talking. Adam tells her about Frau Lenger and his job at her shop. He also tells her about his favorite subjects in school and his love of reading.

At the end of the interview, she offers him the job. Adam can't wait to return home and tell Fritz and Martha the good news.

The following Monday, Adam finishes his chores in the early hours of morning before walking to the library. His breath clouds the air as he walks a steady pace. The rain drizzles from the sky as the clouds hang over the city.

Mrs. Martin is sitting at her desk in the back of the room when he arrives.

"Good morning, Adam."

Mrs. Martin teaches Adam how to catalog the newer books and the system they use for checking out and returning library items from patrons.

By mid-morning, Mrs. Martin is confident that Adam is capable of doing his duties without her supervision, so she withdraws to her office.

As Adam works, he is in awe of the grandeur of the library. Long ladders are used to reach the upper shelves of the massive wooden bookcases. The wood is stained a dark mahogany and the rows of books seem endless.

A tall grandfather clock stands near the checkout desk. The ticking clock is the only sound that penetrates the silence of the library.

That evening, Mrs. Martin reminds Adam that he can check out a book. Adam thanks her, but he isn't sure that he will have time to read between his job at the library and his chores at home. Fritz and Martha are his first priority. He feels that he owes them his life and he never loses sight of that.

23

Elisabeth

Elisabeth watches Friedrich study as she sips her tea. She is grateful that the small flat is warm in the winter months, unlike the flat that she grew up in.

Dieter spends time with Elisabeth and Friedrich as much as possible, but their relationship still remains a secret. Olga seems busy with her own life, but that doesn't mean that she will allow Elisabeth and Dieter to be together. Elisabeth knows that Olga will never allow that to happen.

Elisabeth is grateful for Dieter's visits. She is consumed with anxiety most of the time, and it is becoming increasingly difficult to hide it from Friedrich. She knows that the Americans entering the war promises certain defeat. There is no way that Germany can win this war with so many enemies. Not that it bothers her to see the Nazis lose, but she now fears for her own life and the lives of the people that she loves.

Elisabeth does all that she can to care for Friedrich. She is still grieving the death of her mother and grandmother, and she worries constantly about Adam and Hannah. Henning is fighting in the war and she has no idea if he is dead or alive. In addition to all of this, she lives in fear of Olga finding out about her relationship with Dieter. Elisabeth reminds herself daily to take it a step at a time. That is all she can do.

In February, Friedrich turns fourteen years old. He is so excited to be able to join the Hitler Youth. He is already friends with most of them, but now it's official. Elisabeth smiles kindly and congratulates him, but inside she feels only hate for anything that has to do with Adolf Hitler and his evil Nazis.

Dieter is supposed to come for a visit to celebrate Friedrich's birthday, but he doesn't show. Elisabeth wonders what could have happened. He knows how much it means to Friedrich.

Days later, Dieter arrives at the flat looking troubled. Friedrich answers the door and salutes him with a proud *Heil Hitler*. Dieter apologizes for not being able to see him on his birthday. He hands Friedrich his birthday gift, and Friedrich opens it excitedly as Dieter sits down at the table.

"Friedrich is meeting some friends, so we can talk when he leaves," Elisabeth whispers.

Friedrich thanks Dieter for his gift before heading outside to his waiting friends.

Elisabeth waits for Dieter to speak and braces herself for the worst.

"Reinhard Becker left for Berlin a few days ago," Dieter begins. "He didn't take Olga with him. Last night, when I left work, she was waiting for me outside. She was a mess, drunk and belligerent. She told me that if she couldn't have me she was going to kill herself," Dieter continues. “I don’t care. I hate her for everything that she’s done. I told her that no one would care if she died.”

Elisabeth is stunned by his admission. It’s not like Dieter to be cruel.

“I don’t feel any pity for Olga. She deserves whatever she gets. She threatened to have me arrested and tortured if I wouldn’t be with her. She was screaming and hitting me. It wasn’t long before the Gestapo showed up and arrested her. There was nothing that I could do to calm her down. She was hysterical, Elisabeth. She was out of her mind.”

Elisabeth remains silent.

“I have friends in the Gestapo’s office finding out what they can, but we could be in a lot of trouble if she follows through with her threat. If we are arrested all that we can do is tell the truth and hope that they believe us. I am so sorry for all of this. I put you in this danger and I don’t know how to protect you. I lost my temper.”

Dieter drops his head in his hands.

“Why didn’t they arrest you along with Olga? Why did they let you go?” Elisabeth’s mind races to gather every detail in an effort to predict her future.

“A woman that lives near Olga had been at the shop next door. She tried to help me calm her, but we couldn’t. The woman told the Gestapo about Reinhard going to Berlin; that’s how I found out. She also told the Gestapo that Olga is a drunk and that she’s regularly disruptive to her neighbors. I’m not sure if the Gestapo believed the woman or if they were just in a hurry to get Olga restrained, but when they finally got her into the car they sped off.”

“Did the Gestapo write down the woman’s information?”

“No, he just thanked her and drove off with Olga. It took two Gestapo officers to get her into the car. She was behaving like a mad woman.”

"Her father is a Gestapo officer. That should be our biggest concern right now," Elisabeth reminds Dieter.

"I talked to my uncle. He said that he will take care of Friedrich if anything happens to us. I know that you don't want Friedrich living with Hartwig, and my uncle would take good care of him."

"Thanks, I am going to get Friedrich and tell him what happened. I have no choice. I don't know how much time we have." Elisabeth slips on her coat.

"I'll walk with you. It's not like we have to hide from Olga anymore. Don't give Friedrich too much information. Just tell him that it's a misunderstanding."

The following day, Dieter is standing in the doorway of Elisabeth's flat. Friedrich greets him with his usual *Heil Hitler* before disappearing into Elisabeth's bedroom to allow them privacy.

Elisabeth is in the kitchen preparing breakfast. Dieter pulls her to him and kisses her softly. Elisabeth steps back, confused by his sudden cheerfulness.

"I have good news. Olga has been released, and she didn't say anything about either of us."

"Why didn't she say anything?"

"I don't know, maybe she was too drunk to think clearly, or maybe she finally grew a conscience." Dieter shrugs his shoulders.

"That's not very likely."

That evening, after dinner, Elisabeth finishes cleaning the kitchen before sitting down at the table across from Dieter.

"I'm pregnant."

"We need to get married. We need to do it as soon as possible."

Elisabeth nods her head in agreement. She is angry with herself and ashamed that she allowed this to happen. They have always been so careful. Elisabeth can't help, but feel guilty for bringing a child into the world at a time like this.

Dieter holds her in his arms. He knows what she's feeling. He's feeling it too.

"They are probably going to send you off to war. Your occupational discharge was fine when Germany was winning, but now they are going to need every able bodied man to fight for our country. How am I going to protect Friedrich and our child?" Elisabeth sobs softly.

"One day at a time, Elisabeth," Dieter reminds her.

A month later, Dieter and Elisabeth are secretly married. Dieter's uncle and Friedrich attend. Elisabeth had been sick in the morning, but she is a glowing bride by the time the Registrar officiates that afternoon. Friedrich is pleased that Dieter will be in his life full time now. He misses Henning, and Dieter reminds him of his brother.

Elisabeth prepares a special dinner that afternoon and everyone forgets about the war for a short while.

A week later, Elisabeth arrives at Frau Lenger's shop for a visit. Frau Lenger's health has been declining, so Elisabeth checks in on her every Friday on her way home from work.

"Is there any news on Adam?" This is always her first question for Elisabeth.

"No, I'm sorry."

They spend an hour drinking tea and discussing topics ranging from sewing to current events. They reminisce about the past and share their worries about the future.

Frau Lenger hands Elisabeth a loaf of bread, as she does every Friday. Elisabeth thanks her and heads outside. The evening sun is warm and bright as it slowly sinks into the horizon. It reminds her of Adam and Hannah. She walks home comforted by her memories of lazy summer days by the lake.

Elisabeth is so lost in her thoughts that she forgets to stop at Dieter's flat to pick up a few items for him. They still haven't decided what to do with his flat since it was handed down to him from his grandparents. His flat would be perfect for them, but it is too close to Olga. They have no intentions of pouring fuel on that fire.

Elisabeth opens the heavy wooden door and climbs the stairs to Dieter's flat. It's been a long time. She is reminded of Dieter's mother and the state that Dieter was in after her death.

Elisabeth pushes it from her mind as she climbs the last flight of stairs.

She finally reaches the landing. Her heart races when she sees Olga sitting on the floor in front of his door. She wants to turn back, but it's too late.

"He's not here."

Elisabeth remains still as she studies her, but Olga's face reveals nothing. Elisabeth is met with an empty stare. Only when Olga stands up can Elisabeth see that she has been drinking, but Olga quickly steadies herself.

"Has Henning written to you?" Olga eyes her.

"No, has he written to you?"

"Your brother will die hating me. I'm sure that pleases you," Olga scoffs.

"I don't care either way."

Both are careful to contain their voices to barely a whisper.

"What are you doing here?" Olga asks.

"Friedrich visits Dieter sometimes. He misses Henning. He's not with his friends, so I thought he might be here," Elisabeth lies.

"I came to say goodbye." Olga looks defeated. She gazes at Elisabeth with weary drunken eyes.

"Are you going to Berlin?"

"You really should learn to mind your own business." Olga slightly slurs her words.

"You're right." Elisabeth turns to walk back down the stairs.

"Elisabeth," Olga calls out.

Elisabeth stops and turns back to face her.

"Forget it, it's nothing."

Elisabeth continues down the creaky wooden stairs and makes her way outside. She is surprised to see Olga and even more surprised that she felt nothing as she spoke to her. She felt no fear or anger for the woman that had tried to ruin her life. Olga is her past, a past best left behind.

Days later, Dieter reports to Elisabeth that Olga had committed suicide.

24

Hannah

Hannah sips her tea. Helena is napping, and the flat is quiet. Otto has been working on a way to get his family out of France, but it isn't easy.

Hannah looks out the window to the city below. She still can't believe that the Nazis are actually in Paris. It seems like a bad dream. She had fled Germany and her home to be free of them, now they're parading down the streets of Paris.

Once the Germans took over France, it was clear that the Jews would be treated the same way that they were in Germany. Laws, similar to those of the Nuremburg Laws, were implemented almost immediately against the Jews.

In late August, Marie arrives home from shopping looking troubled.

"The police are going to do another arrest of all Jews in Paris." Marie is clearly shaken as she sits down at the table.

"Don't worry. No one knows that we're here," Itzhak reassures her.

"Yes, they do." Marie looks up at her husband. "Our address is on their list. They don't have our names, but they are coming to this address. Simone was on her way here when I passed her on the street. Her husband saw our address on the list of those suspected of housing Jews. She said that we should flee. Her husband told her to warn us that the police will take Helena, separate her from us, and send her to a camp in Germany. We have to leave here."

Fear washes over Hannah. "Why would they separate the children? Who will care for them?"

"Who is Simone?" Otto interrupts. "Is she a friend?"

"We have been friends with Simone and her husband, Giraud, for years. Giraud has been on the police force for a long time and is well respected," Marie said.

"He is a good man. If he is telling us to flee then we need to heed his warning." Itzhak locks eyes with Otto.

"Where will we go?" Hannah said.

"Marie and I have friends who live in the countryside. Their farm is about sixteen kilometers from Paris. They offered to help us months ago, but we declined," Itzhak said.

"What about Helena? I will not allow the Nazis to harm my daughter," Otto said.

"It's not safe to take Helena into hiding with us," Marie said.

"She needs to be where we can protect her," Otto is adamant.

"She's so young, Otto. How will you keep her quiet?" Marie pleads with him.

"If Helena goes into hiding with us and we are caught we will all be arrested and sent to Drancy. They will take Helena from us, this is the only way to keep her safe." Marie pauses for a moment. "I have friends in the Oeuvre de Secours aux Enfants. They help Jewish children flee France to safer countries. They will take care of Helena and keep her safe. Simone promised to help. She can procure documentation for Helena to travel to Vichy. My friends in the OSE told me that Helena will probably go to America where there are people waiting to care for her."

"We can't give Helena to people that we don't know. There has to be another way," Otto said.

"Don't be a fool, Otto. The Nazis are coming for us all. You've heard what they do to the children," Itzhak warns.

The following afternoon, Itzhak sets the documents on the table in front of Otto. Hannah and Otto pore over each document. Helena's name is changed on the falsified birth certificate to a French name.

Hannah can't believe that this is actually happening. Her heart is breaking as she begins to accept the choice that she is being forced to make. She has heard all of the rumors about the massive killings of the Jews in Poland. Her instincts have been warning her that they are in danger, but she held onto hope that something would save them.

"You don't have much time. You need to decide what you're going to do," Itzhak said.

Otto and Hannah remain silent.

"I can't endanger my daughter." Otto holds Hannah's hand under the table. "What do we need to do to get Helena to Vichy?"

Tears slide down Hannah's cheeks as she tightens her grip on Otto's hand.

The following day, in the early morning hours, Hannah and Otto stand in the hallway outside Helena's bedroom.

"I can't tell her goodbye," Hannah whispers as tears spill down her cheeks. "I can't lose her."

Otto and Hannah weep as Helena sleeps peacefully.

The couple stand in the doorway of their daughter's room for hours until Helena finally wakes from her peaceful slumber.

Hannah and Otto spend the morning holding and playing with their daughter, knowing that it may be the last time that they ever see her.

Hannah couldn't sleep the night before. She wrote a long letter to Helena. In the letter, Hannah tells her daughter how much she and Otto love her. Everything that Hannah wants her daughter to know is in the letter, including lots of memories that Helena will probably forget once she is older. Hannah is determined to give Helena something to hold onto from their past and words of wisdom to take into her future.

Hannah packs the doll that was gifted to Helena from Elisabeth and Adam. She sets it inside the trunk on top of the quilt that Elisabeth had sewn out of her dresses. Hannah also includes Elisabeth and Adam's contact information, and assures her daughter that she can go to them if she ever needs help.

A woman from Oeuvre de Secours aux Enfants arrives to pickup Helena that evening. Hannah has her packed and ready when the woman arrives. Hannah and Otto kiss their daughter goodbye one last time before placing her in the arms of the stranger. Helena screams and reaches out for Hannah to rescue her. She is clearly frightened by the stranger. Hannah smiles to reassure Helena that she is safe, but Helena continues to sob hysterically and pleads for her mother to take her back into her arms.

The woman smiles kindly at Hannah and Otto.

"She'll be alright." The woman reassures them.

Hannah watches from the window as the woman carries Helena down the street. Helena is still screaming and reaching out for her mother as they walk away. At one moment, Hannah thinks Helena caught her eye in the window. Hannah sobs as she watches her daughter disappear down the street in the arms of a stranger.

That night, Hannah and Otto go into hiding. Hannah packs the remaining food in the flat, a small bag of clothes, and personal items. They make their way out of the city, under the cover of darkness, to the meeting place where Itzhak, Marie, and Giselle will be waiting.

The city lights illuminate the night. Hannah and Otto are careful to stay out of sight as they duck through alleys and backstreets to the edge of the city.

Once they arrive at the countryside Hannah turns around to the city behind her and says a silent goodbye to Helena. Hannah has never cared much about religion or spirituality, but at that moment, she prays to God to keep her daughter safe.

She cries in silence under a starless night sky.

It is still dark when they arrive at the farm house, but the morning sun will be rising soon. A man and woman step outside and lead them to a barn.

Once inside, the farmer opens a secret door in the side wall of the loft of the barn and motions for them to go inside. It is dark as Hannah sits down on the floor beside Otto. The scent of hay lingers in the air.

Hannah swallows hard as she sits back against the wooden slats. Otto rests his hand on her leg to reassure her that it is going to be alright.

Hours later, sunlight streams through the slits of wood. There is barely enough of an opening to see outside, but Hannah is relieved that there is finally light. Marie had already made it clear that they needed to be as quiet as mice. Conversation must be limited, and they must only speak in whispers. They will eat once a day, but it won't be much. Food is still scarce, even for the farmers. The Nazis steal from them as well.

Hannah sits in silence until late evening. Her fear is replaced with sadness. She misses Helena. If only she could hold her daughter in her arms one more time. She will never forget Helena reaching for her as she screamed and the look of terror on her daughter's face. She will also never forget watching Helena disappearing down the street with a stranger. She can only imagine how frightened she must have been with strangers taking the place of her family. Hannah cries silently as moonlight seeps through the slits of the barn walls. The pain feels as if it will kill her.

Days go by and Hannah's grief continues to consume her. She leans her head against the wall of the barn and cries silently while Otto holds her in his arms. She wonders if she will ever see Helena again. The guilt she feels for handing her daughter over to strangers is constantly gnawing at her. Hannah has terrible nightmares that the Nazis are tearing Helena from her arms and shooting her or throwing her into blazing fires.

During the day the barn is sweltering, but sometimes fresh air breezes in between the wooden slits of the wall. Hannah is hot and hungry. Marie's friends have very little to share with them. They eat small amounts of vegetables from the garden and bread. Water is kept in a jug inside the secret room.

Sometime in the night, Hannah wakes to the barn door opening below. The wood creaks softly as someone ascends the ladder to the loft. Hannah shakes Otto awake.

"Someone is coming up the ladder," she whispers.

There is a knock on the wall. The farmer slips inside and stands before them. He doesn't have his wife with him this time.

"I just wanted to let you know that the French police have carried out a mass arrest of Jews in Paris. I don't know exactly how many, but it's rumored that there were scores of arrests. You fled just in time. The raids began the night that you arrived. I just received word from my neighbor. He's a communist and a resister. Those that were arrested are being held at Drancy. They are sending all of the prisoners to Germany."

"Why are the Germans taking the Jews when they want to be rid of them?" Marie said.

"I don't know, but I can assure you it's not good," the farmer said.

Hannah can't sleep. She peers out the slits of wood to the countryside. The farmer's light is on inside the house, and the moon is full and bright. Hannah wonders if the farmers are reading or listening to their radio. If she were home that's what she would be doing. She loved reading stories to Helena. Sometimes she would read several in one night.

An hour later, the farmers turn out their light.

Hannah lies down next to Otto and falls into a deep sleep moments later.

The following morning, Hannah starts her period. The farmer's wife offers her some rags to use and discretely places them under some hay near the pot that they use for a bathroom. Hannah is embarrassed to have to ask, but she has no choice. Marie and Giselle are helpful in ensuring that the men are unaware of Hannah's predicament, and that isn't easy considering that they are living in such close quarters. Fortunately, the pot is located on the main floor of the barn under some hay to ensure everyone's bathroom duties are discreet.

Hannah has been in hiding for little over a month, but it feels much longer. The farmers relay news pertaining to the war and current events, but even that communication is not daily. Life in the barn is lonely as she watches the world outside through gaps between the wood in her hiding place.

Hannah wakes to the morning sun gleaming through the slits of the barn. She opens her eyes to find Otto reading. Otto smiles at her before turning back to his book.

She sits up against the wall and watches Otto. She can't understand why he is so peaceful. It seems that losing his daughter, hiding in a barn, and fearing for his life has little affect on him.

Early that afternoon, Hannah is startled by three police cars barreling down the road in the direction of the farm. Everyone moves quickly down the ladder, just as they had rehearsed. Otto scatters hay in the loft to erase any evidence of their existence before following them down. Giselle buries the pot that is their bathroom in a hole in the ground and covers it with hay. They descend the ladder into the cellar beneath the barn.

Inside the cellar, the earth is cool and damp, a welcome respite from the sweltering heat of the barn. Fear eclipses the pleasantness of their new environment as police cars line up outside. Hannah holds tight to Otto's hand.

Moments later, they hear voices. It's the French police.

It's not long before the police and the farmers are inside the barn.

Hannah wonders what will happen if they are discovered. She wonders if she will be tortured by the Nazis or if they will be shot on site by the French police. She hopes that if she's going to die that it's quick and painless.

It isn't long before they hear the cars pull away. The police had conducted their search and found no evidence of Jews hiding at the farmer's residence.

Moments later, the hatch opens and daylight pours into the cellar. The farmer signals that it is safe. Hannah climbs the ladder, when she reaches the top she instantly feels the warm air on her face.

"They are inspecting all of the farms and villages for escaped Jews," the farmer said.

His wife stands quietly by his side.

"We are to report any suspicious activity. The police made it very clear that the consequences for helping Jews will be severe. They warned that it may even be death." The farmer shows little fear of the threat.

"We have put you in a terrible position. If you would like us to leave we understand," Marie said.

"I'm not upset with you. I'm angry that our own police are going along with the Germans. The Germans are our enemy, not the Jews."

The farmer's wife nods in agreement.

That evening, Hannah snuggles next to Otto as he snores softly. She's reminded of the resentment that she felt towards him that morning. She cries silently in the darkness. She has been so consumed with grief that she lost sight of her love for Otto. She vows to never make that mistake again.

25

Elisabeth

The planes buzz overhead as bombs whistle out of the sky. In the autumn of 1942, Munich is under attack.

The sirens wail as Elisabeth, Dieter, and Friedrich seek shelter under the dining room table. Outside, buildings burst into flames. The night sky is illuminated as the fires blaze through the city.

Elisabeth holds Friedrich close. She tries to steady her nerves for the baby living inside of her, but it's almost impossible. The smoke and exhaust fumes breeze through the windows as Dieter hurries to close them. The exploding bombs produce a chemically infused and highly toxic cocktail that quickly contaminates the air. It is an unexpected danger, and few are prepared for the deadly air enveloping the city. Dieter hands Elisabeth his gas mask while he and Friedrich hold wet towels over their mouth and nose.

As Elisabeth seeks shelter under the table there is one thought that comforts her–Adolf Hitler is in Munich.

Although the Fuhrer had escaped attempts on his life before, there's always a chance his luck will run out. She knows that it's not too probable, though. He is sure to have a safe bunker somewhere in the city.

Elisabeth doesn't dare communicate her thoughts out loud. It would devastate Friedrich to find out her true feelings for his beloved Fuhrer.

Finally, the *all clear* siren rings out, and they carefully exit their make shift shelter. Friedrich steps out first and runs to the window. Elisabeth follows, after stretching her legs. She is exhausted. They have been under the table for hours.

Elisabeth feels enormous as she makes her way to the window next to Friedrich. It's not easy to assess the damage, smoke still permeates the air. Dieter kisses her before fitting his gas mask over his head.

"I'll be back."

They watch from the window as he disappears into a cloud of smoke.

Elisabeth peers out to the destroyed buildings and countless fires. She worries about the people trapped underneath the rubble. She is grateful that her family is alive. She wonders if her father survived, but quickly dismisses the thought. She has more important things to do than worry about him.

Elisabeth stands next to Friedrich as they examine the destruction of the city. He looks shocked and horrified.

"It's over now," she consoles him.

Early the next morning, Dieter finally returns. He is covered in soot. Exhaustion weighs heavy on his body as he closes the door to the flat and slowly makes his way to the table.

He sips his tea while Elisabeth prepares breakfast.

"How bad is it?" Elisabeth asks, already knowing the answer.

"It's bad." Dieter won't give her the gory details. Many suffocated to death. Others are buried under the heavy rubble of destroyed buildings. "Assessing from the damage, the bombs were aimed at the affluent neighborhoods. It seems our enemy knows the location of the top ranking Nazi officials."

It is the first time that Elisabeth is actually grateful to be poor.

Elisabeth sets Dieter's plate down in front of him. She's lost in her thoughts as he finishes his breakfast. She wants to say something positive to reassure him that it's going to be alright, but she is certain that he will see right through her lie.

Elisabeth slips into the bathroom and drops her head into her hands. She cries for the people of her city that are dead. She cries for the ones buried alive under the rubble. Hitler and his Nazis promised to restore the fatherland back to its original glory, but they only succeeded in destroying it. Exactly what one would expect from a foundation built on an ideology of hate. Now, the German people will pay for that hate. She knows that this is only the beginning, there will be more pain and suffering exacted on the German people. The flickering light of hope that she will survive is diminishing. She fears that it is only a matter of time before she joins the dead.

Dieter finishes his breakfast, cleans up, and slips into bed. He will need to return to the rescue effort once he is rested.

A week later, Dieter receives notice that his occupational discharge has been revoked, and he is instructed to report for military service in a week. Elisabeth and Dieter suspect that he will probably be sent to Russia.

"The baby is due in a week," Elisabeth cries.

"Well, tell my son that he needs to get here before I leave," Dieter teases.

"Again, you don't know that it's a boy." Elisabeth smiles through the tears.

They both know that he doesn't care if it's a boy or a girl. He just wants his child to be safe and healthy.

"Dieter will be proud to fight for our Fatherland," Friedrich looks up from his book. "I'll help take care of the baby."

"Just concentrate on your studies," Elisabeth said. She doesn't want to hear any more propaganda. It's been a long day.

Two days later, Elisabeth gives birth to a baby boy.

"You were right." Elisabeth smiles up at Dieter.

Dieter kisses her before carefully taking their son from her arms. Their baby boy is fair haired like his parents. Elisabeth thinks he resembles one of the angels from a book that her mother read to her as a child.

"What should we name him?" Dieter said.

"I like Wilhelm." Elisabeth watches her son sleeping peacefully in his father's arms.

"Wilhelm it is." Dieter smiles down at him.

That evening, Elisabeth holds Wilhelm in her arms. The hospital is quiet, and she is growing tired. She worries about what the future holds for her and her son. Dieter will leave his family in a few days as the war rages on. She holds her baby in her arms as he drifts off to sleep. She prays that she can protect him. She also prays that Dieter returns home to them safe and sound. She prays for the war to end soon.

A scowl-faced nurse enters the room interrupting Elisabeth's thoughts. She gently lifts Wilhelm from Elisabeth's arms and carries him out of the room. Elisabeth can't wait to return home where she is free to care for her son without the restrictions set by the hospital.

The next few days, there are no bombings. The city is quiet, but people are traveling in droves to the safety of the countryside. The bombings are typically in the larger cities, so it is safer to flee, if possible. Elisabeth doesn't have that option. She has neither the money, nor the resources, to live in the countryside, but the most important factor is having friends or family willing to open their homes to you.

Dieter holds Wilhelm in his arms as he stands at the window looking out to their war torn city.

"You must let me worry about Wilhelm. You have enough to worry about right now. We have no choice, so you need to do your best to get back to us safely. I will do my best to ensure that we are here waiting for you. That must be our only focus," Elisabeth said.

The following day, Dieter kisses his wife and son goodbye. Elisabeth stands strong as Dieter holds her in his arms.

She watches him climb into a waiting car and wonders how this nightmare is going to end. She wonders if her son will ever know his father.

She watches the car until it disappears down the street. Wilhelm is growing tired, so she gently lays him in his cradle. She sits down in her grandmother's chair, lost in her thoughts.

Resignation settles in and she's all too aware that she's in for the fight of her life.

Cold November winds blow outside as Elisabeth struggles to keep the flat warm. Dieter's uncle shares his coal for heat. He also shares his rations. She doesn't want to accept his help, but he insists. He is a godsend to the harsh conditions that now plague their everyday life.

Elisabeth lost her job at the dress shop months ago. The building where she worked had been destroyed by the bombs. She's now living on Dieter's military allotment and rations.

Wilhelm sleeps with Elisabeth at night, and she loves cuddling with him as they drift off to sleep. Due to the bombings, she is never far from him.

Elisabeth misses Dieter terribly, but rarely will she allow herself to feel it. She knows that she must be strong and focus on her daily life. Worrying will only provide undue stress.

Christmas is fast approaching, but no one seems to notice. Most people are focused on surviving. Constant worry for loved ones either at home, or in the battlefields plagues their thoughts, along with the looming fear that Germany will lose the war.

Adolf Hitler promises to rebuild Munich even better than it was before the war, and the people still believe that he can accomplish it. Most Germans still believe that Hitler is capable of miraculous feats. He had brought the Germans out of the depression and catapulted them to stardom at the Olympics. He wiped away the shame for the loss of the First World War by recreating Germany into a work of prosperity. Adolf Hitler was even Time magazine's Man of the Year in 1938. But, to Elisabeth and others, Adolf Hitler had created a police state comprised of his thugs and psychopaths that abuse their power in order to control and terrorize the German people. She hopes that one of the bombs finds its way to Adolf Hitler's bunker.

In December, Friedrich begins training as an anti-aircraft flak gun assistant. Most of the men have gone off to war, leaving the older boys to fight on the home front. Elisabeth knows the training that Friedrich is receiving is preparing him to join the others in the war. She can only hope that the war will end before that happens.

Elisabeth reads the news about the bombings in Berlin and Hamburg. Cologne is all but destroyed. The British troops bomb by night while the Americans drop their bombs in broad daylight.

Elisabeth still doesn't not know where Dieter will be sent after his military training. She can only hope that it isn't Russia.

Elisabeth walks quickly as the rain pours from the sky. She hasn't seen Dieter's uncle in over a week and that is unlike him. Wilhelm is home with Friedrich, so she must make this visit a short one. One never knows when the enemy will return to the skies above, and she is determined to be by Wilhelm's side when they do.

Elisabeth knocks on the door to his flat. Finally, Uncle Klaus answers. His face is pale, and his body seems weak as he opens the door. He motions for her to come inside. His breathing is labored as he sits down in his chair.

"Have you seen a doctor?" Elisabeth holds her wrist to his forehead.

"Yes. He said the air quality is bad, and it's even worse for an old man with old lungs. If the bombs don't kill us, the air will." Uncle Klaus coughs into his handkerchief.

"Is there anything that I can do?"

"No, I just need to rest."

"Why don't you stay with us?" Elisabeth offers.

"This is my home. I've lived here all of my life and I will die here. How are Friedrich and Wilhelm?"

"Wilhelm has a little cold and Friedrich is doing well. Would you like a cup of tea?"

"Yes, that would be nice, Elisabeth."

"Please, go lie down. I'll prepare the tea."

Uncle Klaus struggles to gather the strength needed to stand up from his chair. Elisabeth helps him to his bed before pulling the heavy blanket to his chest. He drifts off to sleep instantly.

She prepares a pot of potato soup while he snores softly in his bedroom. She must return home soon, but she doesn't want to leave him.

Elisabeth wakes him to eat.

"Your tea is almost ready."

Uncle Klaus lifts the spoon to his mouth and carefully sips the steaming liquid. His hands tremble, but he's able to sip the first spoonful successfully. Elisabeth gently removes the spoon from his hand and dips it into the soup. She blows on it before guiding the spoon back to his lips. He is clearly unable to care for himself, and she wonders how long he's been this way.

"You shouldn't be alone."

"Why don't you and the boys stay here?" Uncle Klaus offers. "This will be yours when I am gone anyway."

Elisabeth ponders his offer for a moment. He needs her help. He can't remain alone with no one to care for him.

"Alright, we will stay with you. Are you sure that we won't be too much for you?"

"You're my family. I would love to have all of you here with me."

Elisabeth knows that the old man is dying, and there is little that anyone can do to stop it. He deserves to die as peacefully and painlessly as possible.

The following day, Elisabeth moves the family into Uncle Klaus' flat. His flat is larger than hers, with two bedrooms and a sitting room. Many of the buildings near his flat have been destroyed by the bombs; he lives outside an affluent neighborhood. Elisabeth stands at the window and stares out to the city below. Wilhelm is asleep in his cradle wrapped in a pale blue knitted blanket. Uncle Klaus' neighborhood has not fared well in the war. Worry rests heavy in her stomach as she scans the destroyed buildings below. Will their enemies return to finish the job? Many high ranking Nazis live only blocks away and their enemy knows it. She turns back for a moment, and rests her gaze on Wilhelm sleeping peacefully. She has no choice but to stay. Dieter's uncle is dying and this is his last wish. She must grant it. She cries silently as the sun gleams through the window. The winter sun brings no warmth as she closes her eyes to its blinding rays.

Soon after Elisabeth moves in she receives a letter from Dieter. She doesn't tell Uncle Klaus.

Dieter is traveling to Russia to fight on the front lines. Elisabeth cries as she rereads his letter. She worries that she will never see him again. She folds the letter, and places it under her pillow. She brushes the tears away. This is not the time to worry about the future. Life is difficult enough dealing with the present. She must push aside her fears and carry on. It is the only way.

Klaus Kiesling dies two days after Christmas. He had drawn up his will almost a year prior to his death. It is clear that he had known he was dying for some time.

Elisabeth cleans his bedroom and packs his personal belongings into a trunk. She carefully places a small stack of family photos inside her wooden box of keepsakes. The wooden box had belonged to her grandmother. Fresh tears spill from her eyes as she stares down at a photo of Dieter when he was a young boy. He closely resembles Wilhelm. She is reminded of her childhood. Henning and Dieter were inseparable. Now, they are off fighting in a war.

Chapter 26
Adam

Warm air breezes through the windows as Adam dries the dishes. Fritz and Martha are talking quietly in the garden as they enjoy a sunny spring afternoon.

Adam sits down at the kitchen table and opens the address book with his mother's handwritten notes. He closes the book and sits back in his chair. Moments later, he stares down at the leather bound address book again and takes a deep breath. He glances out the kitchen door to check on Fritz and Martha before turning his attention back to the book. He finds the page with his uncle's address in Chicago. He picks up his pen and begins writing on the stationary that Martha had given to him. He attempts to explain how much fear and stress they endure every day, but no words can really describe it. He also doesn't want to worry him. Sadness fills his heart as he thinks about his parents. He knows that his uncle will want to know how they are, but Adam can't tell him in this letter.

He can only hope that his uncle is still at the same address.

Later that night, Adam pulls back the blankets and slips into bed. He's exhausted and sleep is always a welcome respite from the stress. He thinks about Elisabeth and Hannah. They are all in danger now. He wonders if they are still alive. He wonders if they will ever see each other again. Memories of his childhood flood his mind as he drifts off to sleep.

Adam is unaware of the letter that Hannah had sent–a letter that he will never receive. It remains lost in the ruins of war torn Europe.

The following morning, Fritz shakes Adam from his sleep.

"Martha has a fever. I called the doctor."

Adam jumps out of bed and goes to her. She shivers under the blankets as Fritz cradles her in his arms. Adam reassures her that the doctor will give her something to help.

The next few days, Martha remains in the hospital. The doctors warn that her weak heart coupled with a virus is cause for significant concern, so she will remain in the hospital until she is fully recovered. Adam visits with her when he isn't working. Fritz holds vigil at her bedside for as long as the doctors will allow. Adam reassures him that Martha will recover, but Fritz seems unconvinced.

"Living under all of this stress can't be good for her." Nancy wipes off the table. "I wish this damn war would end."

"Have you received a letter from your husband?" Adam said.

"No, and I'm fearful every time that there is a knock at the door..." Tears fill her eyes. "I fear it will be a telegram notifying me of his death, or even worse, he's been captured by the Germans."

Adam knows that there is nothing that he can say to quell her fears. He can only be her friend and listen when she needs to talk. That is all that he can do for Fritz as well.

A week later, Martha returns home. She is still weak, but the doctors advise that she should make a full recovery as long as she follows their instructions, including plenty of rest. Fritz is pleased, but he still worries about her incessantly. Nancy and Adam carry Martha's bed downstairs and set it up in the sitting room. She is no longer strong enough to climb the stairs, and Adam doubts that she ever will be again.

Adam reads to Martha at night when he finishes the housework, but some nights they just talk. She reminisces about growing up in Germany and how she met Fritz. There is humor and faith in all of her stories, and it keeps the light of hope flickering for all of them.

A month later, Adam arrives at Nancy's work to walk her home. He doesn't feel that it is safe for a young woman to walk alone in the blacked out city, so he volunteers to walk with her on the days that she works at the Community Feeding Centre. The Ministry of Food created these communal kitchens to feed people who had been bombed out of their homes or people in need.

As they stroll down the dark streets of London, both are grateful that her work is only a short distance from home. Nancy's mother will be waiting at Nancy's house with the children. Adam will walk her home as well.

Adam steps inside the back door to the kitchen. He doesn't want to wake Martha by using the front door.

The kitchen door creaks as he opens it slowly. He walks quietly through the house and finds Fritz in the sitting room. Martha is in her bed asleep. It is odd to find Fritz awake at this hour sitting in the darkness.

"Is everything alright?" Adam whispers.

"Oh, it's fine. I was just thinking," Fritz sighs. "I'm off to bed now."

The house is quiet. Adam boils water for tea and adds coal to the fire for the stove. The house is dark, with only a dim light from the candle flickering on the table. He is reminded of Munich when his father would stay up late working in his office. The dim light from his desk would lull Adam to sleep on cold winter nights.

In June, Adam receives a letter from his uncle. He carefully opens the envelope and removes the hand written letter. His family in America is his last living tie to his parents.

In his uncle's letter, he pleads with Adam to join them in America.

27

Hannah

Hannah is jolted awake. She peers through the slits of the wooden barn. Otto quickly moves next to her and peers out. Cars are speeding down the road in their direction. A cloud of dust trails behind them. They climb down the ladder and make their way into the cellar. Otto quickly closes the door above him after everyone is safe inside.

Hannah's hands are sweaty as she tucks her thumbs into her fingers. She swallows hard and tries to control her rapid breaths. Otto takes her hand as they sit in the darkness.

Soon, voices are shouting inside the barn. Hannah is relieved that the men are speaking French, not German. Items are being thrown around as though they're searching for something. Hannah pleads with God in silence that the officers don't find them.

Moments later, the door to the cellar swings open. Four French policemen stare down at them.

"Come out with your hands up!"

Otto and Itzhak are first to exit the cellar. They are pushed to the ground and kicked by two of the officers.

The officers lead Hannah and her family to the cars waiting outside. The farmer and his wife are arrested as well.

Hannah sits in the backseat next to Otto. She glances over at the car next to them. Marie is seated between Itzhak and Giselle. Marie locks eyes with Hannah before turning her gaze forward. There is nothing to say or do. It's over.

Hannah stares out the window as the cars speed down the winding roads. She refuses to allow tears and show weakness to the officers that have hunted her and her family. She remains silent relishing the fact that she had saved her daughter from the wolves.

The police cars wind through the countryside until they finally reach Paris. Hannah stares out the window at the Parisians going about their daily life.

Finally, they near a U shaped building, several stories high, surrounded by barbed wire. She glances at Otto staring at the guards outside. The cars pull up to the prison. The guards open the doors and signal for Hannah and Otto to exit the car. One of the guards grabs Hannah by the arm and pushes her into a line of women. She turns back to see Otto thrown into a line of men. Itzhak falls to the ground when pushed to the line, but he quickly picks himself up. He lines up behind Otto. Otto turns and locks eyes with Hannah but only briefly. Giselle and Marie line up behind Hannah.

Both lines are marched into a courtyard filled with people. Upon entering the courtyard, the line of men is led to the right. Hannah's line is directed to walk left. Hannah tries to keep an eye on where the officers are taking her husband, but Otto quickly disappears into the crowd.

Suddenly, a fist slams against the side of her head.

"Eyes forward!"

She doesn't look to see the guard's face. She turns her gaze forward and continues to move slowly with the rest of her line.

Hannah follows her line as it winds through the crowd. They pass a small group of children. Unaccompanied toddlers and small children scream for their parents, while crying babies lie alone and helpless on the ground. No one seems to notice the abandoned children. Hannah takes a deep breath. Eyes forward, she is led into the building.

Once inside, the women are separated. She feels Marie being led in another direction, but she doesn't dare turn back.

Hannah is instructed to follow two of the officers. They check her in before leading her to a room.

When they reach the room, Hannah is ordered inside. The two officers close the door before heading back down the hallway.

There are seven other women in the small room. The large window is open allowing the summer air to breeze into the drab looking room. The guards are still screaming orders outside in the courtyard.

A clothes line hangs on one side of the room stretching from wall to wall. A woman is hanging clothes on it as Hannah glances around. The stench of the overflowing chamber pot sitting in the corner fills the room.

"Hello, I'm Leib." A young woman smiles as she steps towards Hannah.

The other women introduce themselves as though on cue.

"Like anything else, you get acclimated to it." Leib sits down on the floor.

Hannah sits down next to her.

Leib explains how the prison works and warns Hannah to stay under the radar of the guards.

"Don't make eye contact. Just blend in with the crowd."

That evening, Hannah stands in line for hours for a bowl of watered down cabbage soup and a piece of stale bread. She searches the crowds for Otto, but he isn't there.

At bedtime, she lies down on the floor next to Leib.

"I noticed that there were only a few children standing in line for soup, but when I arrived I saw many children. What happened to them?" Hannah said.

"They separate the children from their parents immediately upon their arrival and send them to a different camp."

"Why would they separate the children from their parents?"

"No one knows. If you ask questions they will beat you or you just disappear. The guards beat people every day, mostly just for the fun of it. It's beastly. Even the children, they beat them too. It's hard to listen to their screams. I cover my ears and drown it out by humming. I saw a young girl, maybe three years old, kicked to death by one of the officers because she wouldn't stop crying. It was over in a matter of minutes, but I will never get that image out of my head. Keep your head down here, Hannah. If you want to stay safe you must be invisible to them."

That night, as Hannah tries to sleep, she thinks about Otto. She wonders where they have taken him and the rest of her family. She cries silently in the darkness of the room. Her tears form a puddle on dirty floor beneath her.

The next morning, she stands in line for hours only to find that they had run out of soup and bread. She walks back to her room in a daze, careful to blend into the crowd and be invisible. She makes her way through the crowd like a ghost.

When Hannah returns to the room, one of the ladies has washed her clothes and is hanging them on the clothes line. Hannah couldn't care less about washing her clothes.

In the afternoon, there is still no soup. Leib informs her roommates that the guards are still waiting for a delivery that was supposed to have been there two days ago. Leib has friends in high places at Drancy. Hannah is grateful to be her roommate. Her instincts are telling her that Leib is a kind person. She is still cautious about her other roommates though.

Hannah's stomach growls as she sits in the darkness of her room. The others are sleeping, and the room is quiet. Leib snores softly next to her. The moon is bright outside the window. She doesn't cry herself to sleep this night. She lies down on the dirty floor and closes her eyes to the moon's glow. She thinks about the children separated from their parents. She prays to God to keep Helena safe.

In the morning, Hannah stands in line for soup again. She is relieved that there is enough food to fill her stomach, although the soup is bland and the bread is stale. She dips her bread in the watery substance and eats quickly.

She returns to her room. Leib motions for her to sit down.

"I have a message for you," Leib whispers. "My friends told me that there is a man making inquiries about you. He says that he is your husband."

"Otto!"

"I told my friends that I would look for you. He sent a note for you, in case I found you." Leib discreetly slips Hannah a small piece of paper. "Don't tell the others." Leib glances around the room. "I still don't know what roommates can be trusted."

Hannah carefully hides the note inside her sock. She has to wait for a time when it will be safe to read.

The following morning, Hannah doesn't join her roommates in the soup lines. She waits until she is alone and pulls the note from her sock.

Although she's hungry, this is the only way to read the note without anyone catching her.

Hannah smoothes the wrinkled paper between her fingertips. Instantly, she recognizes Otto's handwriting. She weeps as she reads his words. She runs her fingers over the paper knowing that Otto had held it in his hands.

Hannah, I am here with you. I love you. Have you seen M or G?

The note is short and to the point, but Hannah is relieved to find that her husband is still alive. Otto also opens Hannah's eyes to reality. It hadn't occurred to her to try and find Marie and Giselle. A small ray of light penetrates her darkness. She has to find them.

Hannah tucks the note back into her sock and stares out the window. The others must not detect the small amount of happiness that fills her heart. She needs to remain invisible.

That night, as they lay in the darkness, she whispers in Leib's ear.

"Can you find two people for me?"

"What are their names?"

Hannah gives Leib their information. Leib reassures her that she will do all that she can to find them. Hannah thanks her with a squeeze of her hand.

"Don't get your hopes up, Hannah; it will only lead to disappointment."

A week later, Leib whispers in Hannah's ear as the other roommates sleep.

"Giselle said to meet her at the wash station before you get in line for soup in the morning."

Excitement dances in Hannah's stomach.

Hannah wakes before dawn. She waits for the sun to rise, but clouds fill the sky. She makes her way to the wash station, careful not to arise any suspicion. She nears the meeting place and spots Giselle washing her hands in the large filthy tub. Hannah steps next to her. Hannah washes her hands quickly before joining Giselle in the soup lines, neither says a word. They stand close, their hands brush against each other as they follow the slow moving line. They move with the crowd, faceless and invisible. It is imperative that one doesn't draw the attention of the guards or the ones entrusted by the guards to provide information about the other prisoners. There are prisoners that report to the guards regularly about any suspicious behavior. Those prisoners are rewarded for their betrayal while their victims are punished severely.

As soon as they are inside the crowded lines it is safe to speak.

"Have you seen my mother?" Giselle said.

"No, I have a friend that is helping me to find her."

"Let's meet here every morning," Giselle whispers.

"We can't meet at the wash station, they will notice," Hannah warns. "Meet me where those men were arguing a few feet back. Stay with the crowds, but move slowly. If you get here before me don't let the guards catch you standing around, it looks suspicious."

They move like ghosts in slow moving line. Not another word is uttered.

A week later, Hannah steps out of the building and carefully finds her way to Giselle. The woman standing behind Giselle turns and glances back at Hannah. It's Marie. Hannah steps in line behind her and gently brushes her hand against her back for a brief second. Marie touches her hand. They continue to follow the line, stoic, face forward. The women walk with the slow moving lines for hours relishing the precious time that they have together.

When it is safe, Giselle shares how Marie found her. They have been living in rooms on the same floor, both unaware. Marie's connections inside the prison helped to locate her daughter. Hannah can't imagine the fear that Marie carries knowing that her daughter is in this place. Hannah is grateful that she and Otto had chosen to send Helena away. The guilt had plagued her, but now that they have met their fate she is certain that she had made the right decision. Marie's daughter is not that fortunate.

"I will try to find a way to get a pencil so that you can write to Otto. I worry about Itzhak," Marie said.

"I search the crowds for them every day," Hannah said.

Steam billows out of the large soup pots. Bread is stacked in piles on the ground. Hannah places her stale bread on top of the bowl of soup and drinks it quickly. She moves through the crowd, bread hidden in her hand. She'll do it all again at dinner time.

Two days later, Marie slips Hannah a small pencil while they walk in the soup line. Hannah holds it in her sleeve until she returns to her room.

Inside her room, she discretely places the pencil in her sock next to the note.

In the morning, after the others leave to join the lines for breakfast, Hannah replies to Otto's note. She thought about asking him to meet, but that is far too dangerous. If the note falls into the wrong hands it won't be Otto awaiting her arrival.

Hannah writes as small as possible to save room on the paper, just as Otto had.

We're alright. I am with M and G. Itzhak? Stay safe. I love you.

Hannah folds the note as small as possible and slips it back into her sock. That night, she hands it to Leib for delivery.

The following morning, the rain pours down as they stand in the lines for soup. Due to the rain, the soup is even more watered down. Hannah tries to cover her bowl as the rain splashes onto her stale bread. She dips the bread in her soup before tipping the bowl to her mouth and drinking it like water. The cabbage is slimy and tasteless. After she finishes, she returns the bowl and climbs the stairs back to her room.

A few days later, Leib passes Hannah a note from Otto. Hannah slips it discreetly into her sock and waits until it is safe to read.

The following morning, Hannah carefully unfolds the small piece of paper.

Itzhak. Don't know. I love you. Stay safe.

Hannah rereads the words S*tay safe*. She has a bad feeling as the words echo in her mind. She wonders what horrible experience awaits her now.

Two days later, Hannah understands her premonition. She steps out of the building and heads towards the soup lines only to find that the French officers have been replaced with German officers. Fear courses through her body as she carefully weaves through the crowd to catch up to Marie and Giselle.

The crowd is less chaotic. It's as though everyone knows the indubitable evil that the German officers bring.

The German officers are noticeably different from the French. Their leather boots immaculately polished, uniforms smoothed of any imperfections, and their posture perfectly straight. The German officers display a stoic towering stance that accompanies their focused expressions. They study the crowd with marked disdain.

Marie brushes Hannah's hand to relay the fear that cannot be communicated in words. They are now under the watchful eyes of the German officers.

Hannah follows the lines of people as her stomach begins to turn. She takes a deep breath in an attempt to control the vomit that is inching its way up to her throat. She knows that she cannot lose control in front of the officers. She quickly regains her composure and walks like a ghost, hidden inside the faceless crowd.

Hannah receives her soup and walks toward the building, careful to steady her shaking hands. She is finally safe inside. She moves quickly to the lavatory and heaves violently into a filthy sink. Her bread falls to the floor soaking up her spilled soup. She wipes her mouth with the back of her hand before ascending the stairs to her cell.

The following morning, Hannah regains the courage to join the soup lines under the watchful eyes of the German soldiers.

Hannah carefully makes her way to their meeting spot. She joins Marie and Giselle walking in the slow moving line. She takes her place behind them and walks in silence. They keep their gaze forward, their expressions empty. Ahead of them, a German officer is beating a man mercilessly to the ground while the other officers laugh. Hannah continues on her path, ignoring the vile beasts at play.

Hannah concentrates on the sound of the footsteps sloshing through the puddles around her. The rain continues to pour down. She is certain that the soup will be even more watered down than usual as the enormous pots catch the falling rain.

A hand brushes against hers. She turns to see Otto stepping in line beside her. She holds back the tears that try to fill her eyes. Otto stares forward, as does Hannah.

"The Germans made changes to our schedules," Otto speaks in barely a whisper. "I should be here every day at this time."

Hannah explains quickly where they meet every day. Hannah and Otto continue to walk with the crowds in silence, both grateful for the chance to be together. Marie and Giselle are pleased to see Otto as well, but both continue forward as though he's a stranger.

The following morning, Otto is already in line with Marie and Giselle. Hannah catches up with them and touches Otto's hand as she moves in step with them. This time when Hannah walks with Otto her gratitude is replaced with resentment. She hates being kept from the ones that she loves because of the doctrine of a hateful tyrant. She hates it far greater than she hates going hungry.

In early September, Hannah and all of the women on her floor are notified that they are being sent to a work camp the following morning. The German officers advise that they will be allowed soup for breakfast. They will be expected to meet at the first check point towards the entrance of the prison at exactly 6 o'clock. The officers warn that anyone that is late or absent will be found and shot.

Hannah watches Leib for her response, but her cellmate remains stoic.

The following morning, Hannah walks in step with Otto. She waits until it is safe to tell him the news.

"I'm being sent to a work camp today," Hannah whispers.

Her heart breaks as she touches Otto's hand for a brief moment. He doesn't respond. He continues to walk in silence, eyes forward.

Marie and Giselle touch Hannah's hand.

"Stay safe," Marie whispers.

Hannah and Otto approach the soup pots. He holds her hand one last time.

"I love you," Otto whispers.

She can hear his voice tremble as he says it. She squeezes his hand even harder.

"I love you too."

Later that morning, Hannah and the others board a train for the work camp.

28

Elisabeth

Elisabeth and Wilhelm are sleeping peacefully when the wail of sirens jolts them into action. Elisabeth pulls back the blanket and lifts Wilhelm into her arms. She moves quickly down the hallway and ducks carefully under the table. Wilhelm stirs, but only a little. Elisabeth holds him in her arms as the planes buzz overhead.

Elisabeth is certain that Friedrich is at his post shooting back at the RAF bombers. The adrenaline races through her body as she holds Wilhelm against her chest. Wilhelm screams as the bombs explode onto the city. Orange flames light up the night. Elisabeth trembles as she huddles under the table. The building across the street is hit, and the explosion is deafening. The pictures on her wall fall to the floor, dishes shatter in the kitchen. Wilhelm continues to scream.

Elisabeth can't think clearly. It is all a blur as she cradles Wilhelm in her arms. His cries are muffled by the explosions outside. The bombs whistle out of the sky, and the fires blaze out of control. Elisabeth watches the war outside her window and prays that they will survive…over and over she prays.

It seems to go on forever. Finally, their enemies fly off into the distance. Elisabeth's breaths are rapid and shallow as she remains huddled under the table that has been their shelter. Wilhelm is still sobbing as she tries to comfort him. Tears slide down her cheeks as she looks down at her son. They survived.

Elisabeth waits for *all clear* sirens before carrying Wilhelm back to bed. She soothes him back to sleep with a lullaby that her mother sung to her as a child.

She cleans up the dust and debris on the . She is grateful that she still has a home, especially when there are so many others that have been displaced. She wonders if the flat that she had grown up in is still standing and if her father is still alive. Every time she thinks of Hartwig she reminds herself that he is already dead to her. She hopes to never see Hartwig Ehrler again.

Elisabeth continues to sweep up the debris as she pushes the memories of her life in the Ehrler home from her thoughts.

Finally, by early evening, the flat is clean and Wilhelm is playing quietly on the floor in the living room. Elisabeth prepares potato soup and waits for Friedrich to return. Not only is she desperate to find out if her brother has survived the bombings, she hopes Friedrich will know where to find food in the chaos of the war torn city. She tries not worry, but the fear of not being able to feed Wilhelm is not easily pushed from her mind.

In the days to follow, Elisabeth purchases as much food as she is allowed. Friedrich had advised of the only food available, and she was grateful that it all hadn't been destroyed in the relentless bombings. Rationing is even tighter and food is scarce. Munich is quiet now due to many of its residents fleeing to neighboring towns and villages. She wants to flee, but she has nowhere to go. She can only pray that her luck doesn't run out and she can remain in her flat.

Wilhelm sleeps peacefully as Elisabeth lies next to him staring out the window into the darkness. Her body is tired, but her mind is wide awake with worry. She has been in bed for hours, but sleep eludes her. She worries about Dieter and wonders if Wilhelm will ever know his father.

She kneels down next to her bed to pray. She prays for Dieter and her brother to return home safe. She prays for Hannah and her family, and for Adam to be safe.

Elisabeth climbs back into bed. She is grateful that she has always been close to God. Although she doesn't like church, and believes that the bible is a fairy tale, she remains close to Him.

Hold onto God, Elisabeth, and you will never be alone. It was the last piece of advice her mother had given to her.

It is her mother's words that finally lull her to sleep. *Hold onto God, Elisabeth, and you will never be alone.*

In January, Elisabeth and Friedrich listen to the announcement on the radio that German troops have been defeated at Stalingrad. Fresh fear swirls in her stomach. Where are Dieter and Henning? She hopes that they either died in battle or they are fighting somewhere else, anywhere else. The Russians will surely be cruel and inhumane to Germans for the cruelty that Germans had inflicted on their people.

When the announcement concludes, Elisabeth sits quietly holding Wilhelm. Friedrich remains silent as well. They both know that this is a serious blow to the Germans for the government to publically admit defeat.

The following morning, Elisabeth wakes to a cold sore swollen on the right side of her lip. Her worries are coming out whether she wants it or not. As much as she tries to ignore the pain and stress, the body reveals the truth.

Elisabeth prepares breakfast for Wilhelm and Friedrich. The winter winds swirl outside her window and the sky is gray. She rarely peers outside, there is little to see, other than the devastation caused by the bombs.

Hours later, Friedrich is heading out for his military training and Wilhelm is ready for a nap.

Elisabeth tucks Wilhelm into his blankets and kisses his forehead before heading to the kitchen.

Tears fill her eyes as she sits down at the table. Her imagination runs wild with visions of Russian soldiers torturing their German enemy. She sobs with her head in her hands.

Finally, she lifts her head and wipes the tears away. Fresh resentment settles heavy in her heart. She resents Adolf Hitler and those, like her father, who had been foolish enough to follow him. She resents the hate and appetite for power that has caused her world to be torn apart. But what she resents the most, is that humans are capable of such cruel and wicked behavior.

A few days later, Elisabeth receives a letter from Dieter. He reassures her that he is safe. As she weeps, alone in her room, she holds the letter in her hand. She wonders if she will ever receive another one.

29

Hannah

Hannah lies next to a young girl named Susi in the wooden bunk bed. They are on the top bunk with two beds underneath. Susi snores softly as Hannah focuses on the different sounds that fill the room. Many of the prisoners are ill, so they frequent the latrine throughout the night. Others sleep through the constant commotion due to exhaustion from the lack of food and arduous working conditions. Everyone suffers from fatigue except for the prisoners that run the barracks. They are given the power to rule the other prisoners by the SS officers. These prisoners are called *Kapo* or *Oberkapo*. When clothes are delivered to the camp they have first pick. They are also well fed. As well as one can be in Auschwitz. The SS men look the other way, pleased with the politics of the camp. However, if these prisoners fail at keeping the camp running smoothly they are punished severely. Therefore, the prisoners wielding power rule the others with an iron fist.

Hannah has been at Auschwitz for five months, but she still remembers clearly the day that she arrived...

Arbeit macht frei was the sign that welcomed her. An electrified barbed wire fence surrounds the camp. Armed men guard the camp from watch towers and on the ground. The prisoners cannot escape the watchful eyes of the guards. There is no place to hide in Auschwitz.

Hannah's mouth was dry and her head was pounding from dehydration. Inside the train car, people struggled to breathe amongst the crowded conditions and lack of adequate ventilation. Many people didn't survive the journey, and their bodies lay decomposing amongst the living.

Immediately upon her arrival, the stench of death tainted the air. She was then herded into a line to be examined by doctors waiting outside the trains. They inspected all of the prisoners while the orchestra played cheerful music. The music was disturbing as death danced around them. The human ovens billowed smoke from their chimneys as they burned to ash any traces of their victim's existence. Those in line waited to find out their fate. Some children walked hand in hand with a parent or loved one, but most of the children arriving at Auschwitz walked alone in the slow moving lines to their death. The remaining children suffered from the cold, starvation, beatings, and the arduous work conditions alongside the adult prisoners. Babies and small children that weren't murdered on their arrival were left in the barracks to starve to death. This place revealed the true black heart of the Nazi's *Final Solution*. Auschwitz was a testament of their deep-seated hate and the discernible evil that burned inside of them.

Hannah was ordered to join a line. This line was immediately ordered to the showers. The officers screamed while their dogs barked viciously as the prisoners hurried past.

Inside the building, they were ordered to remove their clothes. They undressed quickly as the officers hit and kicked them.

All of their hair was cut off with dull scissors that sometimes pulled the hair out instead of cutting it. Their scalps would bleed, and during the haircut most were also beaten and screamed at by the SS officers that were doing the shearing. It seemed odd to Hannah that only a few of the women cried out from the pain. It was excruciating, but most just took it without uttering a sound.

The women were then ordered to spread their legs and the pubic hair was also cut with dull scissors by the abrasive hands of the SS officers.

Hannah felt her head. Blood caked onto the short strands. She walked back to the line and stared forward.

Soon, they were herded into the showers. The water was ice cold, and she drank as much as she could without getting caught by the officers. Afterwards, the women were given rags to wear and wooden clogs before being directed to stand in line again.

"Move!" The officers ordered. Hannah learned right away that one must do everything quickly in Auschwitz.

The women traveled in a single file line to the barracks. Each was assigned a bed and a number. Next, they were again lined up and led to another building where they were given tattoos of the numbers that each had been assigned. Hannah's tattoo marked the inner side of her left forearm. She was punched in the head as she moved back to the line after receiving her tattoo. She almost fell from the force of the blow, but quickly steadied herself.

Life in the barracks was a daily struggle to survive. The weak were annihilated by the strong. Hannah quickly learned the rules, but it wasn't easy. Her soup bowl was stolen out of her hands in her first days at the camp. At meal time, the same woman would take Hannah's bowl and push her out of the way. Finally, Hannah had enough and pushed the woman to the ground. One swift kick to the stomach was enough for the woman to figure out that Hannah was no longer going to allow her thievery.

Days later, Hannah saw that the woman had found a new girl to victimize. This went on for almost a week until Hannah decided to stand up for the young girl. She had hoped the girl would stand up for herself at some point, but it never happened.

Hannah grabbed the young girl's bowl from the woman and handed it back to her.

The woman turned and found her place back in line.

"These people will treat you as bad as you let them." Hannah warned her before finding her place back in line. That was all that she was going to do for the girl. She needed to learn to stand up for herself, or her chances of surviving Auschwitz would be slim.

Every morning, the dead bodies of those that didn't survive the night were dragged through the dirt and filth before being placed in the pile with the other dead bodies.

The prisoners were allowed to bath once a week. After their showers, they would endure another selection to evaluate who was well enough to continue working. Those that had their numbers written down were taken away the following day. Hannah learned that the selections that she experienced on her first day and all of the others to follow meant that some would live, but most would be sentenced to death.

As Hannah lies awake, listening to Suzi snore, her minds drifts back to her childhood in Munich and the newness of Paris when she had first arrived. She has not seen Marie or Giselle at the camp, although they would be difficult to recognize. Prisoners bear little resemblance to the humans they were before Auschwitz. Hannah doubts that she would recognize her own mother, even if she was standing right in front of her.

Hannah pulls the lice from a strand of hair with her fingernails and smashes them between her fingers. She turns over in her bed to the rows of prisoners surrounding her. The barracks are dark. Someone is groaning across the room. Suddenly, she notices something moving a few bunks away. She strains to see what it is. It's too small to be human. Finally, she can see that it's just a rat. She watches as it scurries across the feet of a sleeping prisoner before dropping down to the floor. It disappears underneath the bunk. She has chills thinking about the long tailed rodent climbing into bed with her.

The following morning, after Hannah drinks her hot beverage, she joins the line for the daily walk to work. The winter air is bitter cold, and the coat that she had been issued is riddled with holes. As she walks, the snow quickly fills her wooden shoes. She feels dizzy, and her heart is having its usual palpitations. Hannah wants to lie down in the snow and sleep forever. She is already exhausted, and she still has a full day of work ahead of her.

Hannah walks numbly through the snow as the SS officers scream obscenities at them. The officers let their vicious dogs close to the prisoners, and sometimes the prisoners get attacked by the dogs that get too close. The dogs savagely attack with no mercy as the officers stand by and laugh. Most prisoners attacked by the dogs do not survive. Some survive the attack only to have the officers pull the dog off before shooting them. It isn't a mercy killing. It's just more efficient to kill the prisoner instantly as opposed to waiting for the prisoner to bleed to death. The SS officers are most efficient.

The hunger and exhaustion are so extreme that Hannah can barely think clearly. Even if she were lucky enough to get her hands on a book, she doubted that she could read it. Even the simplest of tasks are difficult now. She can feel herself slowly dying. The Nazis are working and starving them to death. Work will set you free, and the freedom is death.

The following evening, Hannah is instructed to go to the infirmary. She is led outside the barracks by a gruff looking Polish woman.

Hannah walks quickly, struggling to keep pace with the woman that has come to collect her. Hannah has just returned from work duty, and it has already been a long walk back to the barracks. She trudges through the snow every morning and evening in her wooden shoes and bare feet.

As Hannah walks, she can only think about the food that she will be missing. Suddenly, fear swirls in her stomach. The infirmary means certain death. Her heart races, and her head spins. She struggles to keep from fainting as the adrenaline pounds her weak heart.

Hannah enters the building and is instructed to stand at the reception desk. Hannah eyes everyone in the room, but no one notices her. They are all busy with their work. She narrows her eyes to the woman behind a desk, lost in paperwork. She seems familiar. The Polish woman that brought Hannah to the infirmary speaks in a hushed tone to the woman behind the desk. The woman looks up and eyes Hannah. It's Leib. Hannah recognizes her right away. Other than the bad haircut, Leib looks about the same as she had in Drancy. She isn't gaunt like the others and she appears somewhat human.

Leib motions for Hannah to sit down.

"I worked it out so that you would have a position here."

"How did you get this job?" Hannah said.

"I always have connections. At Auschwitz, it's important to *organize.*"

In the world of Auschwitz, *organize* has its own definition.

That evening, Hannah eats dinner with Leib and the soup actually has a couple of small pieces of potato in it. Hannah is grateful that her friend has thought of her. Not just for the soup and the job, but as a reminder that good people still exist, even in a place like Auschwitz.

That night, Hannah can only think about Otto. She prays that he isn't at Auschwitz. She misses him terribly. She falls into a deep sleep with memories of lying safely in his arms.

Hannah reports for work after standing in roll call for three hours in the snow. She can barely feel her feet as she makes her way to the infirmary. Her face is red and raw from the cold wind.

Hannah wipes her runny nose with her sleeve before she opens the door to the infirmary. She is instantly welcomed by the heat radiating from the stoves. Leib is seated at her desk reviewing paperwork.

"Put this on your face," Leib said.

Hannah isn't sure what it is, it feels like oil. She soothes it on her skin with her fingertips. The relief is immediate.

"Thanks." Hannah smiles slightly. At that moment, she wants to break down and cry at Leib's kindness, but she remains stoic. That kind of weakness cannot be shown or felt in Auschwitz if you want to survive.

Hannah spends the morning filling out cards for patients that have come to the infirmary. Most are just in need of ointment. No one wants to go to the infirmary. The weak or sick are always sent to the gas chambers, so the prisoners know to keep their illnesses a secret.

Leib warns Hannah about the doctors, especially Dr. Mengele. He is exceptionally disarming.

"He seems kind and caring, so the patients feel comfortable telling him the truth about what ails them. He then places their names on the list, without even a second thought. He's a wolf in sheep's clothing," Leib warns. "He does horrible experiments on the children. He sticks needles into their eyes and injects them with his concoctions. He does surgeries with no anesthesia, including sewing twin children together. He's a sadistic man."

Hannah is horrified. Again, she is grateful that she had sent Helena away. She hopes that wherever her daughter is she is safe.

That evening, Hannah lies awake in bed. She thinks about God. She no longer prays. She doesn't believe in Him anymore. No God would stand by and allow a place like Auschwitz to exist.

"I'm having trouble breathing." Susi interrupts her thoughts.

"It's going to be alright." Hannah tries to soothe her.

There is nothing that Hannah can do. She worries that her friend is having a heart attack, which is how many of the prisoners die. Some prisoners die on the job or while traveling to or from work; others pass away in their sleep. That is the way Hannah hopes to die, peacefully in her sleep.

Hannah worries that she will be the next casualty. She knows that her heart isn't working properly and she hopes that her new job at the infirmary will provide enough of a respite to heal. She has to do what she can to survive this place so that she can find her daughter and family. Hannah is determined to get out of Auschwitz alive.

The following morning, Susi doesn't stir. Her lifeless body lies in the bed next to Hannah. She motions for help to get her body down from the top bunk. No one says a word as they work together to take Susi's corpse outside to the pile of the dead.

Hannah stands in roll call watching the SS guards beating and screaming at their prisoners. The evil beasts bask in their power to execute cruelty to their fellow human beings. It is revolting and disturbing to witness. These beasts killed Hannah's friend and took away her family. These beasts throw live children into raging fires and kill their families. These beasts rule this place.

Hannah finally arrives at the infirmary. Leib is sitting at her desk reviewing paperwork.

"The German army surrendered at Stalingrad," Leib whispers.

That is all that she says before turning her attention back to her work. Hannah feels a light of hope at the news as she sits down at her desk. The excitement that they both feel is masked by their usual stoic disposition.

That afternoon, a nurse named Rachela asks Hannah to accompany her to a barrack where it is reported that a woman is in labor. Dr. Mengele instructs that the newborn be brought to him directly.

"Do you know why I chose you?"

"No." Hannah walks in step with her.

"My instincts tell me that you can handle this better than the others. I need someone that will do the job efficiently and hide their true feelings. The lives of these women depend on it."

Hannah swallows hard.

As they enter the barrack, they move quickly towards a woman writhing in pain. She is silent, but her face is contorted as she endures another contraction.

In silence, the women give birth to their babies, most of which are severely premature. What the mother's don't know is that Rachela kills the babies with an injection before they are fully out of the birth canal. The babies die within seconds. The mothers are told that their babies are stillborn.

For the newborn babies of Auschwitz, Rachela is their Angel of Death.

"They can't keep their children. If they do, the mother and child will be sent to the gas together. to save the women." Rachela advises as they walk back to the infirmary. That is all she says about it. That is all there is to say. She remains unapologetic for saving the lives of the women and killing their newborn babies.

Hannah walks back to the barracks later that night. She hears footsteps behind her.

"Why aren't you in your barrack?" The officer towers over her.

"I work in the infirmary." Hannah is shaking as she stares down at the ground, careful not to look the officer in the eye.

His fist crashes against her face. She falls hard to the ground. The snow crunches beneath her as he kicks her in the stomach and head. Blow after blow Hannah tries to recover, but it isn't long until she is lying face down in muddy snow, motionless.

"Get to your barracks!"

Hannah stands up with one wooden shoe on her foot, the other lost in the snow. She walks back to the barracks, barely conscious, but aware that if she doesn't return to the barracks on her own she will surely be killed.

A young woman helps Hannah up to her top bunk. Hannah doesn't know the woman, she looks to be around the same age, but one can never tell.

The kind woman introduces herself as Hilde to a barely conscious Hannah. Hilde stays with her all night. Hannah has nightmares and wakes a few times, but she quickly falls back to sleep. Hilde holds Hannah in her arms the entire night.

The following morning, Hannah tries to recall the events of the previous night, but she can only remember her nightmares. She was throwing live babies into the fires of Auschwitz.

30

Adam

Gray barrage balloons float in the skies over London. The balloons are a new form of protection from the low flying German bombers that are now relentlessly firing onto the city. The Germans are losing the war, and they are determined to take their enemies down with them.

Adam finishes hoeing the garden and sits down to rest. He stares up at the sky to the peaceful balloons that hover overhead. The sun is bright and the air is warm. He leans back against the fence and closes his eyes to the sun. He falls asleep on the ground with the hoe sitting beside him. It had been a long night in the bomb shelter with Fritz. Martha had passed away two weeks ago. Her heart couldn't handle the stress of living under wartime conditions any longer.

Fritz is still reeling from the blow of losing the love of his life. He now speaks very little and remains upstairs in his bedroom most of the time. Adam delivers trays of food to him, but Fritz barely touches it. Adam leaves him alone. He understands Fritz's grief because he still feels it every day-with every breath. He often wonders if time really does heal the pain, or if that's just something people say.

Adam wakes from his nap and walks sleepily to the kitchen to prepare dinner. He places the kettle on the stove and peels a small wrinkled potato to go in the soup.

That night, after all of the chores are completed and the house is cleaned, the sirens sound. Adam is just putting on his pajamas. He angrily curses out loud at Adolf Hitler before quickly making his way to Fritz's bedroom.

Adam and Fritz disappear inside the shelter. Adam snuggles under the blankets while Fritz sits up listening to the doodle bugs overhead. Doodle bugs are unmanned bombs. When the buzzing stops, there is an ominous silence. That's when you know that they are about to hit the intended target–the silence. Right before impact, the engine shuts off. One never knows if you are the intended target until it's over.

Finally, in the early hours of morning, the *all clear* sirens alert the city that it is safe to exit their shelters. It is finally over. Adam and Fritz have survived to live another day.

That afternoon, Adam receives a letter and another care package from his uncle. He sits down at the table and excitedly tears open the postmarked envelope from America.

The letter is three pages long front to back. The letter begins with an inquiry about his parents. Adam still isn't sure how to tell his uncle the terrible news. His uncle also inquires about his own son living in Berlin. He asks Adam do whatever he can to find him.

The letter also includes all of the information that Adam will need to begin the process of immigrating to United States, including contact information for an organization in Chicago helping European Jews fleeing to America. Adam's uncle warns that it won't be easy. The United States has strict regulations on immigration now.

"Is that a letter from your uncle?" Fritz sits down across the table.

"Yes. I still don't know how to tell him about my parents.

"Did he say anything about you joining him in America?"

"Yes, he said that it won't be easy. America has strict quotas on immigration. I know this from personal experience."

"Adam, you do whatever it takes to get to America. I know that you had planned on staying here with me, but I can take care of myself. Please go to your family. You have paid your dues with Martha and me, although we felt you owed us nothing."

"You and Martha are my family, too."

Fritz just smiles his kind smile and takes a deep breath. "I miss her." A single tear slowly slides down his cheek.

"Me, too." Adam brushes a tear away.

Adam pours Fritz a cup of tea. They sit in silence as the sun streams through the kitchen window.

Fritz finishes his tea before heading back upstairs for a nap. It has been a long day for the grieving old man.

The next weekend, Adam walks with Nancy to work. The skies are gray and it looks as though it will rain at any moment.

"I finally received a letter. He's in France." Nancy beams up at Adam. "He seems to be doing well."

Adam can see the relief on her face. It's a light of hope in their darkness.

"I wonder how much longer this war will go on," Nancy said.

"I'm sure you can't wait to see your husband."

"You have no idea."

Shortly after they arrive at Nancy's work, the sirens ring out. The Germans bomb them relentlessly now. Adam and Nancy run to the tube station for shelter. They join the large crowd gathered inside, huddled in the shelter underneath the city. He hopes that Fritz made his way to the shelter on his own. He rests his head against the cold wall and closes his eyes.

Hours later, they step out of the shelter into the darkness of the blacked out streets.

The air is polluted with smoke and chemicals from the bombs. They quickly put on their gas masks.

The city isn't as dark as they get closer to home. The flames from the fires illuminate the night sky of their neighborhood.

Adam and Nancy approach their street. Adam runs toward the houses with Nancy close behind. Fear grips them both as Adam worries about Fritz, and Nancy worries about her children and mother, alone at her house.

It's the Scholz's house that is ablaze with flames. The fire workers hold Adam back as he screams for Fritz.

Nancy runs to her children standing with her mother on the side of the street.

Adam bends down to catch his breath.

"Is he alright?" Adam asks through the mask.

"We don't know. There was no one in the shelter. How many people were inside the house?"

Fear washes over him as his mind races with questions. At that moment, the remaining part of the house collapses. The blaze spits fiery sparks into the night air.

Adam sits down on the ground, no longer moved by the pandemonium that surrounds him. He removes his mask. With his head in his hands, he sobs. He cries for Fritz. He cries for all of them. The pain is so overwhelming that his stomach feels uneasy as the tears drench his face and hands.

He stands up and hurries behind a bush. The vomit escapes with such force that it strains his chest. His body heaves violently as he drops to his knees.

Adam lies down on the cold ground. The smell of vomit permeates the smoke filled air.

Adam finally sits up to find Nancy standing over him.

"Are you alright?"

Adam stares out to the fiery embers that had been his home.

"Why wasn't he in the shelter?" Adam said.

"I don't know." Nancy watches the fire workers still working to contain the fire. "Come with me to my mother's house. It's no use sitting here, and who knows when the Krauts will be back. You need to get away from here, at least tonight." Nancy holds out her hand.

"I have nowhere to go. Everything that I own burned in the fire." Adam begins to sob. "They took everything! They took my parents, my family, my friends, my home, Martha and Fritz–they took everything!"

Nancy sits down on the grass next to Adam as the fires illuminate the night sky.

The following morning, the sun shines bright, as if the horrific events of the previous night had all been a bad dream. Adam quickly regrets removing the blackout blinds.

Nancy knocks softly on his door before stepping inside.

"I brought you a cup of tea." She sits down beside Adam on the bed. "I want you to stay with me. I don't have a lot of room, but we will manage. The boys would love to have you and so would I. I'm lonely and you're alone, so we would be helping each other. At least, until you go to America."

Adam sips his tea and stares out the window.

“I’m grateful that I always keep my uncle’s letter in my pocket, or I would have lost that too. Thanks for the offer. I will take care of all of the cooking and chores, and I will give you my paychecks from the library.”

“No, you don’t need to do that. Keep your money. We will work together on the cooking and chores and I don’t want to hear any more about it. Our only focus will be getting you to America, and that’s not cheap, so save your money. Oh, and surviving this damn war.”

“It didn’t even occur to me until now. All of the money that I had saved is gone, up in flames with everything else.”

“Yes, but you still have your life.”

In the weeks to follow, Adam spends his free time at various government offices replacing his documentation that had burned in the fire. It isn’t easy, and the lines are long, but he finally has everything that he needs in order to prove who he is and that he is legally allowed to reside in England.

June ushers in the summer air. The sun is bright, but Adam knows not to trust an English sun. It can pour down rain at any moment. He slips on his shoes and joins Nancy in the kitchen preparing breakfast.

“I think I’m ready to go next door and sift through the ashes for any remaining items that may have survived the fire. I doubt that I’ll find anything, but I think it’s time I face it.” Adam stands at the back door.

“Do you want me to come with you?”

“No, I’ll be alright.”

The metal roof of the shelter is covered in black soot, but inside everything remains untouched. Adam climbs inside and sits on the bunk where he would lay across from Fritz and Martha. He holds the blanket that had belonged to his parents. He can feel Fritz and Martha there with him.

“I should have been here. I’m so sorry,” Adam sobs. “I’m so sorry.”

Later that afternoon, Adam emerges from the shelter. A man stands where the kitchen door had been.

"Can I help you?" Adam tries to compose himself, but it is futile.

"Are you Adam Herschel?"

"Yes."

"William Burnett. I am the Scholz's solicitor. Please accept my condolences. I was very fond of Fritz and Martha."

"I don't understand the term *solicitor*."

"I am their legal counsel."

Adam waits for Mr. Burnett to offer information as to why he is there and how he knows Adam's name.

"I would like to meet with you at my office to go over the Scholz's last will and testament. They named you as their sole beneficiary."

Adam stares at the man in disbelief. Fritz rarely left the house. When did he have time to meet with his solicitor? Why didn't he tell him about the will?

"Are you available Tuesday morning?"

"Yes."

"I'll see you then."

Adam watches Mr. Burnett walk to the street and climb into his car. He watches the car until it disappears in the distance. Tears slide down his cheeks. For a brief moment, he thinks he feels Fritz standing next to him.

On Tuesday morning, Adam sits in Mr. Burnett's office with Nancy by his side.

Mr. Burnett shuffles through the documents on his desk until he finds the paper that he is searching for in the pile.

It takes Mr. Burnett close to an hour to read aloud and explain the Scholz's will. To Adam, it seems very complicated, and he is grateful that Mr. Burnett has devoted the time to go over each and every detail until he is certain that Adam understands all that has been bequeathed to him. Mr. Burnett explains the debts that are to be paid and what will remain after those obligations have been met. In the end, it is clear that Adam can live comfortably on the money that Fritz and Martha left for him. He isn't rich, by any means, but he won't starve. He is grateful, but feels undeserving.

Mr. Burnett and Nancy wait for Adam's reaction, but he remains silent.

"Fritz also left you a note." Mr. Burnett again shuffles through the papers on his desk. "He added it shortly after Martha's death."

Adam holds the note in his hands as he forces back the tears. Fritz begins his letter with a quote from one of Martha's favorite authors.

Guard well within yourself that treasure, kindness. Know how to give without hesitation, how to lose without regret, how to acquire without meanness. –George Sand

A tear slides down his cheek as he reads the rest of the note.

Hold onto the goodness inside of you, no matter how difficult or terrifying it may be. That is where your true strength lies.

Fritz

Fritz, as usual, had been short and to the point.

Adam folds the note and slips into his pocket.

Adam is lost in his thoughts on the way home. He wonders if he is strong enough to get past his bitterness and resentment towards the people that destroyed his life. The good in him seems to be fading into the darkness of his hate. Again, he had let Fritz down.

31

Elisabeth

Elisabeth prepares Wilhelm's breakfast while Friedrich cleans his boots in the living room. Cool air drifts through the windows. Soon, autumn will be welcoming another Munich winter.

It has been months since Elisabeth received a letter from Dieter, and she worries that he is hurt or dead, although she continues to push those thoughts from her mind.

She cleans the breakfast dishes as Wilhelm plays on the floor. Friedrich puts his gun away before joining Wilhelm.

Elisabeth can see that Friedrich's enthusiasm is slowly being replaced with fear. He has seen too much to pretend the glory of the Third Reich will prevail. Even young Friedrich now has doubts about Germany winning the war, but he still adores Adolf Hitler.

"I saw father a few days ago," Friedrich said.

"Where did you see him?"

"He came into the beer hall."

"I told you to stay away from those places."

"I know, but I had no choice. When a senior officer tells you to do something you don't question it."

"Your senior officer ordered you to drink at the beer hall?"

"He didn't order us. It had been a long day of bombs being dropped around us and enemy aircraft above us. He was just trying to build up morale. I only had two beers and then I came home."

"Alright, what did Hartwig say?"

"He was wallowing in self-pity while I paid for his drinks."

"Let me guess, his children left him for no reason, and now he's all alone and penniless."

"He also claims that he's too old to work now."

"He isn't working?"

"That's what he said. You can't believe anything that comes out of his mouth. He would have said anything to keep me paying for his drinks."

"I don't care what happens to him. He's never cared about anyone, but himself, his entire life. He made his bed, now he can lie in it."

The following week, Elisabeth receives the news that she has been dreading.

The words repeat in her mind...*we regret to inform you...heroic death.*

Dieter had been killed on the battlefield in Russia.

Elisabeth's world in the days that follow are dreamlike. Friedrich tries to talk to her, but she can barely hear him. Everything sounds as though it's underwater.

The flat is unkempt. It takes all that she has to care for Wilhelm and prepare meals. She sleeps more now than she ever has, yet exhaustion still weighs heavy on her.

Weeks after the news, Friedrich voices his concerns to Elisabeth.

"I know that losing Dieter has been hard on you, Elisabeth, but you have to think of Wilhelm."

Elisabeth sits down across from Friedrich at the table. Tears fill her eyes. She drops her head into her hands and sobs uncontrollably.

"I don't want to live without him," Elisabeth cries. "I can't do this anymore. I lost Dieter, the bombs keep falling, and I am afraid all of the time. I worry about you and Wilhelm every day. I can't bear to lose you too."

"Just concentrate on surviving right now. I'll help with the flat and Wilhelm."

Weeks later, Elisabeth wakes in the night to Wilhelm sobbing next to her. She picks him up and rocks him in her arms. He's burning with fever. She rests a cool cloth on his forehead. She soothes him with a lullaby and rocks him in her arms until he finally falls back asleep.

The following morning, the doctor confirms what Elisabeth had suspected, Wilhelm has an ear infection. Medicine is in short supply, but by some miracle, he has the medicine that Wilhelm needs.

Elisabeth walks through the rubble and debris back to the flat. Wilhelm sleeps peacefully, wrapped in a blanket in her arms. Elisabeth looks around at her war torn city as she walks carefully through its streets. Skeletons of buildings, buildings that have been reduced to rubble, and streets covered in debris, are all that remain of the beautiful city that has been her home all of her life. Chalk written names and addresses on buildings that are no longer inhabitable surround her. It is the only way that people can communicate to their friends and loved ones where they have gone.

Elisabeth sits down on a pile of rubble. Tears fill her eyes as she cradles Wilhelm in her arms. She thinks about Adam and Hannah. She needs her friends now, more than ever, and she suspects that they probably need her. Elisabeth prays every night for God to protect

Adam, Hannah and all of the other people that she loves, but as she looks around at the ruins of her city she wonders if God will answer her prayers. He didn't save Dieter.

Elisabeth cries the rest of the way home. She doesn't care if anyone sees her. It doesn't matter anymore. She is grateful for the tears; it has taken a long time for them to come. It is time to stop holding on so tight and just let go. Forcing away the pain is only making it worse.

That night, as they lie awake in bed, Wilhelm coos softly. His tiny hands twirl Elisabeth's braid. She strokes his soft blonde hair while she watches him slowly drift off to sleep.

Elisabeth cries as she thinks about Dieter. Though her heart is filled with gratitude for Wilhelm and Friedrich, the grief is still a shadow over her world. Dieter had been the first loving and safe man that she had ever known. He was the love of her life. She still struggles to accept that he is never coming back.

In November, Friedrich is notified that he will be joining the war. It is clear that Germany's enemies will soon be entering the Fatherland and every able bodied male, even young boys, are expected to fight to the death.

Elisabeth sits quietly at dinner across the table from Friedrich. He seems unmoved by the news that he will have to fight in the war, but Elisabeth knows that he must be afraid. She wants to tell him to hide, but boys found hiding are hanged. There is no way out for Friedrich.

"You're just a boy," Elisabeth finally interrupts the silence.

"I've been trained well, I 'm ready to fight for our Fatherland. One never knows how all of this will turn out, but I will fight until the bitter end, if that's what it takes."

Elisabeth sighs. Friedrich has no idea what he is really fighting for and she sees no point in telling him. Adolf Hitler had grandiose plans to take over the world and it backfired. While Hitler is tucked safely away in a bunker, he is sending young boys and old men to fight to their death in a war that is already lost.

Elisabeth hugs Friedrich before he heads off to bed. He will be leaving first thing in the morning. She holds her brother tight, knowing that it may be the last time that she will ever see him. She doesn't cry; it wouldn't be fair.

Elisabeth pulls away and smiles at Friedrich as if to reassure him that no matter what happens they will be alright.

The following morning, Friedrich carries Wilhelm through the rubble to the meeting point with Elisabeth by his side.

Elisabeth is surprised to see long lines of old men and boys ready to travel to their assigned destinations, a look of resignation written on their faces.

Friedrich kisses Wilhelm's head before handing him over to Elisabeth. He hugs them both before heading to the check-in table.

Elisabeth holds back tears as she watches her brother join the others.

"Elisabeth." A familiar voice interrupts her thoughts.

Elisabeth turns around to see Hartwig standing in front of her.

"If you came to say goodbye, he's over there," Elisabeth points.

"No, I'm going with him."

It never occurred to her that Hartwig could be deployed with all of the other men. Elisabeth had forgotten about Hartwig entirely.

"So, this is my grandson." Hartwig smiles down at Wilhelm.

Elisabeth takes a deep breath. She can't be unkind to her father knowing that he is probably going to his death. She didn't allow him in her life because of his ill intentions toward her, not as a way to punish him. Sometimes, we have to love people from afar in order to protect ourselves from their darkness.

"Yes, this is Wilhelm."

"I better go." Hartwig looks deep into her eyes for a moment.

"Goodbye."

"Goodbye, Elisabeth."

With that, he walks slowly in the direction of the check-in table.

Elisabeth turns her focus back to Friedrich. Memories flood her mind of when he was young, and the nights that he would sleep in her bed when he was just a baby. The times that she soothed away his fears as Hartwig terrorized the family in the other room. She can't protect him now.

Elisabeth waits until Friedrich disappears out of sight before she makes her way home through the rubble.

She has a feeling this will be the last time she ever sees her brother.

32

Hannah

In November of 1944, the cold winter has descended upon the prisoners of Auschwitz. Hannah makes her way to roll call and stands in the icy snow with the others that have survived the night.

The *Kapo* yells his usual commands.

Hannah moves swiftly to the infirmary.

The air is bitter cold, and she is grateful for the coat that Hilde had given to her. Although Hannah now fairs a little better than the others, she is still starving to death. She hasn't had a period in over a year. The heart palpitations still occur daily, but not as often.

The human stoves at Auschwitz now burn all day and night. The red sky lights up the night as the sour stench of burning bodies fills the air.

Hannah is unmoved by the death that surrounds her. She now steps over their emaciated and lifeless bodies with indifference. It had taken some time to become numb to this hell, but one must to survive. Her indifference worries her that she, too, is turning into a monster.

In early November, Dr. Mengele strolls into the infirmary with a small boy that walks close to him. Hannah has seen the boy before; he seems to be special to the doctor. The boy is well dressed and clean. He also seems well fed, as with many of the doctor's victims. Those that are chosen for experiments receive better treatment than the other prisoners before their savior, Dr. Mengele, becomes their merciless killer.

Dr. Mengele is the most sadistic man Hannah has ever met. He is a demon with a black soul armed with the looks and charm of an angel.

Dr. Mengele hands the small boy a piece of chocolate and pulls him up on his lap. The doctor then shuffles through paperwork as the boy quietly enjoys his gift.

An hour later, Dr. Mengele finishes his work and scoops up the sleeping toddler in his arms. The doctor waves goodbye to one of the nurses and strolls out of the infirmary.

Two days later, the boy is dead. It was Dr. Mengele that had placed the boy in the gas chamber himself. The boy's cries for help didn't save him. The wicked doctor strolled away whistling a tune.

Hannah sits in front of the oven in the infirmary thinking about the boy as the rats scurry around in search for food. The rats come out at night and steal the stale bread from under the pillows of sleeping prisoners. Some have no idea that it's actually the rats stealing the food, so they blame their fellow prisoners for the theft.

Hannah slips on her coat and heads back to the barracks. As she gets closer, she notices the officer that had beaten her before. She keeps her head down.

"What are you doing out here?"

The scent of alcohol permeates the frigid air between them.

"I work in the infirmary."

"Why are getting back so late?" The officer staggers towards her.

"This is the time that I always return."

The officer grabs Hannah by both arms and pulls her close.

"Do you think they will save you, Juden?" The officer whispers through clenched teeth, referring to the Russian Army. "No, they will not."

Hannah trembles under his grasp.

Suddenly, the sirens wail. The officer steps back and turns in the opposite direction. The drunken officer seems to forget about Hannah as he moves quickly in the direction of the guard towers.

Hannah stands frozen in the snow as her rapid breaths escape her trembling lips.

That night, she lies awake in bed going over her path to the infirmary. She designs a new plan for her journey to and from work. She needs to be more careful going forward, or she will not survive long enough to be liberated.

New Year's Day 1945, is a day that Hannah knows she will remember for the rest of her life.

In previous years, the German officers would celebrate the New Year with an all-night party. The orchestra would play, and the drinks would flow as they shot off their guns and drunkenly sang songs. This year is different.

Hannah finishes cleaning the floors and sits down at her desk.

Leib arrives with a partial loaf of bread.

"How did you get that?" Hannah said.

"Haven't you heard?"

Leib takes Hannah's hand and leads her outside.

"The Germans are scared. They will not be checking on us tonight."

Hannah looks around. There are no officers in sight. Large snowflakes fall silent from the sky. An uneasy feeling settles in her stomach. The silence of the camp is an ominous warning.

Hannah ignores her anxious feelings and parties with the others that work in the infirmary. They sing, laugh and talk quietly about liberation. When the clock strikes midnight, they kiss and hug. Everyone holds onto the hope that these are their last days in Auschwitz.

Hannah cries as Leib hugs her. Hanna knows that she owes Leib her life, and she has no idea how she will ever repay her.

"I am so blessed to know you and call you my friend," Hannah whispers to Leib.

"Me, too," Leib smiles through her tears.

In the days that follow, the sirens continue to warn the Germans that their enemies are fast approaching. Russian planes buzz overhead as the sounds of exploding bombs draws near.

In early January, Dr. Mengele, with the assistance of German officers, bursts into the infirmary. Everyone stands at attention. Fear swells in Hannah's stomach.

"Get me all of the records and paperwork that you have on all of the prisoners. All of it."

"Don't try hiding anything," the officers warn.

The Nazis running the camp are now the ones living in fear. The Russians are quickly descending upon them. Now they are the hunted. Everyone knows what the Russian Army will bring to the Germans. Joseph Stalin demanded that his people show the Germans no mercy, just as the Germans had shown the Russians.

Dr. Mengele's hands shake as he sifts through paperwork. Soon, all of the documents are collected. The doctor and his officers exit the infirmary with the evidence of the atrocities that they have committed.

"They're afraid," Leib said. "I hope they all die a horrible death."

"They deserve worse than that," a nurse chimes in. "They deserve to live in Auschwitz."

A few days after Dr. Mengele's visit, Hannah, along with crowds of women and children, are marched out of Auschwitz. Freedom has again eluded her.

Hannah trudges through the snow in her wooden clogs. As she walks, she wonders where the officers are taking them. She knows that the Russians must be approaching. The bombs behind them are getting louder. Hannah prays that they will be liberated soon. She just needs to hold on a little longer. Freedom is still in her grasp.

The lines of people march into the night. The dead are stepped on or kicked out of the way by the German officers. Hannah can't tell if the dead are from her group or a previous one. It doesn't matter; her only focus is to survive this hell.

Hours later, Hannah can barely feel her feet. The wooden shoes and thin socks offer little protection from the blistering cold. Hannah follows the person in front of her and keeps her focus on the back of the gown the woman is wearing. It is the only way that Hannah can pretend that she isn't totally exhausted. She blocks everything out, but the black gown and the pale skin showing through the holes.

Soon, the sun begins to glow over the horizon. The exploding bombs fade into the distance, but Hannah holds on to hope that the Russians will catch up to them. The woman in the black gown is beginning to struggle, and Hannah prays that the officers don't notice. If you are caught lagging behind, you are shot, no exceptions. Hannah helps the woman a couple of times, but she needs to reserve her energy.

Hours later, the woman in the black gown falls to the ground and doesn't get up. Hannah steps over her and continues her march.

Seconds later, gun shots ring out behind her. She doesn't look back.

Hannah is now following a young girl, judging by her height, she looks to be around eleven years old. Hannah sighs. No little girl deserves this. Hannah looks above the young girl to the back of someone else. The stranger that keeps Hannah's focus wears a brown coat with holes that allow the stuffing to fall out. Hannah keeps a close eye on the coat. She does not waiver in her determination to keep marching. People are dying around her, and she almost allows herself to lose hope, but she pushes the negative thoughts away and keeps her focus on the brown coat. The German officers continue to shoot the weak. Hannah pretends not to hear them.

By mid-morning, Hannah can no longer hold back the diarrhea that she has had for the last two days. Her bottom is still raw. The German officers are all around, but Hannah can't hold it anymore. If she were healthy enough to cry tears, she would cry at the stinging pain that she feels as the warm acidic substance finally seeps out against her raw skin. Hannah glances down at the black water streaming down her legs. If this had happened before, when she was a human, she would have been embarrassed, but she hadn't been a human since she arrived at Auschwitz.

As she walks, she wonders what would have happened if she would have gone to the infirmary instead of lining up for roll call. She regrets that she didn't hide. She suspects that if she would have stayed in Auschwitz she would probably be free soon. She hopes that Leib and her friends had been smarter that she had been. She scoops up another handful of snow and lets it melt in her mouth. She's growing weaker and the heart palpitations are getting worse. She prays that the Russians catch up soon.

As they march through the Polish villages, some of the villagers throw bread from their windows for the prisoners when the officers aren't looking. Hannah cannot believe that people actually care about them. It really feels as though they had been long since forgotten. Sorrow fills her heart. She prays again that they will be saved.

Hannah isn't sure if she has walked for an entire week or just days, but the prisoners are now being loaded onto trains. She wants to sob. She can no longer hear the Russians in the distance. She can only imagine what Adolf Hitler and the Nazis have planned for them now.

She hurries onto the train as the German officers scream and hit them. She is pushed to the floor as the crowd rushes into the train car. She struggles to get up, but she doesn't have the strength.

Hannah suddenly feels someone pull her up. As she rises to her feet she thanks the woman. The woman leads her to the window.

"If you remember, from your trip to Auschwitz, this is the best spot for air. My name is Lilly."

"I was hoping the Russians would save us. I'm Hannah."

"Don't give up yet."

Hannah and the woman say nothing more as the train barrels down the track to their fate.

Four days later, Hannah wakes feeling weaker than usual. The night is dark as she stands up to feel the cold air blowing through the window. Dead bodies lie all around. Hannah holds onto the bars on the window and breathes in the cold air.

The woman that pulled Hannah up is still alive and Hannah is grateful. The woman's kindness gives her hope that somehow it is going to be alright. She feels sorry for the others that had died on the march and those now lying dead around her.

Hannah had kept an eye on the young girl that had walked ahead of her during their march, but one morning the little one didn't wake up. Hours later, the German officers forced the prisoners to throw the dead from the train. Hannah had to look away.

She feels guilty for the relief she feels that there is no longer a suffocating amount of people on the train. She is left to wonder how long she will be able to remain alive.

The sun is slowly rising in the distance. Hannah stares out to the countryside. She feels lightheaded and slightly delirious, but she is certain the train is in Bavaria. Fear washes over her. They have returned to Germany. No one can save them now.

"What is it?" Lilly sees the fear on Hannah's face.

"We're in Germany."

The train arrives at another camp later that evening. The prisoners are quickly herded off the train and into lines. The German officers continue their usual brutal treatment as they scream at their prisoners.

The dogs bark ferociously, along with their masters. Hannah is convinced that her weak heart can't take much more.

This time there is no roll call. There are rows of buildings surrounded by electronic barbed wire fences. It is much like Auschwitz, only smaller.

Hannah looks around at the skeletons standing by the fence, awaiting their arrival. Behind them, the same sign from Auschwitz... *Arbeit macht frei*.

The tattooed number of each prisoner is documented before the prisoners are led to the barracks.

Hannah is instantly aware that this work camp closely resembles Auschwitz, including the stacked wooden bunk beds. She can't help, but wonder, why the Germans hadn't just finished the job and shot them all.

That night, the lice crawl all over Hannah's body. She tries to brush them off, but they return almost instantly.

Hannah wants to find out her location. She senses that they are close to Munich. She has to find a way to escape. She knows that her body can't hold on much longer, but it is almost impossible to slip through the German officer's hands. She prays again that they will be saved. As she drifts off to sleep, her mind is filled with memories of her life. Love fills her heart.

The following morning, the sun is bright in the clear blue sky.

Hannah's lifeless body lies peacefully on the top bunk. She died in her sleep in the early hours of morning as the sun rose over Germany.

Hannah died at Dachau concentration camp, located only a few miles from Munich, on March 5th, 1945.

33

Adam

Nancy and her family are outside in the streets celebrating with the rest of the British people. Germany surrendered unconditionally on May 7, 1945. The war is over.

Adam stands at the window looking out to the dimly lit city. It has been a long time since the city lights illuminated the skies of London instead of the blazing fires caused by the bombs. The blackout rules have ended. The black painted blinds are removed from the windows. It is finally over.

Adam watches the crowds below. He can't join them. No one would accept a German joining in their celebrations. He had lived through all that they had and maybe even more, but it doesn't matter. All that matters is that he's a German.

He sits down on the bed as the faint light streams through the window into his darkness. He thinks of the countless lives lost. Many are celebrating tonight, but the grief for all that has happened and all that has been lost will return. Adolf Hitler, the Nazis, all of the people that helped, and all of the people that remained silent, are to blame for the events that took the lives of so many innocent people.

Adam sighs as he stares back out the window. He thinks about Elisabeth and Hannah and their secret place. In his mind, he is there again laughing and talking under a clear blue sky. The sun kisses his face as the water splashes against the rocks. He can still feel the cool grass beneath his feet. His parents are safe at home. A life that had seemed so hard, he would trade anything to be back there again.

A tear slides down his cheek. He promises himself, in that moment, that he will hold onto that light for the rest of his life. He will never forget the days before Adolf Hitler and his Nazis.

34

Elisabeth

Elisabeth stares out the window to the apocalyptic view outside. The American soldiers had entered Munich with little resistance, and now the green camouflaged men parade down the streets. Most Germans are too tired and indifferent to care that the Americans are there, but Elisabeth eyes them with distrust.

Elisabeth studies the woman across the street cleaning her clothes. The wall to her building is almost completely gone; leaving her flat open for the world to see inside.

Elisabeth steps away from the window. She walks to the bedroom to check on Wilhelm. She smiles down at her son as he sleeps peacefully.

Wilhelm begins to stir, as though he feels his mother's presence in the room. She sits down on the bed next to him as he stretches sleepily.

That afternoon, Elisabeth and Wilhelm walk across the street to the partially destroyed building.

Elisabeth ascends the stairs behind Wilhelm, making sure that he holds onto the wooden handrail.

She has never met the woman from across the street, but she has to see if there is anything that she can do to help.

Elisabeth knocks on the door to her flat.

Soon, the woman appears, exhaustion written all over her face.

"I live across the street. My name is Elisabeth Kiesling, and this is Wilhelm."

"Please come in." The woman motions for them enter. "My name is Inna Engel."

Elisabeth lifts Wilhelm up and holds him in her arms. It isn't safe to let him roam around the flat.

"The Americans are here," Elisabeth said.

"Yes, and it seems the German women can't get enough of them." Inna shakes her head. "Please sit down. I'll make some tea."

Everything in the flat seems normal, except for one major wall that would have faced out to the street. The entire wall had crumbled from the bombs, but the rest of the flat remained untouched.

Inna pours the tea and offers Wilhelm a piece of chocolate.

"I haven't seen chocolate in a long time," Elisabeth said.

"A soldier gave it to me a few days ago when I was on my way to the market. I think they believe that they can bribe us into giving them anything they want. The Americans may seem nice, but I don't trust them." Inna sits down at the table across from Elisabeth. "Are you married?"

"Yes, my husband died on the Russian front," Elisabeth mouths the words, careful not to garner Wilhelm's attention from his chocolate.

"Mine, too. I have a son and daughter that were taken to the Hitler Youth camp. I tried to keep them with me, but it was not allowed. I receive letters from them, but not often. I hope they return soon, but for now, it's just me living in this war torn city," Inna sighs. "Did you grow up here?"

"Yes, not far from here. And you?"

"My family lived a short distance away. My husband grew up in this flat. We lived with his mother until her death a few years ago. I fear that if I leave the flat someone will take it. There is no law and order anymore. People take what they want. Is your family still here in Munich?"

"My mother and grandmother are dead, my brothers are soldiers, and so is my father, so I don't know if they're still alive."

"Well, I can promise you that you're not alone. Hitler and his Nazis have destroyed us all."

Elisabeth is shocked to hear Inna talk about Adolf Hitler in such a negative way. Speaking with any kind of condemnation towards the Nazi government had been outlawed for years, punishable by death.

"You look shocked. Are you a Nazi?" Inna narrows her eyes to Elisabeth.

"No. This is the first time that I have ever heard anyone speak negatively, in the open, about Adolf Hitler." Elisabeth pauses for a moment. "I guess there's not much anyone can do to us now. It's such a relief that he's dead."

"The young people had more courage to stand up to the government than we did," Inna said.

"I was horrified at what the monsters did to Hans and Sophie Scholl." The smile fades from Elisabeth's face. "I kept one of their leaflets. I knew that it could get me killed, but I held onto it, as though it was some sign of hope, and maybe a reassurance that I wasn't the only one seeing what the monsters were doing to Germany."

"I saw a leaflet in the street one morning, but I was too terrified to pick it up. I understand why you held onto it. I was a coward for so long. I was afraid of what they might do to my family if I stood up. I regret the choices that I made, and I fear the shame will always be with me."

The following morning, Elisabeth arrives at work. Everyone needs to help rebuild the city. It's arduous work, but it's the only way. The work is done daily, mostly by women.

A neighbor in Elisabeth's building helps with Wilhelm. Elisabeth has known the older woman since she had moved into the flat and Wilhelm enjoys being with her, which is a relief.

Elisabeth and Inna work side by side ten hours a day lifting the heavy stone and debris. Even elderly women help with the cleanup.

The American soldiers sometimes stop and talk to the women working, but Elisabeth and Inna keep to themselves.

In May, Elisabeth receives news that Hartwig had been killed in the line of duty and Friedrich had been captured by the Red Army. Elisabeth rereads the words over and over again. While Wilhelm sleeps in the bedroom, she sits down on the kitchen floor. In the darkness she sobs. Friedrich was more like a son than a brother. She wants to find him and rescue him from the Russians, but no one can save him now.

By dawn, Elisabeth pulls herself together and walks to the living room window. She watches the sun rise over the destroyed city. The American soldiers march below, singing their victory chants, as they do every morning.

She numbly walks into Friedrich's bedroom and sits down on the bed. Glancing around the room she spots the wooden toy that Henning had made for him when he was young.

She runs her fingers over the soft wood. Tears drip onto her hands.

"Don't cry." Wilhelm's voice interrupts her thoughts.

Wilhelm climbs onto the bed next to Elisabeth and leans his head against her arm.

Elisabeth kisses him on the head before brushing the tears from her cheeks.

"Are you hungry?"

She prepares his breakfast, pushing the sadness aside so that her son can no longer see it.

Elisabeth boils cabbage and potatoes as Wilhelm plays on the floor. The flat is quiet as the sun bursts through the windows. As she watches Wilhelm, she feels a twinge of guilt. She knows that she should be grateful that she survived, that her son survived. She thinks about their future, if they have one. They still need to survive the desperate living conditions. She has to hope that she can keep her son alive. People are still dying under the harsh conditions, and there is little medical care if you became ill.

Elisabeth straightens in her chair and stares out to the sun drenched city. Her mother's words echo in her mind... *In the darkness there are miracles.*

Elisabeth watches her son. He is her miracle. In this moment, she knows that she has to hold onto hope, even if she doesn't believe it. She needs to keep moving through the darkness until she finds her way to the light.

35

Adam

The sun is bright in the sky as the train roars down the track. Adam stares out the window to the farms in the distance. It has been a long journey to America, and Chicago is only a few hours away.

It has been a little over a year since the war ended, and life is taking him in a new direction.

Adam sits silently, listening to the people around him speaking in an American accent. He smiles inside. He had spent so much time perfecting his English accent, now he'll need to replace it with an American one.

Nancy had been kind enough to allow him to stay with her, but his uncle finally found a way for him to join him in Chicago.

Adam understands that it will be a long process to receive US citizenship, but he agrees with his uncle; he needs to hold onto the family that is still alive. Millions of Jews had been killed by the Nazis. Some families were wiped out entirely with no one to carry on their name.

As the train approaches Chicago, Adam's eyes grow wide. He stares out to the skyscrapers reaching up to the sky.

Adam steps off the train. There are lines of railroad tracks and other trains all around him inside the dimly lit station.

Adam walks to the doors. A policeman holds it open with a smile.

Adam steps onto the marble floors that lead to an enormous room with a vast ceiling made of glass. The sun streams into the room as he sits down on a bench. His uncle will be there to meet him after work, so Adam is prepared to wait for a short time.

He rests his suitcase between his feet. A single suitcase is more than enough to carry what is left of his belongings.

Soldiers are still returning home. Adam watches the family reunions as the soldiers enter the station. It makes him even more excited about seeing his uncle again, but also reminds him of those he lost. A feeling of sadness washes over him. He can only hope that life in America will bring some happiness.

An hour later, Adam is in his uncle's arms and his uncle is squeezing him tight, almost too tight.

"I'm so pleased that you're here." Uncle Nysen smiles as the tears spill down his cheeks.

"Me, too." Adam chokes back a sob.

Adam's tears aren't just for the gratitude that he feels for his uncle. His uncle resembles his father so much that he almost has to look away.

Adam follows his uncle as they walk to the elevated trains. He looks straight up at the skyscrapers surrounding him, dizzied by their enormity.

"Your aunt is preparing a wonderful dinner. You must be hungry. You look terribly thin, Adam."

His uncle is clearly concerned with his wellbeing. Adam is very different from the boy that he had left in Munich.

They walk five blocks from the elevated train platform to a small brick house with neatly manicured bushes in the front.

"This is your new home, Adam." Nysen Herschel smiles proudly.

Uncle Nysen holds the door, and Adam is met with the delectable scent of chicken roasting in the oven. Adam's Aunt Else rushes to hug him.

"I prepared a feast, and it looks like you could use it." She looks him up and down.

His uncle leads him to his bedroom, but assures him that their bedroom is right down the hall if Adam should need anything. Adam sets his suitcase on the bed and opens it.

"I'll call you when dinner is ready." Uncle Nysen closes the door.

Adam peers out the window to the children playing outside. The fresh air breezes in as he sits down on the bed. Between the long journey and the excitement of the city, he is exhausted. He can't wait to slip under the soft blankets and lose himself to sleep.

"Would you like a radio for your room?" Uncle Nysen peers his head in the door.

"If you have an extra one that would be nice, otherwise, I'll be fine."

He still has to hold back tears when he is in his uncle's presence. Adam fears that if he allows all of the pain to flow he will never stop crying.

"Oh yes, I have an extra one in the basement." Uncle Nysen sets off to retrieve it.

After dinner, Adam draws back the blankets on his bed. The sun is slowly fading, so he switches on his lamp and closes the curtains.

"Don't you have pajamas, Adam?" Aunt Else said.

"No, I will buy some tomorrow.

"Would you like to wear a pair of your uncle's?"

"No thanks, I will be al."

"Alright, get some rest."

Before Aunt Else can close the door Adam's uncle returns to make sure he is comfortable.

"Good night, Adam. We're so pleased that you're finally here." Tears fill his eyes again as he closes the door behind him.

The following morning, Aunt Else accompanies Adam to exchange his English currency for American dollars, and they stop by the tailor where Adam will be working.

Hal Rosen and his wife Emily own the tailor shop and they are dear friends of Nysen and Else's.

"They were very kind to us when we arrived from Germany. You will like them, Adam. They are good people."

As soon as Adam steps inside the shop vivid memories flood his mind. The sewing machines hum in the back room just like they did at Frau Lenger's shop.

"Hello Adam, it is a pleasure to meet you." Hal steps forward to shake his hand.

Emily Rosen emerges from the back and introduces herself as well.

Both can see that Adam is in need of food and rest. His face is pale and his body thin.

"I think that you need to eat, young man," Hal surprises Adam by speaking in German. "You need to put on some weight. Don't worry, take your time and rest. You have a job waiting for you."

"Thank you, I am so grateful for this opportunity. I can start any time."

"How about 5 a.m. on Monday morning? That will give you almost a week to rest and acclimate to your new home."

Later that afternoon, Adam and his uncle walk to the lawyer's office. Adam has all of his documentation in hand, and his uncle reassures him that his lawyer is one of the best.

Adam's lawyer sits behind a large mahogany desk eyeing Adam intently. Adam hands him the documentation and waits to find out the next step in the process, but his lawyer says very little.

"It will be helpful that your papers are from England. I will be in touch."

Adam's uncle reassures him that it will be alright as they walk home.

"He seems like a grumpy old man, but he is very good at what he does."

Adam understands that it will take some time, but all that he really wants is a place to call home without the fear of being deported.

In the weeks to follow, Adam works hard at the shop. Working in Hal and Emily's shop is similar to working in Frau Lenger's. Hal had immigrated to Chicago from Germany when he was very young. Adam is growing closer to Hal and Emily, but he is still quite guarded.

He doesn't go to the synagogue, and Uncle Nysen seldom bothers him about it. Adam struggles with his spirituality, especially after hearing all of the reports of the concentration camps. He cannot understand how God stood silently by and allowed the hounds of hell to torture and kill millions of innocent people.

"You mustn't try to figure God out. Just know that he loves us," Uncle Nysen advises one evening at dinner.

Adam is still awaiting news about his mother. He can only hope, by some miracle, that she is still alive.

In late October, Adam receives a letter from Nancy. She writes that all is well and thanks him for the gifts he had sent to her and the boys. He also sent them a postcard with a picture of the Chicago skyline when he had first arrived. Nancy commented on how amazing it must be to live there. Adam is still amazed every time he rides the elevated train downtown. Every day, he is reminded that he is living his dream, but there is hard work ahead of him. He has finally made it to America; now he can only hope that he will be able to stay.

Adam purchases some oil paints and begins painting in his free time. It helps to calm his mind. He spends much of his time alone, much to his Aunt Else's disapproval. She wants him to meet a nice girl and marry.

In November, Adam writes letters to Hannah and Elisabeth. He no longer has their addresses, but he knows the street that Elisabeth had lived on and he remembers the street of Hannah's last address. He doesn't know the building numbers, but he hopes that the letter service will be able to deliver the letters to them anyway.

As Adam writes the letters, he is again reminded that the Nazis are no longer in power. He can say anything that he pleases without endangering himself or his friends, unlike the first time that he had written to them. It is a relief that Adolf Hitler had committed suicide. Adam only regretted that the evil Fuhrer hadn't done it before he killed millions of people.

November brings gray skies, cooler temperatures, and the Nuremberg trials.

What is most shocking is that Hermann Goering believes that the Nazis will remain in power, with him as their leader. It is baffling the arrogance and stupidity that the Nazis exhibit. Hermann Goering and the other Nazis really believe that they will win the trial, but the truth is that they will probably be hanged.

"They have no shame!" Else switches off the radio and disappears into the kitchen.

Adam glances at his uncle. A look of disgust grapples Nysen's face.

Their son and his family had been killed by the Nazis, starved to death in a concentration camp.

"I hope they all hang," Adam said.

"Let God deal with them, Adam," Uncle Nysen said. "We must move past our resentment. We are only hurting ourselves."

"I hope they hang, too." Else sits down in her chair and narrows her eyes to Nysen. "They deserve much worse."

Nysen pats his wife's knee as she cries softly. Nysen gently pulls her into his arms and holds her. Adam retreats to his bedroom as the tears slide down his face.

Adam slips on a sweater and heads outside. He grabs a rake from the garage and eyes the leaves that blanket the ground. He needs to get them picked up before it snows or the yard will be a mess in the spring.

He piles up the leaves and douses them with a small amount of fuel. He stands back and watches the orange flames spread across the brittle leaves. Some of the fire sparks into the air, but most of it remains contained to the narrow pile on the side of the street.

Adam removes his gloves and holds his hands over the fire. As he warms his hands, he wonders if Elisabeth or Hannah will ever receive his letters. He wonders if he will ever hear from them again. He wonders if they are still alive.

By the end of December, there is still no news on Else Herschel, but the Jewish organization that is helping Adam's uncle has members in Germany investigating her disappearance, and the disappearance of many others.

The organizations and individuals that took the initiative to help the displaced survivors searching for their missing family, and those from all over the world searching for their loved ones, had a daunting task ahead. The Nazis had done all that they could to destroy any evidence of their atrocities.

Adam watches the blowing snow outside his window. The bitter winds make an ominous sound.

He is surprised to find that not knowing is worse than knowing his mother's fate.

He wonders if he will ever hear from Hannah or Elisabeth again.

36

Helena

Helena sits on the edge of her bed holding the doll that Elisabeth and Adam had given to her, the pages of Hannah's letter by her side. The blanket that Elisabeth had sewn out of Hannah's dresses is folded neatly inside the wooden chest at Helena's feet.

Andreas, Helena's husband, sets a steaming mug of coffee for her on the nightstand. "I think you should try to find them."

She stares out the window to auburn and gold leaves blowing gently on the trees. The sky is gray and there is a chill in the air. The warm light from the lamp glows softly lighting their bedroom. A small fire still burns in the fireplace from the previous night.

Andreas stands at the window sipping his coffee.

"Do you think I'm being ungrateful for what my parents have done for me?" Helena searches his face.

"Your parents have always been honest about your past. How many times have they reminded you that your real parents must have loved you very much to have made the choice to give you up? Your real parents saved your life. You would have died with them if they hadn't made that sacrifice. They will understand that you want to know more about the people who loved you that much."

"I don't want to hurt anyone."

"You're not going to hurt them, Helena." Andreas sits down beside her. "Are you afraid of what you might find?"

Helena is quiet for moment.

"This is going to hurt. I know that. I remember them, Andreas. I saw my mother crying in the window when they took me away. It's a faint memory, and sometimes I question whether it's real or just my imagination, but I don't question how much I loved them. My love for them will remain safe in my heart, always." Helena sips her coffee. "I could be worrying for nothing. I may find out that Elisabeth and Adam didn't survive." Worry burrows deep in her brow as she stares down at her slippers. "Those soulless Nazis killed so many in their reign of terror. I don't understand how so many stood by and did nothing. My God, even the children weren't spared." Helena raises her head. "If they are alive, I have to find them. I have to find them for my mother. I have to do this for her. She told me, in the letter, about their promise. They promised to always to stay together. I must keep her promise for her."

The following day, Helena hires a private investigator, the same private investigator that her adopted parents had hired to find Hannah and Otto. It took him over a year, but he found them. He broke the news to Helena and her parents that Hannah had died in Dachau and Otto had died in Auschwitz. He had died in the gas chambers a year after his arrival to the camp.

37

Adam

Adam removes the stray threads from his pants before walking to the front of the shop. He peers out the window to the city outside. The sun is bright in the sky as the air conditioner hums in the back room. He sits down on one of the winged chairs that adorn the shop window and sips his coffee. The city is just waking, but he's been awake since four o'clock. Adam reclines back in his chair. He is reminded of Frau Lenger's words–*In the morning, everything is ahead of you. The promise of a new day.*

Gracie rests her chin on Adam's shoe.

"Are you ready for a nap?" Adam smiles down at the fluffy white poodle at his feet.

Adam enjoys the morning sun for a few moments, but he needs to finish cleaning up. The customers will be there soon.

"Adam, where is the fabric delivery?" Anna peers out the doorway of the back room.

"I already put it away."

"You can head out if you want. We've got it from here."

"Are you sure?" Adam glances back at Anna.

"Yes, boss."

Adam takes another sip of coffee and stares out the window.

Adam and Gracie walk their usual path home, Gracie sniffing the usual spots, marking her territory as she does every day. Children play in the distance as people make their way to work. The city is finally awake. Adam lifts Gracie into his arms before climbing the stairs to his Greystone. He feels gratitude swell inside of him. Every time he walks up those stairs he feels it.

He sets Gracie down inside and closes the door behind them.

"You're early." Peter bites into his toast. "Do you want some breakfast?"

"No, I think I'll sit out back and have another cup of coffee."

"I'm working today," Peter said.

"That's fine. We'll let the writer write, huh Gracie?" Gracie jumps up on Adam's legs.

Peter works better when the house is quiet, and Adam and Gracie are happy to oblige, with the exception of Gracie's fierce determination to bark at any squirrels that she spots from the sitting room window.

Adam met Peter a few years after he arrived in the United States. They kept their relationship a secret for a long time. Both of their families were vehemently against homosexuality, so it was easier just to hide it. Live in shame. A decision they both regretted. No one was worth that. Not even family.

Adam's uncle and aunt are both deceased now, so he has no living relatives. Peter's father lives in the city and is still able to care for himself at age eighty seven. Peter's father knows about their relationship now, but they had hidden it from him for years. Peter finally told him a year after his mother died. His father doesn't understand it, but he accepts it. He has even grown to care for Adam. Peter and Adam treat his father to dinner twice a month and visit him every weekend. They've offered many times for him to move in with them, but he insists on remaining in his own home. So, as long as he is able to care for himself Adam and Peter relent.

Adam walks out to the vegetable garden and picks a couple of large ripe tomatoes. His mind drifts back to Munich. He can see clearly, the fields of asparagus that he would pick with Elisabeth and Hannah in their secret place. He has been feeling tired lately, and the past seems to be his constant companion. Peter had warned him years ago that it would catch up to him, but Adam thought he could out run it.

The first years in the United States were a period of rebuilding for Adam. He set out to build a new life. He felt that he owed it to his parents and to the many others who had lost their lives. He had survived, although it still didn't make sense to him. He couldn't understand why he had been spared; there was nothing special about him. So, he lived inside the confines of his new life and left the past behind. Peter had asked many times if they could travel to Europe, but Adam vowed never to return. Peter finally relented and traveled to Europe with his mother. Adam also gave up looking for Hannah and Elisabeth. He suspected that they were dead, and in his heart he knew it to be true. The flat where Elisabeth had lived was destroyed in the bombings. Hannah disappeared, like many other Jews. All of the roads led to a dead end, so he stopped searching. He stopped searching because he wanted the past to disappear, and take all of the trauma and pain with it. He still had nightmares from time to time. He could still hear the bombs falling from the sky as he struggled to wake from the nightmares in the middle of the night. There were times that he would wake sobbing, but he couldn't remember the dream.

"Adam, are you alright?" Peter stands next to him in the garden.

"Yes, I'm fine." Adam looks up at him.

"I just asked you three times if you want me to take something out for dinner." Peter studies him.

"Oh, I didn't hear you. Sorry. It's been a long day."

"Maybe you should get a checkup. You've been like this for weeks. You're not yourself."

"I had a checkup in January. I'm fine. I'm just getting old."

"Adam, if there's something going on I want to help."

Adam drops his head and a tear falls onto a green tomato hanging from its vine. He cries softly as Peter holds him in his arms. He can't explain it to Peter. He doesn't understand what is happening. He can't put it into words. All he knows is that he is feeling the pain that he can no longer push away. The ghosts from his past surround him and he's terrified of what they bring.

That evening, after many tears and a long nap, Peter joins Adam at the table outside. Adam sips his glass of wine, Gracie cuddles on his lap.

"I bought this for you." Peter sets a wrapped gift in front of him.

Adam carefully unwraps his present.

He sets the wrapping paper aside, and holds the journal in his hands.

"I know that you don't like to talk about your feelings, but maybe this will help you find out what's hurting you. It's private. You don't have to share anything with me or anyone else. This is just you writing down your thoughts, your feelings. I don't know. I think it might help." Peter smiles and holds Adam's hand for a brief moment. "Will you just try it for two weeks? I mean a proper try. That's all I ask."

Adam stares down at the journal. He wants to say no. He wants to tell Peter that he's afraid.

"Ok, two weeks."

The following morning, Adam picks up his journal. Gracie follows him down the hallway to his study. He closes the door and sits down at his desk. Gracie lies comfortably on a shaft of sunlight on the floor. Adam picks up his pen and opens the journal. He writes the date at the top right corner. He pauses for a moment before setting the pen back down.

After careful deliberation, he picks up his pen and begins to write.

Suddenly, the words begin to flow as though they had waited a lifetime to be written. His pen moves quickly across each line on the page working hard to keep up with his thoughts. The truth inks onto the paper in quick succession. Adam turns the page and continues to write as the tears stream down his face. He brushes them away with the back of his hand and continues writing.

Finally, he sets his pen down. He had written seven pages front and back. The ink on the last page is still wet as he reclines back in his chair. He glances over at Gracie napping in the sunlight and takes a deep breath. He tries not to disturb her slumber as he lies down next to her. He closes his eyes to the sun, soaking in its warmth. Gracie licks his face before returning to her nap.

In the next few weeks, Adam writes in his journal every day. The truth that had been buried is finally finding its way to the light. The daily fatigue is diminishing as well.

"The Beatles are on tonight." Peter steps out the back door.

"All of that screaming." Adam shakes his head as he pulls weeds in the garden.

"I'd be one of them if I were there," Peter laughs.

That evening, as they watch the Beatles perform on their black and white television, Adam's mind wonders back to Germany.

"The world sure has changed," Adam says during a commercial.

"Do you mean there was a world before the Beatles?" Peter feigns shock.

Adam is reminded of the hysteria of the German people for Adolf Hitler, and the crowds that would fill the streets for him and his soldiers. They had an unwavering belief that he was going to restore Germany to greatness. Many believed he was God like.

Adam sips his tea and sits back in his chair. The truth is that Adolf Hitler destroyed much of Germany and Europe. The truth is that in the end, he sent young boys and old men off to a war that was already lost. The truth is that Germany will always be remembered, first and foremost, for the Nazis and the atrocities that they committed. The truth is that one man wanted to rule the world and he didn't care if it was at the expense of all humanity.

Peter turns off the television and sits down on the floor. "What are you thinking about?"

"The past," Adam sighs.

"You don't have to hide that stuff from me. I can handle it. You don't need to protect me from your past," Peter said.

The anxiety begins to swirl in Adam's stomach. The adrenaline moves at a steady pace as Adam swallows hard. "They took everything from me," Adam begins. "They took the people that I loved. They took my belief in the kindness of humanity. They created a terrifying world for me to live in. They took away my God; a God that I loved. I can no longer feel Him. I don't believe in his love anymore. His love should have saved all of those people. He can't possibly exist."

"Don't lose hope. You may find Him again on the other side of this grief. That's what this is. You couldn't figure out what was happening to you. You're grieving and it's about time too."

Adam cries softly in Peter's arms long into the night.

38

Helena

Helena wakes in the night. Andreas snores softly next to her. She glances at the clock. Another 4 a.m. wake up call. She stares up into the darkness, and takes a deep breath. Astra stands up at the end of the bed and stretches. Wagging her tail, she waits for Helena to get out of bed.

"Ok, let's go," Helena whispers before kissing her head.

Helena quietly retrieves her clothes and steps into the bathroom to change.

It is dark as she slips on her shoes and steps outside into the brisk morning air.

Astra runs ahead into the forest with Helena close behind. The sun will be rising soon. Her breath fogs the air as she follows Astra down their usual trail through the dense trees. The lake will be in sight soon. Helena thinks about Adam. Her private investigator had found him; it had taken just under a year to complete his investigation. Adam had survived the bombings in London before relocating to the United States.

The sun begins to rise. It glows in a warm orange hue illuminating the morning sky. The lake reflects the sun like a mirror. Astra plays in the cool water near the shore as Helena finds her usual spot on the rocks.

Her mind returns to Adam. She has no memory of him, only what her mother had written in her letter. Hannah had described him as sensitive, kind, and gentle. She said that Adam and Elisabeth would have stood by her even if the whole world was against her. Helena will never forget those words. She wonders if Adam remembers her mother. She can't imagine that he could have forgotten her. They grew up together. She wonders if Adam is still the lovely person that her mother had described in her letter, or if he was a different person, afflicted with the affects of war and the Nazis. She was informed by the investigator that Adam's parents had been imprisoned and that Adam had fled Germany on the SS St. Louis. What if she finds a broken or bitter man? She wonders if Adam will resent her coming into his life. She now understands what has been waking her in the early hours of morning. She is terrified that she could hurt him by bringing up his past. A past she is certain holds pain, and likely, trauma.

Helena stares out to the lake. The sun is now warm on her face. She has to make a decision. What would her mother want her to do?

39

Adam

Rain pours from the sky, melting the remaining snow. Adam waters the seedlings that sit on a table in his kitchen in front of the window. The spring air drifts through the window as he opens it slightly.

"They're starting to sprout." Peter points to the fresh green buds that have risen up from the dirt. "Are those cucumbers?"

"No, that's tomatoes. The cucumbers usually take a bit longer. We need more sunny days." Adam watches the rain drops stream down the window. "I'll plant the lettuce and onions this week if I can get some dry days."

Adam lifts Gracie up in his arms and gives her a kiss. "If this rain ever lets up we'll go for a walk."

"I'm going to make bread this afternoon," Peter said.

"I think I'll make some soup to go with it." Adam sets Gracie down on her blanket. "Did I ever tell you that I ate a lot of soup when I was growing up?"

"No. Was your mom a good cook?"

"Yeah, she was when we had food. We ate cabbage and potato soup most of the time. I vowed to never eat soup again once I could afford to eat solid food," Adam sighs. "Things change."

Adam opens the back door and peers out to the garden. The rain taps lightly against table outside. "I think that I'm lucky in a way. I'm still grateful for all that I have. When you grow up the way that I did, with very little, you must remember where you came from. It will always keep you grateful."

"I like that you talk about your past now." Peter sits down at the table with his coffee. "I understood, but your past was always a secret between us." Peter sips his coffee. "I wish I could have met your parents."

"I wish I had pictures. They all burned in the fire the night that Fritz died." Adam sits down across from Peter. "That's alright, in my mind, I can still see them. Hannah and Elisabeth thought my mother was pretty, I just thought of her as my mom. My dad was funny."

Adam's smile fades. "He was before the Nazis."

"I still can't imagine how terrifying it had to be living in Germany at that time. The Nazis scare me now."

"There was a great deal of anger and hate."

Moments later, the doorbell rings, and Gracie runs to answer it.

"Gracie, quiet." Adam picks her up and holds her in his arms as he opens the door. Gracie continues to bark at the woman standing in the doorway. The rain taps loudly on her umbrella as thunder rumbles in the distance. Adam and the woman remain frozen in the doorway.

Peter is now standing behind Adam.

"Can I help you?" Peter said.

Helena stands in the rain staring up at Adam.

"Can I help you?" Peter asks again, but Helena takes no notice of him.

Adam stands frozen in the doorway holding Gracie. Gracie is still barking at the woman, but Adam can barely hear her. The room begins to spin.

"Adam." Peter grabs his arm in an effort to break him free of his trance.

"Hannah." Adam begins to sob.

Peter slips Gracie out of Adam's arms before Adam falls to his knees.

Helena drops her umbrella and kneels down next to him.

"It's okay," Helena reassures him. "I'm sorry. It's okay."

"Hannah." Adam repeats.

"No, it's Helena."

Adam continues to sob as Helena holds him in her arms. Peter stands above them holding Gracie. Gracie is quiet now. The only sound to be heard is the rain tapping on the abandoned umbrella just outside the door.

"Come in out of the rain." Peter shakes the rain off of the umbrella before helping Adam and Helena to their feet.

Adam follows Peter into the kitchen. Helena is close behind with Gracie sniffing her heals.

"She won't bite," Peter said.

Helena sits down and holds out her hand for Gracie to investigate.

"Her name is Gracie." Peter pours Helena a cup of coffee. "Adam, are you alright?" Peter glances over at Adam before setting Helena's coffee down in front of her.

Adam swallows hard and takes a deep breath. "Yes, I'm sorry."

"No. I'm sorry," Helena begins. "I should have called you first. I watched you from across the street of your shop yesterday. You were so happy. You're so wonderful with the customers, especially the children. I had worried that the past might have changed you, but I could see that you were exactly as my mother had described. I felt confident after seeing you that you weren't the broken man I had worried you might have become. I'm sorry for spying on you, but I didn't want to take a chance. I didn't want to hurt you. I feel awful." Tears fill Helena's eyes.

Adam stands up and rests his hands on her shoulder. "There is nothing for you to feel awful about, sweet girl. You look so much like your mother." Adam begins to cry. "My God." Adam has to sit back down.

"I didn't know. I don't have any pictures of her or my father. We couldn't travel with any pictures; it might have given us away. In my mother's letter, she said that she packed them for me, but it wasn't safe."

Adam looks fused. "They took you from Hannah and Otto?" Fresh tears stream down his face. "Are they alive?"

Helena is silent for a moment. "No. I'm sorry, Adam."

Adam drops his gaze to floor as a tear slides down his cheek. "I knew it. I could feel it. I knew she was dead." His breaths are steady, but fresh pain is flowing in waves throughout his body. He takes another deep breath. "Helena, would it be alright if I got some air?"

Helena nods.

"I just need a little time alone." Adam glances at Helena then Peter.

Adam steps out of the back door. The rain pelts his face as his breath fogs the air. He walks to the vegetable garden and takes a deep breath. He needs to pull himself together. "Please help me." Adam stares up to the sky. "Please help me," he cries.

Adam sits down at the table outside. As the rain pours down from the sky, a new found peace slowly washes over him. Adam can feel God there with him.

"Adam." Peter stands in the doorway. "Please come inside. You're going to catch a cold."

Adam takes another deep breath before standing up from the table.

Peter hands him a towel as he steps back inside. Helena is still seated at the table. He can see that she regrets her decision to visit him.

"I'm glad you're here," Adam reassures her. "It's eerie. I have recently spent a lot of time trying to heal from my past, and then you show up at my door." Adam's eyes fill with tears. "I believe in fate. This has happened exactly as it should, my dear girl."

Adam walks to the stove. "I'm making potato soup. Would you like some?"

"Thank you," Helena said.

Helena and Peter spend the afternoon eating, drinking wine, and listening to Adam's stories from the past. He shares every detail that he can remember about where he, Hannah, and Elisabeth had grown up, their friendship, their hardships and Otto. He wants Helena to know every detail about her parents and her family.

"I remember them," Helena looks as though she's trying to convince them, but they believe her. "I loved them so much. Even though my adoptive parents gave me a good home and much love, somewhere inside of me there was something missing or hurting. I can't explain it. I feel like I've been walking around with a broken heart from the moment that I lost them. I loved them so much." Helena pauses for a moment. "You still have such a strong accent. It somehow sounds familiar to me."

Adam laughs. "I've spent years trying to acclimate, but my German accent just won't leave me."

"I'm glad. I should be getting back to my hotel. It's been a long day."

"Please stay here with us. We have plenty of room," Adam said.

"Family shouldn't stay in a hotel," Peter adds.

"Do you have an extra toothbrush?"

"We have a couple in the linen closet. I have a pair of pajamas that I just bought for Adam. They'll be a little big, but they haven't been worn. There are fresh towels in the bathroom next to your room. Anything else that you need we will get for you," Peter smiles. "If you would like, you can go up and have a bath. I'll put the kettle on."

"Thank you." Helena stands up from the table. Gracie follows her upstairs. Helena has made a new friend.

Later that night, Adam pulls back the blankets on their bed.

"She's fast asleep." Peter quietly closes their bedroom door.

"It's been a long day for all of us." Adam slips into bed and turns out the light.

The following morning, Helena joins Adam and Peter for breakfast.

"It's just coffee and porridge." Adam sets a steaming cup of coffee on the table for Helena. "I can make you something else," Adam said.

"No, this is fine." Helena sips her coffee.

"There's something on your mind," Adam said.

Helena stares out the window. The sun is bright in the sky. "It was a long night. It's a lot to process."

"Well, you rest. We'll all rest."

"I'm going to the hotel this morning to pick up my things. You really don't mind me staying here?"

"We want you here, Helena. Stay forever if you want."

"I'm not sure how my husband and my dog would feel about that. And, I'm on a flight to Munich on Monday."

"Munich?"

"Yes. I'm going to see Elisabeth."

"I don't understand." Adam straightens in his chair.

"We thought she was dead." Peter sits down next to Adam. Confusion washes over both of their faces.

"No, she's in Munich." Helena looks equally confused. "I thought you knew."

"She's alive?" Adam said.

"Yes. I haven't spoken to her. I thought I should do a little more investigating on my own. What you and Elisabeth have lived through...I want to be careful not to add any more pain."

"You're certain she is alive?" Adam said.

"Yes, she has a son. Her husband died in the war. Her father and brothers also died in the war. She never remarried." Helena opens her bag and pulls out a folder. "Here's the information that I was given. Helena spreads the documents out on the table, moving Adam's folder, containing his information, to the side.

Adam eagerly reads each document.

"She married Dieter! She couldn't stop them!"

"Who couldn't stop them?" Peter said.

"Olga." Adam continues to pore over the documents. "I told you both about her."

"Olga is the girl that bullied my mother, right?"

"She bullied all of us." Adam continues reading. "Yes, she's the one that I told you about, the one that tried to cut Hannah's hair off." Adam sets the papers down and turns his attention back to Helena and Peter. "She was in love with Dieter. She was horrible to Elisabeth. She married Elisabeth's brother."

"What?" Helena looks confused.

So begins the story of Olga, Henning, Dieter, and Elisabeth.

The room is quiet when Adam finishes. The only sound to be heard is the clock ticking on the wall.

Finally, Peter speaks. "She would have had them tortured and killed? I mean, she wasn't just trying to scare them?" Peter looks horrified.

"No, she meant it."

A look of disgust washes over Helena's face.

Adam holds up one of the documents and rereads Elisabeth's address. "She doesn't live far from where we grew up."

"Do you want to come with me?" Helena said.

Adam looks down at the papers scattered on the table. "Yes. I do."

Adam and Helena arrive in Munich early Tuesday morning. The sun is bright in the sky as they step up onto the tram. Adam watches the people getting on and off. It is all so familiar, a world he thought he had left behind, but now he is breathing its air.

"Are you ok?" Helena whispers.

"Yes." Adam looks out across the city.

The tram begins to glide down the track. Adam tries to take in every inch, every building, and every person. The air is warm with a hint of a spring chill. He knows the chill will be gone by afternoon. He knows this place. This is home.

There is a knock at Adam's hotel room door.

"Are you ready?" Helena steps inside.

"I'm apprehensive," Adam said.

"We can wait. If you want to rest, that is fine. I don't know what state we will find her in, I'm afraid. It's important that you're ready, Adam." Helena sits down in the chair by the window.

Adam stands near the window peering out to the city below.

"I'm ready."

Adam and Helena are close to the boutique where Elisabeth is believed to work.

"What should we do?" Helena is clearly nervous.

"Let's have a coffee over there." Adam points to the café across the street from the boutique.

"Wait!" Adam grabs Helena's arm and gently pulls her back. "We have to make sure she doesn't see us. She might recognize me and she would definitely recognize you since you look so much like Hannah. Let's go around the corner and enter the café from a different direction."

Adam and Helena cautiously enter the café. Adam finds a safe table near the window.

"I wonder if she's in there." He peers across the street to the boutique.

"What if she's not? Do you want to go to her last known address? I don't want to frighten her."

"We won't frighten her. Elisabeth doesn't scare easily, but she will be shocked, to say the least."

"Is that her?" Helena points to a woman leaving the boutique.

Adam narrows his eyes and moves closer to the window.

"I think that's her! What should we do?" Adam stands up quickly. "Let's follow her!"

"We have to be careful not to let her see us." Helena follows him outside.

Adam and Helena step outside the café and cross the street. Adam glances inside the boutique as they walk past.

"Put your hat on," Helena said.

Adam hastily places his hat on his head and pulls it down slightly in the front.

"Let's slow down a little." Adam slows his pace.

"What if we lose her?" Helena walks in stride with him.

Elisabeth disappears around the corner. Adam and Helena quicken their pace.

Adam and Helena round the corner just in time to see Elisabeth step inside a bakery.

"This is the weirdest thing that I've ever done," Adam said.

They stand shoulder to shoulder, both watching the door to the bakery.

"I would like to agree with you, but I did this last week in Chicago," Helena grins.

"You really are your mother's daughter," Adam shakes his head with a smile.

Elisabeth steps out of the bakery carrying a small package. She crosses the street as Adam and Helena follow a block behind her.

They remain unnoticed by Elisabeth as they follow her to a park. Elisabeth sits down in the grass before opening the package. She takes a bite of the pastry and stares out to the lake.

Adam and Helena sit down in the grass facing the opposite direction. They turn to watch her from afar, but close enough to clearly see her face.

Adam remains quiet as Helena waits for his instructions.

"I never thought that I would see her again." Adam is now feeling the enormity of this miracle.

Helena holds Adam's hand for a moment before turning back to Elisabeth.

"You can do this, Adam."

Adam dries his tears and stands up. He holds out his hand to Helena and pulls her up.

They walk slowly towards Elisabeth. The water from the lake splashes softly on the rocks as the sun beams down from the sky.

Elisabeth turns her attention to them. Her eyes narrow as she studies the two strangers.

Elisabeth stands up carefully as tears spill from her eyes. She walks towards them. Adam and Helena step closer. They pull Elisabeth into their arms as they all cry.

"I thought I lost you! I couldn't find you!" Elisabeth speaks in German to Adam. Her voice is shaky as the tears stream down her cheeks.

"I thought you were dead." Adam is sobbing. "I thought you were dead." He repeats in German.

Elisabeth shakes her head as she cries. All that Adam can see is the young Elisabeth, his friend. He can see her so clearly as the tears stream down her face.

"Helena?"

Helena nods her head as the tears stream down her face.

"My goodness, you look so much like Hannah." Elisabeth pauses before searching their faces. "Hannah and Otto... are they alive?"

Adam shakes his head and sobs.

Elisabeth covers her face with her hands and sobs.

Moments later, she looks up at Adam. "I'm ok, just give me a second."

Adam translates Elisabeth's German to English for Helena.

Elisabeth brushes her tears away and smiles at them. "I'll speak in English. Let's sit down for a moment."

Adam holds their hands as they stare out to the lake.

"We kept our promise," Elisabeth speaks in English. "And, Helena kept Hannah's."

"Thank you, my sweet girl." Adam squeezes Helena's hand before turning his attention to Elisabeth. "Helena found us."

Elisabeth hugs Helena. "I hope Hannah and Otto are with us right now. I can still hear her laughter. I can still see her smile. She was the most courageous person that I ever met. I will continue to miss her every day for the rest of my life."

Adam can't stop the tears or the pain that is finally releasing itself from him. "I should have tried harder to find you. I'm so sorry."

Elisabeth looks into his eyes. "I don't care. I'm just so happy to see you, to hear your voice, I missed you terribly." Her eyes are a watery sea of green. "I'm never going to let you go." Elisabeth hugs him. She then turns to Helena. "I don't know how I can ever repay you."

"I told her that she is our family now." Adam looks like a proud father.

"She always was," Elisabeth smiles.

Helena reaches into her bag and pulls out a small box. She opens it revealing the doll that Elisabeth had sewn for her when she was a little girl.

"I didn't know that you still had that?" Adam feels a fresh pain as he holds in his hands the clothes that his mother had sewn.

"I wanted you and Elisabeth to see it together. I have the quilt that Elisabeth made out of my mother's dresses at home. It was too large to travel with, but I will bring it the next time I come to visit. I also have this letter." Helena places the folded letter in front of Elisabeth and Adam. "I'm going for a walk. I think you should read this together."

Elisabeth scoots closer to Adam before unfolding the letter. Tears fall silent down Adam's cheeks. He recognizes Hannah's handwriting. It's flowery and beautiful, just like Hannah.

Page after page, Hannah details Helena's family on both Hannah and Otto's side. Sprinkled in, are funny and sometimes sad stories about each member. Hannah left no stone unturned. She wrote about her love for Otto and what a wonderful husband he was to her. She also wrote about Otto's love for Helena. She wrote about growing up with Adam and Elisabeth. She said it was some of the happiest times of her life. She wrote the last address that she had for both of them. She told Helena that if she ever needed anything Adam and Elisabeth would help her. She gave Helena advice about happiness and love. She also wrote about hate and what it was like living in Germany with the Nazis. She ends the letter with the confession that she was unsure of her choice to send Helena away into the arms of strangers, but she couldn't take a chance of her daughter falling into the hands of the heartless Nazis.

They finish reading the letter, and Elisabeth places it carefully on the grass.

"I didn't know that she thought I was strong. I didn't feel strong." Elisabeth looks out to the lake.

Adam is quiet. "Are you happy?"

"I lead a quiet life, and I think I've found some peace. Are you happy?"

Adam thinks for a moment.

"I've built a good life. I have a loving family, though it's quite small," Adam smiles. "That doesn't matter. Yes, I think I am happy. I'm learning that my past is part of who I am, and I can't run from it. I'm tired of running. I'm just going to take life as it comes."

Helena returns from her walk and sits down beside them.

"I just want you to know that I will keep my mother's promise. You are all that I have left of my family. I don't ever want to let you go. I will always be there for both of you, just as my mother would have if she had survived."

"I think we should make a new promise." Adam reaches for Helena and Elisabeth's hands. "I promise to celebrate the lives of the people that we loved and lost. I would like us to get together, when we can, to celebrate them with the memories that live in our hearts. Even your memory, Helena, and I do believe it was a memory. I don't think it was your imagination. The memory of seeing Hannah in the window as you were taken away is painful, but it is also love. Your parents gave you away to save your life. That memory should always be a reminder that you were truly loved by them."

"I promise." Helena looks into Adam and Elisabeth's eyes.

"I promise." Elisabeth squeezes Adam and Helena's hands.

"I promise." Adam meets their eyes, just as he had long ago with Hannah and Elisabeth.

40

Elisabeth

Elisabeth opens the curtains to the sun drenched city outside. Morning is still her favorite time of day. She walks quietly to the kitchen and prepares coffee.

"Do you remember how impossible it was to get coffee?" Adam sits down at the table.

"Yes. It's hard not to have a grateful heart when you grow up the way that we did. I feel like I'm rich now. Of course I'm not even close, but to me, I'm rich."

"Yes, I know what you mean," Adam smiles. "I'm glad that Helena was able to stay a few extra days."

"I am too."

"I still can't believe that you married Dieter. It seemed that fate always found a way to keep you apart."

"In the end, it did." The smile fades from Elisabeth's face.

"I'm sorry. I shouldn't have brought it up."

"No more of that. We decided that we're not running from our past." Elisabeth pats his hand. "I love Dieter. I'll always love him."

"Is that why you never remarried?"

"There weren't a lot of men around after the war. I spent my time rebuilding this city and raising our son. There was no time for anything else." Elisabeth walks over to the window and looks out. "It was all destroyed. I'm lucky to be alive. The bombing raids were relentless. I still have nightmares. I'll never forget the smell of the bombs."

"I know." Adam stands by her side.

"Life can change you." Elisabeth looks out to the city. "I don't think that I will ever love anyone the way that I loved Dieter. I don't want to. I'm alright being alone."

"Are you sure about that?"

Elisabeth shakes her head. "No, I'm not sure, but what's wrong with a safe life?"

"There's nothing wrong with living a safe life. We survived some dangerous and dark times. I'd say we've earned it." Adam picks up a framed black and white photo of Elisabeth's family when she was young. "Your father was terrifying."

"Yes, he was." Elisabeth glances down at the picture. "Dieter protected me from him. Unfortunately, he couldn't protect me from Olga."

"What happened to Olga? Is she still alive?"

"No, she took her own life shortly after the war began. She lived a tumultuous life leading up to her death. She cheated on Henning with a brute and lost herself in the bottle." Elisabeth pauses for a moment. "I lived here during the war with Wilhelm and Friedrich. This flat belonged to Dieter's uncle. We had one of our meetings here. Do you remember?" Elisabeth said changing the subject.

"Oh my goodness, yes, I remember. Wilhelm reminds me so much of Dieter. He even has some of his mannerisms. I'm so glad that he found time to spend with us during our visit." Adam looks up from Dieter's picture. "Do you remember when Dieter surprised us at Hannah's flat on that foggy day?"

"I'll never forget it."

"Do you like your job at the boutique?"

"Yes, but I own the boutique. I took it over from the owner. I worked for her for many years. Her son and husband had died in the war, and she had no other family. She passed away, and I found out that she had left it to me in her will." Elisabeth is lost in her thoughts for a moment. "Do you want to see your house?"

"It's still standing?"

"Yes, even your tree is still standing."

That afternoon, Elisabeth and Adam travel to their old neighborhood. Adam takes pictures of his house, the tree, and the lake. Elisabeth takes him to where Frau Lenger's shop had stood, but it has since been replaced with another building. They spend the afternoon picnicking in their favorite place. It's different now, but it doesn't matter. They are together.

That night, Elisabeth looks out to city lights. Adam is asleep, and the house is quiet. She stands at the window in the darkness. He'll be returning to Chicago in the morning. She dreads having to let him go. She fears she will never see him again. Her mind wanders back to her childhood. She thinks about Hannah. She wants to cry, but she can't, the pain holds on. She thinks about Friedrich, the way he would play with her braids with his tiny hands. The memories flow through her mind in quick succession, one tied to another. Finally, she sits down in her mother's chair. The city lights dimly light the room. She looks around at the framed photos from her past. She has a few photographs of Dieter, they are her most cherished, but she also has photographs of her grandmother Heilwig, her mother, and brothers. They're a reminder of another time, long ago. She knows now why she didn't want to remarry. She couldn't bear losing one more person.

She decides, at that moment, that shutting love out is not the way she wants to live her life. Though she will not search it out, if fate brings her someone to love she will try to let it in.

The following morning, Elisabeth hugs Adam one last time. "I don't want to let you go."

Adam steps back and places his hands on her shoulders. "We will see each other in June when you come to Chicago. No matter what happens, this was a . Helena finding us was a miracle. We're still here, we're together, and that's a miracle. Remember the promise."

Elisabeth holds back her tears. "I'll always remember the promise. Take care. I'll see you in June."

She stands at the large window of the airport watching Adam's plane take off. She watches until it disappears into the sky.

In June, Elisabeth and Helena board separate flights to Chicago.

Elisabeth, Adam, and Helena stay true to their promise. They remain close for the rest of their lives. Elisabeth and Adam are there for Helena as she spends years struggling to conceive a child, and they are by her side when she is blessed with the miracle of a baby girl. Helena names her Hannah.

Helena and Elisabeth help Peter nurse Adam through cancer. Later, following the news that he was cancer free, Adam and Peter sell everything and move to Munich. Adam wanted to grow old with his best friend, and Peter happily agreed.

Elisabeth never remarried. Destiny had proved her right, but she was wrong about Dieter being the only man that she would ever love. She loved her son and her brothers. She loved Adam, and she grew to love Peter, and Helena's husband, Andreas. Love doesn't always meet our expectations. It will never measure up to our vision of perfection. That's what makes it beautiful. Love doesn't need to be perfect, and we don't need to be perfect to give it or receive it. Even those that live in the darkness, they can still find the light of love. It doesn't judge or punish. Love is perfect in its imperfection.

Made in United States
Troutdale, OR
04/03/2024